Under Sealed Orders

By H.A. Cody

Introduction by
Ted Jones

Formac Publishing Company Limited
Halifax

Formac Publishing Company Limited recognizes the support of the Province of Nova Scotia through the Department of Communities, Culture and Heritage. We are pleased to work in partnership with the province to develop and promote our culture resources for all Nova Scotians. We acknowledge the financial support of the Government of Canada through the Canada Book Fund for our publishing activities. We acknowledge the support of the Canada Council for the Arts which last year invested $157 million to bring the arts to Canadians throughout the country.

Library and Archives Canada Cataloguing in Publication

Cody, H. A. (Hiram Alfred), 1872-1948, author
    Under sealed orders / by H.A. Cody ; introduction
by Ted Jones.

(Formac fiction treasures)
First published: Toronto : McClelland & Stewart, c1917.
ISBN 978-1-4595-0333-5 (pbk.)

    I. Jones, Ted, 1939-, writer of supplementary textual
content II. Title. III. Series: Formac fiction treasures

PS8505.O2U53 2014   C813'.52   C2014-904334-1

Formac Publishing Company Limited
5502 Atlantic Street
Halifax, Nova Scotia, Canada
B3H 1G4
www.formac.ca

Printed and bound in Canada.

MIX
Paper from
responsible sources
FSC® C004071

Presenting Formac Fiction Treasures

Series Editor: Gwendolyn Davies

A taste for reading popular fiction expanded in the nineteenth century with the mass marketing of books and magazines. People read rousing adventure stories aloud at night around the fireside; they bought entertaining romances to read while travelling on trains and curled up with the latest serial novel in their leisure moments. Novelists were important cultural figures, with devotees who eagerly awaited their next work.

Among the many successful popular English language novelists of the late 19th and early 20th centuries were a group of Maritimers who found, in their own education, travel and sense of history, events and characters capable of entertaining readers on both sides of the Atlantic. They emerged from well-established communities that valued education and culture, for women as well as men. Faced with limited publishing opportunities in the Maritimes, successful writers sought magazine and book publishers in the major cultural centres: New York, Boston, Philadelphia, London and sometimes Montreal and Toronto. They often enjoyed much success with readers at home, but the best of these writers found large audiences across Canada and in the United States and Great Britain.

The Formac Fiction Treasures series is aimed at offering contemporary readers access to books that were successful, often huge bestsellers in their time, but which are now little known and often hard to find. The authors and titles selected are chosen first of all as enjoyable to read, and secondly for the light they shine on historical events and on attitudes and views of the culture from which they emerged. These complete original texts reflect values that are sometimes in conflict with those of today: for example, racism is often evident, and bluntly expressed. This collection of novels is offered as a step towards rediscovering a surprisingly diverse and not nearly well enough known popular cultural heritage of the Maritime provinces and of Canada.

H.A. Cody

INTRODUCTION

Along the shores of Washademoak Lake, Queens County, New Brunswick, there is a tiny village simply called Codys, which bears the family name of one of Canada's most successful popular novelists — Hiram Alfred Cody, who was born there on July 3rd, 1872, a direct descendant of Loyalist roots. Over one hundred and forty years have now passed and the house of his birth, *Hillscote*, still stands, high above the fields that slope toward the lake. In recent years the Cody homestead has been restored, with much of the original style being recaptured, and it has been designated a Provincial Historic Site.

Between 1908 and 1937, twenty-five books appeared under the signature of H.A. Cody. Twenty-two of them were novels, two were biographies, and one was a collection of poems. Along with Ralph Connor, Gilbert Parker, L.M. Montgomery, and Stephen Leacock, Cody's name was on bestseller lists throughout Canada, the United States, and England. In bookshops and on the internet today, collectors browse for hard-cover, first-edition Cody books that have long since been out of print. The twenty-five titles suggest an impressive sweep of backgrounds and genres, ranging from *An Apostle of the North* (1908) to *Rod of the Lone Patrol* (1916) to *Storm King Banner* (1937).[1] But H.A. Cody was prolific far beyond his books. His poems, plays, short stories, non-fiction articles, sermons, and novel serializations were published in many of the leading periodicals, newspapers, and church magazines of the time, including in *The Church Bell*, which he edited and published throughout his life. And, as it is with most writers, at the time of his death he left a number of unpublished manuscripts, including many articles, two novels, two poetry collections, and his unfinished autobiography.

The young "Hilie" Cody began to show signs of a future literary career at an early age. When he and his two sisters, Mary (1865–1935) and Julia (1869–1974), were small children, they started a little handwritten "family" paper called *The Jolly Band*. Cody supplied the local news and the poetry under the name of Mr. DeWinkle, a *nom de plume* given to him by his sisters because of his excessive winking habit (a trait he carried with him all his life). By the time Cody was twelve, he was keeping a small notebook journal in which he was carefully recording the important events of his daily life, such as visits to his line traps, accounts of his finances, various adventures with his horse and wagon, experimental dialogue, and rhyming couplets. This small black-covered notebook with its neatly penciled entries still survives, along with the forty annual hard-covered journals that came later, whereby he never missed a daily entry in pen and ink.

Of the three children born to miller and lumberman George Redmond Cody and his wife, Loretta Augusta (Doney), Julia lived to be 105, thus giving me an opportunity to interview her a few years before her death. At that time, she clearly remembered how her father wanted his only son to go on to higher education after attending the one-room village school. The son, however, had other plans. According to his 1943 autobiographical notes:

> *It was the summer of 1889 when I*
> *was seventeen that I decided to go to*
> *Sussex, twenty miles away, with a young*
> *neighbor, to drill. The militia trained*

*there every summer and I was keen
to join the Princess Louise Regiment. I
had my long-legged boots made, and
my horse in readiness to go, when word
came that the drill was put off until
fall. This, so far as I know, had never
happened before. I have often wondered
what it would have meant to my life if
I had gone to Sussex that summer, for
it was then that I made up my mind to
study for the Ministry. My father and
uncle [Hiram, his father's brother and
Cody's namesake] were anxious for me
to do so, but, as I have mentioned, I
wished to be a hunter or a trapper or a
machinist. That fall I left home and went
to Saint John and entered the Grammar
School.*

From the old Saint John Grammar School, he went on to
King's College, Windsor, Nova Scotia, where he was a student under Professor Charles G.D. Roberts, a cornerstone
of Post-Confederation Canadian Literature, who encouraged
Cody's literary ambitions and who influenced Cody's early
work. When Cody became editor-in-chief of the profession-
ally published *King's College Record*, his own prose pieces
began to appear alongside those of his mentor, Professor
(later Sir) Charles G.D. Roberts. Their paths also crossed at
the Haliburton Literary Club, the Quinctilian Debating Society,
the Athletic Association, the Three Elms Cricket Club, and the
Student Missionary Society, in all of which Cody was an active
member.

Cody successfully completed his B.A. examinations in June

of 1896, and, at that time, his first published poem appeared in a national publication. He was on his way to New Brunswick's Miramichi area to spend the summer as a lay reader when the following incident occurred:

> *Professor Roberts came to my room in a*
> *hotel in Fredericton, where I was staying*
> *for the night, to congratulate me. He had*
> *read the poem and had seen my name in*
> *the hotel register. That touch meant very*
> *much to me.*

The title of the poem was "The Indian's Grave" and it was printed in *The Canadian Magazine* (Toronto). Cody returned to King's a year later, as was the custom, to receive his degree and to be valedictorian of the 1897 class. In 1908 he received an M.A. degree from King's, his first book being accepted as his thesis. His last visit to his *alma mater* (relocated in Halifax on the Dalhousie University Campus after the Windsor campus had been destroyed by fire in 1920) was in 1939, when an honorary degree of Doctor of Divinity was conferred upon him.

At Christ Church Cathedral, Fredericton, on December 20th, 1896, H.A. Cody was ordained deacon. A few weeks later he took up his first rectorship:

> *The Bishop told me that I was to go to*
> *the Parish of Greenwich, so I arrived*
> *there on Monday, January 4th, 1897.*
> *It had been a cold morning when I*
> *left home with Tom Worden, a river*
> *boatman. I drove my horse, Tom Thum,*
> *hitched to a sleigh which my father had*
> *made, towing a two-wheel cart. Tom*

Worden had his own horse and pung,
bringing my trunk and box of books.
We landed that evening at Oak Point.
The weather had changed and it was
raining. Leaving my sleigh in Jas. N.
Inch's barn, I hitched Tom Thum to my
cart and drove down the road to the Rev.
D.W. Pickett's, where I was expected.
Cold, tired, hungry, and forlorn, I
received a most hearty welcome, and
that house was a home to me for the next
seven and a half years.

From the little rectory at Oak Point on the lower St. John River Valley, Cody launched *The Church Bell.* He started a circulation library, taking a number of books with him wherever he went as he extended his ministry into several parishes, even organizing the building of new churches. He also created a large collection of homemade lantern views to accompany his weekly church sermons and his church-hall lectures. At the end of each day, he went to his journal, a special column being added to record the distances he had travelled, on the average between twenty and thirty miles daily. His experiences on rough roads, through all kinds of weather, and his involvement with hundreds of rural folk, later formed the basis for a popular series of articles entitled "Thrills of a Country Parson".

In May 1904, H.A. Cody went to the Yukon, responding to an appeal for a travelling missionary under William Bompas, the famous pioneer bishop of the North. Cody made his headquarters at Whitehorse, but spent most of his time visiting miners and Natives in the outlying stations, using pack-horse and canoe in summer, dogsled and snowshoes in winter. His faithful Native guide and interpreter, Jimmy Jackson, always went with him. His experiences inspired him to write poems and articles which he submitted to various North American magazines, often accompanying them with photographs that he had taken and developed himself. Then he would wait at the wharf for the steamer and the published results from "the outside," along with mail from home. A vast correspondence was carried on with his relatives and friends in the East, who, like himself, were waiting for his first visit home from the North in the summer of 1905.

Upon his return to the Yukon in the fall of 1905, the following item appeared in *The Whitehorse Star* newspaper: "Rev. H.A. Cody, who left ten weeks ago on a visit to his old home in New Brunswick, but primarily to forsake the ranks of single life, will arrive with his bride on this evening's train." He had married Jessie Margaret Flewelling (1884–1967) of Oak Point, a member of his Greenwich parish congregation and a dedicated Sunday School teacher. They were to live in the Episcopal log rectory at Whitehorse, Cody having been appointed rector of the little log Christ Church next door. During the next four years, many people in the Yukon were to enjoy the Codys' friendship and hospitality. After Sunday evening services, a number of the Mounties of "H" Division would call at the rectory, along with prospectors, miners, young ladies of the community, and a young bank clerk by the name of Robert W. Service, who wrote his first book, *Songs of a Sourdough*, while he was in Whitehorse. Service was also Cody's vestry clerk at the little log church and, following the monthly vestry meetings, the two of them would have long chats about literary matters.

As well, H.A. Cody's first writing to achieve national acclaim was written at Whitehorse. It was a 5,000-word essay, entitled "The Yukon Territory," about its history, resources, and future possibilities, and it was submitted as part of a Yukon Council contest open to the public. The writer with the *nom de plume*

"Quik Pak" (ancient Russian for Yukon River) was awarded the first prize of $200 and it was soon made known that H.A. Cody was the winner, his essay being published in three installments in *The Dawson News* (July issues of 1906). This essay's success was followed by H.A. Cody's first book, a biography of Bishop Bompas, entitled *An Apostle of the North*, simultaneously published in 1908 by Seely in England, Briggs in Canada, and Dutton in the United States. It received many favourable reviews, including the *New York Times'* encomium:

> *A story of hard work done in establishing the kingdom of righteousness in the wilderness of the far Northwest has been tenderly told . . . A saintly man, and a sympathetic, clearly drawn portrait of him, it is illustrated with a multitude of excellent half-tones.*

At the end of 1909, the Codys and their first son (Douglas) left the Yukon, returning home to New Brunswick and the rectorship of St. James' Stone Church in Saint John. But the North was not forgotten. In 1910, a children's version of Bishop Bompas's life was published under the title *On Trail and Rapid by Dog-Sled and Canoe*. At the same time, Cody's first novel appeared — a romantic adventure story set in the North and aptly titled *The Frontiersman*. According to *The Canadian Author & Bookman*, "it was THE BIG BOOK in Saint John that Christmas," and, for the next two decades, shoppers headed their Christmas list with "the new Cody". Yet, although Cody always did his best to deliver, he was writing for a fickle public. His second novel, *The Fourth Watch*, a New Brunswick story set in the quiet rural landscape of the lower St. John River Valley familiar to him from his Greenwich parish years, enjoyed good sales but was dismissed by Toronto's *Saturday Night* as being "hard to take seriously" given its clerical author-ship. Thus, for his third novel, *The Long Patrol: A Tale of the Mounted Police* (1912),[2] Cody returned to the thrilling experi-ences of the North, prefacing it with the dedication:

> *To that noble body of men, the Royal*
> *North-West Mounted Police, by one who*
> *for several years lived among them and*
> *shared their hospitality in the far-flung*
> *Canadian Northland.*

His three publishers waited impatiently for the manuscript, Cody working late at night so as not to neglect his family nor his church. He hired a local typist and then he asked a member of his con-gregation to do the proofreading. The final step was a visit to the post office.

Although it was heavy with melodrama, *The Long Patrol* became a bestseller with the public and a hit with the critics. As a result, Cody joined two press-clipping agencies, one in Toronto and one in New York, receiving numerous reviews that were immediately placed in the large scrapbooks kept throughout his literary career. During this period, Cody and the pseudonymous Canadian writer Ralph Connor were often compared and even advertised together, as was done in *The Toronto Mail & Empire* at the time:

> *The public appetite for stories of the*
> *Royal North-West Mounted Police seems*
> *to have been slaked not at all. Quite*
> *a number of very bad books have*
> *appeared recently dealing with this*
> *field . . . Happily, the two publications*
> *here under notice are of a worthier*

sort. Ralph Connor, who adds to his
long list of eminent Canada studies in
Corporal Cameron of the North West
Mounted Police, *and H.A. Cody, who has*
written The Long Patrol, *have first-hand*
experience of the men and things and
places whereof they tell.

Like Cody, Connor was a clergyman (the Reverend Charles William Gordon, 1860–1937). Born in the Scottish area of Glengarry County, Ontario, Connor was to serve as a Presbyterian minister in the west, in France as a padre in WWI, and as Moderator of the Presbyterian Church during his later career. His pen name gave him the freedom to write with forcefulness and realism, a freedom which H.A. Cody was never to experience. For years, Connor and Cody were both to be household names and fiction-writing contemporaries known for their novels of muscular Christianity. And they were to enjoy "a certain vogue" — writers of the West at a time when Western stories were very popular.

Cody's next two novels were also set in the North — *The Chief of the Ranges* (1913) and *If Any Man Sin* (1915). The former tells the story of the Yukon before European invasion, concentrating on two particular Native tribes. The latter tells the story of a young preacher who has committed a serious offence against somebody in his parish, and, having been defrocked, escapes to the Peace River country to repent. As with all his books, Cody often struggled to get the right title, working with all three of his publishers, exchanging many letters discussing various possibilities for one that would work. Although the title of *The Chief of the Ranges* remained unchanged since its inception, *If Any Man Sin* might have appeared as *The Outcast, The Price, Beyond the Pale,* or *The Seat of the Scornful.*

The heroine in *The Chief of the Ranges*, the daughter of the Chief, was inspired by a young Native girl called Owindia whom Bishop and Mrs. Bompas had taken to live with them and with whom Cody had become acquainted. A Métis trader named Natsatt (noticeably influenced by James Fenimore Cooper's Natty Bumppo) and an old Ranger called Dan (coincidentally, the grandfather of Owindia) are the only non-First Nations men in the story. A relationship develops between Owindia and Natsatt, advertised on the dust jacket of the book as a "powerful" love-interest "pulsating" through the novel — "in fact, IS the story!" *The Milwaukee Journal* backed up the book cover's promise, noting in its review:

> *Mr. Cody has been suggested as a new*
> *James Fenimore Cooper, an ambitious*
> *position which it is possible to imagine*
> *that he might fill. For he manages to*
> *thrill us and yet keep us well within*
> *the boundaries of possibilities . . . in*
> *very much the way Cooper did with his*
> Leather Stocking Tales.

For his next two novels, H.A. Cody returned to New Brunswick for his settings, *Rod of the Lone Patrol* appearing in 1916, and *Under Sealed Orders* being released in 1917. He continued to rise at four in the morning and, using only two fingers, peck out his stories on an old Underwood typewriter that he had brought back from the Yukon. Nearby on the study floor was his collie dog, Laddie. In the summer, he would write in longhand, stretched out on the veranda hammock, with his cat, Malta, curled up beside him. Summers were spent at Oak Point, Cody having acquired the vine-clad rectory of his first parish for a country home. It was situated near the banks of his beloved St. John River and he called it *Bide-a-wee*. Four more children were born to the Codys — three boys (Kenneth, Norman, George) — and a girl (Frances). On warm summer evenings, the favourite family novel to be read aloud at *Bide-a-wee* was *Rod of the Lone Patrol.* When the next generation (grandchildren) came along, this book continued to be the most requested. Although the story is concerned with quiet, wholesome village life, which is a great change from the Yukon and the absorbing problems found in the North, the attractive feature was the fact that the whole story is based on the Boy Scout Movement. There were many positive reviews, such as this one from *The New York Evening Sun:*

> *The Boy Scout stories never fail to please*
> *young gentlemen and ladies in the stages*
> *of knickerbockers and pigtails. The Boy*
> *Scouts for the past half dozen years have*
> *been the most popular theme in juvenile*
> *books. This year caps a glad climax.*
> *There is, for instance,* Rod of the Lone
> Patrol *by H.A. Cody — a scout story*
> *which is splendidly written, beyond the*
> *usual juvenile in every way.*

The book is appropriately dedicated to Cody's little sons, "who are anxious to become Boy Scouts".

On the other hand, the adult novel *Under Sealed Orders* was a different kind of story with a rather misleading title, but probably a better title than the others that Cody and his publishers had considered: *The Devil's Poor, The Sport of Fools, The Heart of Leaping Power.* The chosen title has a ring of military or state affairs about it, but the mysteriously sealed orders really refer to the affairs of an elderly and poverty-stricken immigrant whose rich brother in England makes reparation for past injustices. The inspiration came from an article in the March 1916 issue of *The Canadian Magazine*, written by Cody's Saint John friend and fellow author, A.M. Belding. The title of the article was "The Devil's Poor — A Mild Form of Slavery as Practised in New Brunswick." The article referred to a policy in New Brunswick (as in other provinces) where overseers of the poor were appointed in each parish. If taxes could not be collected to support the poor, and, if there were no almshouse in the parish, the overseers made arrangements with local people to keep the paupers for an annual sum of money paid by the parish. It was a contract system whereby the paupers were "farmed out" for common labour, and whereby the overseers were supposed to make follow-up visits to see how each pauper was being treated. In many cases these administrative visits were never made and, as a result, the paupers were left to the mercy of their owners. But nothing was worse than the public auction aspect of a pauper's placement. The pauper was publicly bought by the lowest bidder; however, the small sum of money that was bid was paid by the parish to the bidder for the upkeep of the pauper. Everyone gained except the pauper, who lost his or her freedom, identity, and dignity for a fixed period of time.

Cody saw this terrible custom as a manifestation of man's inhumanity to his fellow man and he was ready to act upon it by letting his novel become a protest in print that would reach many readers. To sugarcoat the pill, however, he introduced mysterious and historical themes running throughout *Under Sealed Orders*, making it a detective story, the answer to the puzzle remaining "under sealed orders" until the final chapters. There is also a large cast of characters that Cody attempts to develop from chapter to chapter through actions and dialogue, although the latter appears to be unrealistic and even wooden at times. Fortunately, the storyline takes over and the reader is eager to know more about the selling of paupers, a rural community divided, and the dark, sealed secrets. *Under Sealed Orders* was given a splash of advertisements in Canada, England, and the United States by all three of Cody's publishers, one of the ads even appearing on the dust jacket of Ralph Connor's new book *The Major*. As a result, *Under Sealed Orders* was widely read, garnering a number of favourable reviews, especially in the United States.

For example, *The Brooklyn Eagle* entitled its review "A Canadian Mystery Story" and said that H.A. Cody "has written another of his out-of-doors novels with his usual cleverness for sharp interest, well-sustained, and some admirable sketches of character-drawing." *The San Francisco Chronicle* thought it was "remarkable for its presentation of a very fine character in an old man, an idealist, who dreams all manner of dreams." *The Chicago Continent* was impressed with "the dramatic thread of mystery". For *The Cincinnati Times-Star*, the book was, "after a fashion, a detective story without professional detectives . . . written with the charming simplicity of the old times, a rarity in these days." *The Philadelphia Press* concluded its comments with this statement: "Love, mystery and a constant out-of-doors atmosphere, what better ingredients could be required for a successful piece of light fiction." *Book News Monthly* used the term "Thoreau-like" and said it was "a story filled with uncommonly attractive people that it does one good to know." *The Pittsburgh Gazette Times* praised Cody for "writing interest stories, stories that might as well be true as to be fiction." Regardless, the story "is entertainingly set forth," said *The Boston Herald*. And *The Atlanta Constitution* referred specifically to the interesting dedication: "To all 'Spuds,' successful or unsuccessful; to all 'Fools,' wise or unwise; and to all of 'The Devil's Poor,' not forgetting authors."

Unfortunately, Cody did not have a clipping service in England, but, in Canada, *Under Sealed Orders* picked up encouraging reviews from across the country. *The Montreal Star* said the novel had "a mystery and a murder," and *The Montreal Witness* thought it was "good, clean entertainment of the popular sort." Saint John's pride in having a local writer of international recognition was reflected in all of that city's daily newspapers (*The Times, The Telegraph, The Globe, The Standard*). *The Globe* even did two reviews, the first saying that "Rev. H.A. Cody has written a new story, a novel of considerable power, which shows a marked advance in technique and in construction. Mr. Cody long ago passed the apprenticeship period and with his later stories has taken a foremost place among Canadian writers of fiction." However, it was *The Saint John Times*, appreciating the "distinct New Brunswick atmosphere" of *Under Sealed Orders*, that zeroed in on the real reason why Cody wrote this particular story:

> *One rises from a reading of the book with a feeling that the author desires to do much more than write a readable book. Such a custom as that of selling the keep of paupers to the lowest bidder, now happily past, although some localities in this province are still very far from making proper provision for indigent persons, is held up by Mr. Cody to deserved scorn, while the petty meanness of selfish and narrow-minded and malicious persons are made to stand out in hateful contrast to the finer elements of human character.*

The first two chapters of *Under Sealed Orders* set the tone for the entire novel. In Chapter One, entitled "The Lure of Falling

Water," the reader is introduced to the book's main character, a well-bred and intelligent gentleman by the name of David Findley, who appreciates the current pastoral setting and the future energy source of a beautiful waterfall. By Chapter Two, entitled "To the Lowest Bidder," Mr. Findley is labelled a "crazy pauper" and is ridiculed by the community as he is about to be "let" in a pauper auction on May 30th to the lowest bidder, with his board, lodging, and clothing to be provided for a period of one year. The pauper auction is to take place in front of a local store where a notice has been attached to the door and it has been signed by three overseers of the poor. The end of May has been chosen for the auction instead of the usual end of December because the community wants to get "Crazy David" placed as soon as possible. And they do — with a brute of a farmer, who is realistically described by Cody as ignorant and illiterate, bidding only $100 to take the thin and feeble old man in ragged clothes to a farm to be put to work. But, as the story unfolds and more characters are introduced, there are many plot twists and contrivances, as with all the Cody novels. The reader wants to know what eventually happens to David Findley and the kind people who believe in him and who become his friends and guardians. It is interesting to note that, ironically, all these genuine friends gain financially as the story draws to a close and that "Crazy David" in some respects has "the last laugh" with respect to the pauper system and its public auction. Moreover, by the end of the novel, not only has the reader enjoyed a mystery and an entertaining story but all in the community have learned a universal lesson.

Under Sealed Orders had resonance when it was released in 1917 because there were still parishes in New Brunswick where paupers were "farmed out" or "auctioned off." And this antiquated and abusive system continued until the late 1920s. Because of increased taxes, not everyone agreed that complete institutional care for paupers might be the best approach; yet, when the almshouse system was finally adopted throughout New Brunswick, it remained in operation until the early 1950s. Indeed, in the beginning, almshouses were only to be homes for paupers, but they were soon filled with the aged, the infirm, and the insane. As a result, shades of Dickensian England emerged from time to time. Men, women, and children of all ages moved in, crowding together in a building that would never be large enough, the ordinary decencies of life scarcely being preserved. Many of these paupers could not read or write and, to make matters worse, the local newspapers kept referring to them as "inmates". Over a period of time, prominent people of the parish were appointed to be commissioners and keepers of the almshouses and, in many cases, long overdue improvements were made.

Walter Learning and Alden Nowlan's highly successful premiere of their controversial play, *The Dollar Woman,* at Theatre New Brunswick in January of 1977, reminded Frederictonians of the dark history of these pauper auctions. Set in a small New Brunswick town in the Sussex area in the 1880s, *The Dollar Woman* portrayed the dramatic showdown between a well-intentioned overseer of paupers and a crusading newspaper editor at what is supposed to have been the final pauper auction in the province's history. In the background, a community is divided as the last female pauper is sold for a dollar. In February of 2012, the Black Box Theatre of St. Thomas University in Fredericton staged a 35th anniversary revival of *The Dollar Woman* with great success.

Even as H.A. Cody's early novels were being released in new editions, multiple reprints, and serializations, fifteen more fiction books were to be published, including his most popular in 1922 — *The King's Arrow* (with the subtitle "A Tale of the United Empire Loyalists" and the dedication "To My Ancestors of the

United Empire Loyalists Who Came to the St. John River, May, 1783"). McClelland & Stewart were Cody's new Canadian publishers and they were able to get *The King's Arrow* serialized in *The Family Herald and Weekly Star*. From England, Sir Ernest Hodder-Williams, chairman of the prominent publishing house of Hodder & Stoughton, which handled the British sales of the book, wrote a personal congratulatory note to Cody: "It is a very real pride and pleasure to be associated with the publication of your work." Also, from England, came a glowing review in *The London Times Literary Supplement*, concluding with the statement: "Love at first sight and a whirl of events calling out all the heroism and loyalty of the hero make up a thrilling and picturesque tale." Today, the story continues to live on with the name of *The King's Arrow* Arena in the military town of Oromocto, New Brunswick.

In 1925, H.A. Cody's only book of verse, *Songs of a Bluenose* (49 poems), was published by McClelland & Stewart. It has become a collector's item in the 21st century. In 2007, a sequel was published under the title *More Songs of a Bluenose* (110 poems), being released on the 135th anniversary of H.A. Cody's birth. In honour of the event, a memorial celebration was held in Gagetown, New Brunswick, not far from Cody's birthplace at Highfield. Many of his grandchildren were in attendance, one of them being Dr. Thane Cody (1932–2014), who arrived from Florida. It was Thane who had joined forces with the Queens' County Historical Society to edit and publish the sequel. His introduction to the book concludes with these comments: "H.A. Cody's creative mind was displayed time and again in his novels, but I think even more so in his poems. There are poems dealing with religion, nature, love, war, the sea and ships, human nature, and humour. Some of the poems are as relevant today as they were in the 1930s and 1940s. I hope that those who read this collection will enjoy this poetic journey back in time as much as I have."

During the ten years that remained to H.A. Cody after the publication of his last book (1937), he continued to be an active member of the Boy Scout Movement and a governor of the Saint John Male Orphan Home. He still belonged to the Fortnightly Club and the Canadian Club, and he was made an honorary member of the Canadian Authors' Association "In consideration of his notable contribution to Canadian historical fiction." In an address given to an Archdeaconry Conference in 1942, he said: "On the morning of July 3rd of this year I woke and found myself 70 years old. It was something startling, although I knew it was coming. But it gave me a strange feeling to think that I had reached the three-score years and ten of which the Bible speaks. When one reaches that age, he is justified in looking back a little to consider the years that are past, and the changes which have taken place."

H.A. Cody was seventy-five when he died on February 9th, 1948. From the little stone church where he had been rector for thirty-three years, he was taken to Fernhill Cemetery, the harbour of the old grey city of Saint John a short distance away. Perhaps he met Death according to his own description in the last stanza of his poem "The Conqueror":

> *We knew he smiled, the Great Heart*
> *lying there,*
> *As only victors smile at ended strife.*
> *For silent now with light on his cold lips,*
> *He smiled at death, for death to him*
> *meant life.*

— Ted Jones

Ted Jones is the author of *All the Days of His Life, A Biography of Archdeacon H.A. Cody*, published by The New Brunswick Museum, 1981.

ENDNOTES

1. Other titles by Cody include: *An Apostle of the North* (1908); *The Frontiersman* (1910); *On Trail and Rapid by Dog-Sled and Canoe* (1910); *The Fourth Watch* (1911); *The Long Patrol* (1912); *The Chief of the Ranges* (1913); *If Any Man Sin* (1915); *Rod of the Lone Patrol* (1916); *Under Sealed Orders* (1917); *The Unknown Wrestler* (1918); *The Touch of Abner* (1919); *Glen of the High North* (1920); *Jess of the Rebel Trail* (1921); *The King's Arrow* (1922); *The Trail of the Golden Horn* (1923); *The Master Revenge* (1924); *Songs of a Bluenose* (1925); *The Fighting-Slogan* (1926); *Fighting Stars* (1927); *The Stumbling Shepherd* (1929); *The River Fury* (1930); *The Red Ranger* (1931); *The Girl at Bullet Lake* (1933); *The Crimson Sign* (1935); *Storm King Banner* (1937)

2. Two other titles were considered: *The Ragged Edge* and *The Hound of the North*.

CONTENTS

CHAPTER I

THE LURE OF FALLING WATER

It was evening and a late April wind was whipping down the valley. It swayed the tops of the tall pine and spruce trees as they shouldered up from the swift brook below. It tossed into driving spray the water of Break Neck Falls where it leaped one hundred feet below with a thundering roar and swirl. It tossed as well the thin grey hair, long beard, and thread-bare clothes of an old man standing upon a large rock which towered high above the stream.

The entire scene was wild and made weird by the approach of night. But the old man did not seem to notice anything except the falling of the waters. His eyes glowed with an intense light as he kept them fixed upon the leaping and swirling columns below. His face was like the face of a lover turned toward the object of his affection.

For some time the man stood there drinking in the scene before him. Then he took a step forward which brought him perilously near the edge of the steep rock. His lips moved though no sound could be heard for the tumult of the falls which was rending the air. What connection had such a man with his surroundings? No boor or clown was he, for the simple dignity of face and manner marked him as one of Nature's true gentlemen.

It was almost dark when he at last reluctantly left the rock and entered the thick woods where a trail led away from the falls. Along this he moved with the unerring instinct of one who had travelled it often and was sure of his bearings. But ever and anon he paused to listen to the sound of the falling waters which followed him like the voice of a loved one urging him to return.

"Yes, you want me," he at length cried, as he once more paused. "I hear your voice calling, and I know its meaning. Others need you, too, but they do not know it. You have been calling to them for years, but they have not understood your language. It was left for me to listen and take heed. They will some day, and then you will show your power. I can see what you will do, beautiful falls, and the changes which will come to this fair land when your luring voice is heeded."

He stood for awhile as if entranced after uttering these mystic words. Then he continued on his way and night wrapped more closely about him her dark mantle. He had to walk very cautiously now for the trail was rough, and there were sharp stones and roots ready to strike his feet and trip him up.

At length the trail ended and he reached the smooth surface of the broad highway. Along this he sped with the quick elastic step of one who has seen a vision. The fire of a great idea was burning fiercely within him which caused him to take no heed to his surroundings.

He had not gone far, however, ere some strong impulse caused him to pause again and listen to that fascinating sound of falling waters far off in the distance. It was on an elevation in the road where he stopped, and here the shadows which enwrapped the forest were not so heavy. The lingering light of departing day was still in the west and touched this part of the highway with its faint glow. It brought out into clear relief the silhouette of the old man as he stood there with his right hand placed to his ear so as not to miss the least sound drifting down the valley.

So intent was he upon what he heard that he did not notice the sounds of approaching footsteps, so when a man stopped a few yards away and watched him curiously, he was completely unaware of his presence. "Ring on, sweet waters," he cried. "Your voice follows me no matter how far I go. I alone can understand your language, and know what you are saying. All are deaf but me. They hear but do not know your meaning." He ceased, and again listened for a few seconds.

A strange half-mocking laugh startled him, and caused him to look quickly around. Seeing that he was observed, he was about to hurry away, when a man stepped forward.

"Pardon me," he began. "I did not mean to offend you. But your words seem so strange, that I could not help laughing."

"And were you listening to the voice?" the old man eagerly asked. "Do the falling waters speak to you as they do to me? Is that why you are here?"

"Yes, I hear them," was the reply. "But they do not bring any special message to my mind."

"And they do not tell you of power, of the wonderful things they are ready and willing to do when men will heed what they are saying?"

"No, I can't say that they do. They make a noise up there among the trees, but I do not know what they are saying."

"Strange, strange," and the old man placed his hand to his forehead. "You are like all the rest, then. You hear but you do not understand."

"What do you hear?" the newcomer asked, thinking that he was talking to a weak-minded creature.

"I hear great things, which will be for the welfare of the whole community. The waters tell me what they will do. They will make life worth living. They will give light and power to the people all along the river and revolutionise their daily tasks. Instead of hard labour by the sweat of the brow, the waters will do the work. People will be happy, and have time for the beautiful things of life. Grinding toil and sorrow will be banished forever."

"Umph! So that is what you hear, eh? What is the good of hearing such a voice, if you have no power to make it come true?"

"But the people will hear and understand," the old man insisted. "I am telling them about it."

"Yes, I know you are, and they think you are a fool for your efforts. They laugh at you, and call you crazy."

"But they will come to see that I am right. They, too, will hear the voice, and then they will not be able to resist its pleadings."

"If you had the money they would listen to you, for that is the only voice people will heed to-day. If you came here with an abundance of gold, people would hear anything you asked them to in the falls up yonder. But because you are poor, like myself, your ideas will have no more weight with them than the lightest feather. Back your visions with money and people will crowd around you, and you will be heeded. But try to get along without money, and, bah! you are a fool."

Scarcely had these words left his lips ere a raucous honk up the road startled him. Then an auto with blazing lights leaped out of the night. The old man was standing right in its way, unconscious of his danger. Almost instinctively two strong hands clutched him and hurled him into the ditch as the car swept past. Shouts of merriment sounded forth upon the night air from the occupants of the car. The fright they had given the two by the side of the road evidently gave them much amusement. Their laughter caused the rescuer to straighten suddenly up, and clutch the old man fiercely by the arm.

"Did you hear them?" he asked, and his voice was filled with suppressed emotion.

"Yes," was the reply. "They are only thoughtless youths having a good time, I suppose."

"It's just what money does, though. I know who they are, for I caught a glimpse of them as they sped past. It's money that talks with them; that is the only voice they hear. They will ride over the less fortunate, and crush them down as worms beneath their feet. They have been doing it for ages, and look upon it as their right. What do they care about the meaning of the falling waters when they are always listening to the voice of money. Curse them. Why should they revel and sport with ill-got gains, when honest men can hardly get enough to keep breath in their bodies."

The young man was standing erect now on the side of the road. His companion shrank away somewhat fearful lest he should turn upon him and smite him.

"You seem to have suffered," he at length remarked. "You appear to be annoyed at people who have money."

"And why shouldn't I?" was the savage reply. "Haven't I suffered at their hands, young as I am? Haven't I been scorned by them to the limit of all endurance? Haven't they made a mock of me for years, calling me names behind my back? And why? Just because I happen to be poor, and have tried honestly to make my way in life. But there, enough of this. What's the use of talking about such things? It will do no more good than the voice of the waters which you are continually hearing."

Along the road the two walked in deep silence. The old man found it hard to keep up with his companion, and he was at last forced to fall behind. Soon he was alone, and then his thoughts went once more back to the falls, and the glorious vision which was in his mind.

It was only when he reached a small building by the side of the road that he stopped. Pushing open the door, he entered. All was dark and silent within. The strange loneliness of the place would have smitten any one else with the feeling of dread. But the old man never seemed to mind it. Fumbling in his vest pocket, he found a match. This he struck and lighted a tallow dip which was stuck into a rude candle-stick upon a bare wooden table. One glance at the room revealed by the dim light showed its desolate bareness. Besides the table there were two small benches and a wash-stand, containing a granite-iron basin. A small broken-down stove stood at one end of the room, by the side of which was a couch. Not a scrap of mat or rug adorned the floor. There were no blinds or curtains to the cheerless, windows, and not a picture adorned the walls.

But the old man did not notice the desolation of the place. It was quite evident that he was beyond the influence of earthly surroundings for the moment. Going at once to the couch, he brought forth a roll of paper hidden away beneath the pillow. Carrying this over to the table, he sat down upon one of the benches and spread the paper out before him. By the light of the candle it was easy for him to study the carefully-made lines upon the large sheet. Eagerly he scanned the drawings, and then placing the forefinger of his right hand upon one central point, he moved it along one line extending farther than the rest until it stopped at a small square in which was the word "City." This action gave him much satisfaction and a pleased expression lighted up his face. "Power, power," he murmured. "Ay, quicker than thought, and bright as the sun shining in its strength. Great, wonderful! and yet they do not realise it. But they shall know, and understand."

Along the other lines he also ran his finger, pausing at the end of each where was marked "Town," "Village," or "Settlement." He talked continually as he did so, but it was all about "glory" and "power." Over and over again he repeated these words, now in a soft low voice, and again in a loud triumphant manner.

At length he rose from the bench, crossed the room, opened the door, and stepped outside. Not a star was to be seen, and the wind was stronger than ever. It was keen, piercing. But the man heeded neither the one nor the other. He was listening intently, and the faint sound of Break Neck Falls drifting in from the distance was to him the sweetest of music.

And as he stood there a sudden change took place. His dead drooped, and he leaned against the side of the building for support. A shiver shook his body, and as he turned and entered the house his steps were slow, and he half-stumbled across the threshold. He looked at the wood-box behind the stove, but there was not a stick in it. He next opened the door of the little cupboard near by, but not a scrap of food was there. Almost mechanically he thrust his hand into his pocket and brought forth a purse. This he opened, but there was nothing inside. Half-dazed he stood there in the centre of the room. Then he glanced toward the paper with the drawings lying upon the table, and as he did so a peculiar light of comprehension shone in his eyes.

CHAPTER II

TO THE LOWEST BIDDER

There was an unusually large number of people gathered in front of Thomas Marshall's store one morning about the last of May. Women were there as well as men, and all were talking and laughing in a most pleasant way. The cause of this excitement was explained by a notice tacked on the store door.

The Board, Lodging, and Clothing of David Findley, Pauper, will be let to the lowest bidder for a period of one year, on Wednesday, May 30th inst., at Thomas Marshall's store, Chutes Corner, at 10 o'clock A. M.
Signed
J. B. FLETCHER, T. S. TITUS, O. R. MITCHELL
Overseers of Poor

This notice had been posted there for about two weeks, and had attracted the attention of all the people in the parish. It was out of the ordinary for such a sale to take place at this season of the year. Hitherto, it had occurred at the last of December. But this was an exceptional case, and one in which all were keenly interested.

"I hear he is stark crazy," Mrs. Munson was saying to a neighbour, Peter McQueen, "and that he has a funny notion in his head."

"Should say so," McQueen replied. "Any man who has lived

as he has for months must be pretty well off his base. Why, he didn't have a scrap of food in the house when he was found by Jim Trask one morning the last of April. Jim has been keeping him ever since."

"Isn't he able to work?" Mrs. Munson inquired.

"Seems not. I guess he's a scholar or something like that, and did some book-keeping in the city until he drifted this way. He must have had a little money to live as long as he has. He's always been a mystery to me."

"And to everybody else, I guess."

"Yes, so it appears. But it's a great pity that we've got to be burdened with the likes of him. Our taxes are heavy enough now without having to take care of this strange pauper. We've got too many on our hands already for our good."

"But do you know anything about that queer notion of his, Pete?" Mrs. Munson asked.

"Ho, ho, I've heard about it, and I guess it's true all right. He's in love with Break Neck Falls, and makes regular trips there every day, and sometimes at night. Jim followed him once, and saw him standing upon that high rock right by the falls. He kept waving his hands and shouting to the water, though Jim could not make out what he was saying. He has some writing on a piece of paper which he keeps very close. He has told, though, that his plan will do wonderful things for the city and the whole surrounding country. He once said that we don't know what a valuable thing we have right in our midst. I guess we've lived here longer than he has, and should know a thing or two. It is not necessary for a half-cracked old man to come and tell us of our possessions. But, say, here he is now, coming along in Jim Trask's farm waggon."

As the team drew near, all eyes were turned in its direction, for the first glimpse of "Crazy David," as he was generally called. There was no difficulty about seeing him for he was sitting by Jim's side on the rough board seat. He looked much older and careworn than the night he had awakened from his dream, and found his wood-box, cupboard, and pocket-book empty. He had sat huddled on the seat for most of the way up the road, but when near the store he lifted his eyes and fixed them curiously upon the people before him. There was something pathetically appealing in the expression upon his face. He seemed like a man trying to recall something to his mind. He appeared strangely out of place in that rough farm waggon. Even his almost ragged clothes could not hide the dignity of his bearing as he straightened himself up and tried to assume the appearance of a gentleman. The people saw this effort on his part, and several wondered and spoke about it afterwards.

At first the old man did not seem to realise the purpose of the gathering. But when he saw the auctioneer mount a box alongside of him and call for bids, the truth of the entire situation dawned upon him. He was to be sold as a pauper to the lowest bidder, so he heard the auctioneer say. For an instant a deep feeling of anger stirred within his bosom, and he lifted his head as if to say something. But seeing the eyes of all fixed upon him, he desisted.

"What am I offered for the keep of this old man?" the auctioneer cried. "The lowest bid gets him."

"Two hundred dollars," came from a man not far off.

"Two hundred dollars!" and the auctioneer turned fiercely upon him. "You're out for a bargain, Joe Tippits. Why, he's worth that to any man for a year's work. He'll be able to do many an odd job. Come, you can do better than that."

"One seventy-five," came from another.

"Too much," the auctioneer cried. "The parish can't stand that."

"One fifty, then."

"That's better, Joe. Try again. You're a long way off yet."

"I'll take the critter fer one hundred dollars, and not a cent less."

At these emphatic words all turned and stared hard at the speaker. A perceptible shiver passed through the bystanders, while several muttered protests were heard. "Oh, I hope he won't get him, anyway," Mrs. Munson whispered to a neighbour. "Jim Goban isn't a fit man to look after a snake, and if he gets Crazy David in his clutches may God have mercy upon the poor old man."

"One hundred dollars I am offered," again the voice of the auctioneer rang out. "Can any one do better than that? One hundred dollars. Going at one hundred dollars. I shan't dwell. One hundred dollars and sold to Jim Goban for one hundred dollars."

This inhuman traffic did not seriously affect the people who had gathered for the auction. When it was over, they quickly dispersed, to discuss with one another about the life Jim Goban would lead Crazy David. It was an incident of only a passing moment, and mattered little more to them than if it had been a horse or a cow which had been sold instead of a poor feeble old man.

It was the custom which had been going on for years, and it was the only way they could see out of the difficult problem of dealing with paupers.

When Jim Goban reached home with his purchase, dinner was ready. There were five young Gobans who stared curiously upon David as he took his seat at the table. Mrs. Goban was a thin-face, tired looking woman who deferred to her husband in everything. There was nothing else for her to do, as she had found out shortly after their marriage what a brute he was.

David was pleased at the presence of the children and he often turned his eyes upon them.

"Nice children," he at length remarked, speaking for the first time since his arrival.

"So ye think they're nice, do ye?" Jim queried, leaning over and looking the old man in the eyes.

"Why, yes," David replied, shrinking back somewhat from the coarse face. "All children are nice to me, but yours are especially fine ones. What nice hair they have, and such beautiful eyes. I suppose the oldest go to school."

"Naw. They never saw the inside of a school house."

"You don't say so!" and David looked his astonishment. "Surely there must be a school near here."

"Oh, yes, there's a school all right, but they've never gone. I don't set any store by eddication. What good is it to any one, I'd like to know? Will it help a man to hoe a row of pertaters, or a woman to bake bread? Now, look at me. I've no eddication, an' yit I've got a good place here, an' a bank account. You've got eddication, so I understand, an' what good is it to you? I'm one of the biggest tax-payers in the parish, an' you, why yer nothing but a pauper, the Devil's Poor."

At this cruel reminder David shrank back as from a blow, and never uttered another word during the rest of the meal. The iron was entering into his soul, and he was beginning to understand something of the ignominy he was to endure at this house.

"Now look here," Jim began when they were through with dinner, "I've a big pile of wood out there in the yard, an' I want ye to tote it into the wood-house an' pile it up. I'll show ye where to put it. I'm gittin' mighty little fer yer keep, an' I expect ye to git a hustle on to help pay fer yer grub an' washin'."

"Don't be too hard on him, Jim," Mrs. Goban remarked. "He doesn't look very strong."

"Don't ye worry, Kitty, I'll attend to that. I know a wrinkle or two."

David was accordingly taken to the wood-house and Jim explained to him how and where he was to pile the wood. "Ye needn't kill yerself," he told him in conclusion. "But I want ye to keep busy, fer when that job's through I've got something else on hand. Ye can sit down when ye feel a little tired, but don't sit too long or too often, see?"

For about half an hour David worked patiently at the wood, piling it as neatly as possible. The work was not hard, and he was quite satisfied with his task. He was alone, anyway, and could think about his beloved falls. His hands, however, were soft, and ere long they were bruised and bleeding from the rough sticks. At length a sharp splinter entered his finger, and he sat down upon a stick to pull it out. In trying to do this, it broke off leaving a portion deeply embedded in the flesh, which caused him considerable pain. Not knowing what to do, he sat looking upon the finger in a dejected manner.

"What's the matter? You seem to be in trouble."

At these words David looked quickly around, and saw a young girl standing by his side. Though her dress was old and worn, her face was bright, and her eyes sparkled with interest.

"Here, let me take that splinter out," she ordered, as she sat down by his side, and drawing forth a needle, began to probe into the flesh. "There, I've got it!" she cried in triumph. "My! it's a monster. You'll have to be more careful after this. You should have gloves."

"Thank you very much," David replied. "To whom am I indebted for this kindness?"

"Oh, I'm Betty Bean, that's all."

"And you live here?"

"No. I'm just dying here."

"Dying!" David exclaimed in surprise. "Why, you don't look like a dying person."

"Maybe I don't, but I am. I'm just staying here because I have to. My mother's a widow, and I want to earn some money to help her, and as this was the only place I could get I had to take it."

"So you do not like it, then?"

"Who would like any place where there is such a brute as Jim

Goban? My, I'm sorry for you. To think of any man getting into his clutches."

"But surely I won't be any worse off than you are."

"I'm not so sure about that. You see, I'm about boss here, and do and say just what I like."

"How's that?"

"Well, I'm the only person Jim can get to work here. All the girls for miles around know what kind of a creature he is, and they wouldn't come for any amount of money. They're scared to death of him. But I'm not, and I tell him right to his face what I think of him, and the way he treats his poor wife. He would like to horsewhip me, but he knows that if I leave no one else would come in my place. But I'm glad now that I am here so I can look after you."

"Look after me!"

"Yes. I guess you'll need me all right. I know who you are, and I'm sorry for you. I'm going to stand between you and Jim Goban. He's scared to death of me, for I'm the only one who dares give him a tongue-lashing, and I do it whenever it is necessary, which is quite often."

"You're a brave girl," and David looked with admiration upon the slight form by his side. "How old are you?"

"Fifteen last March. But one's age is nothing. I've done a woman's work ever since I was ten. I stand up for my rights now, though. When I first came here Jim was bound that I should work all the time. But at last I told him that I was going to have every Saturday afternoon off, especially in summer, so I could go home or out upon the river. Can you row?" she suddenly asked.

"A little," was the reply.

"That's good. Now, look, I'm going to take you out in the boat next Saturday, and you're going to meet somebody there you'll like."

"Somebody I like," David repeated. "Who is it?"

"It's a woman, that's who it is. But I'm not going to tell you her name. She only came here last week, and she is so fond of the water, and spends so much time upon it. Oh, you'll like her when you see her. She's a beauty, with such lovely eyes and dark hair. And she's not a bit stuck up, either. She just talks in a friendly way, and makes you feel easy all over. There, now, I guess you'd better pile some more wood. I have a bit of work to do, and when I'm through I'll come out and give you a hand. I like to be with you. I know we're going to be friends."

The girl rose, and was about to leave. She paused, however, and looked inquiringly into the old man's face.

"Do you smoke?" she asked.

Into David's eyes came an eager expression, which Betty was not slow to see.

"I know you do," she cried, "but you have no tobacco."

"I have a pipe," and David fumbled into a pocket of his coat. "But I haven't had a smoke for weeks, because —"

"I know, I know," the girl hastily replied. "I'll get you some in a jiffy."

She was gone only a short time when she returned, and handed David half a fig of tobacco.

"There, take that," she said. "It's a piece Jim left on the kitchen window-sill."

"But is it right for me to take it?" David asked.

"Sure it's right. Didn't Jim agree to feed and lodge you for one year? You can't live without tobacco. It's a part of your food, see? If Jim says anything about it, I'll soon settle him."

"You are a good girl," David returned, as with trembling hands he hastily whittled off a few slices of tobacco with an old knife, and filled his pipe. "This will put new life into me. I can never repay you for your kindness."

CHAPTER III

ONE, AT LEAST, RINGS TRUE

With the small boat pulled well upon the beach, Lois Sinclair stood for a few moments looking out over the water. Her eyes were fixed upon a little boat in the distance containing two people, an old man and a young girl. The wind, which was steadily increasing, tossed her wavy, luxuriant hair over her brow, while several tresses fell across her cheeks, flushed by the recent rowing. She knew that she should be home, for supper would be waiting and her father would be impatient. But she hesitated. Her thoughts were out there on the water where she loved to be. The twang of the wind as it swept through the trees along the shore, and the beat of the surf upon the gravelly beach were music sweet to her ears.

At length, with one more lingering glance out upon the river, she turned and walked along a path leading from the shore. She moved slowly, for she was not at all anxious to reach the house situated about two hundred yards beyond. And yet it was an attractive house, well-built, and cosy in appearance, designed both for summer and winter use. A spacious verandah swept the front and ends, over which clambered a luxuriant growth of wild grape vines. Large trees of ash, elm, and maple spread their expansive branches over the well-kept lawn, providing an excellent shade when the sun was hot. Altogether, it was a most delightful spot to spend the summer months away from the smoke and confusion of the city.

The place, however, did not altogether appeal to Lois

Sinclair. If she had needed rest, the situation would have been ideal. But it was activity she desired, and not luxurious ease such as so many crave, especially two young men lolling on the verandah awaiting her coming. Even though one was her brother, she could not restrain a feeling of contempt as she looked upon their white faces, soft hands, and immaculate clothes. Why should men, she asked herself, be so ready and willing to give themselves completely up to effeminate habits when their blood was hot within them, and the great Open was calling them with such a strong insistent voice?

The young woman's arrival brought one of the young men to his feet, with the offer of a hammock.

"Please do not trouble yourself," she told him. "I must hurry and get ready for dinner. I know that father is very angry with me."

"He is not the only one who is angry, I can assure you," Sammie Dingle remarked. "We have been furious with you for leaving us this afternoon when we needed your company so much in the car. I cannot understand how you can enjoy yourself alone out on the river in that nasty boat."

"No, I suppose you cannot," Lois replied, and so infatuated was Sammie with the young woman that he did not notice the slightest sarcasm in her words.

"Hurry up, Lois," her brother ordered, "I'm almost starved. Dad's got it in for you."

"All right, Dick," was her reply. "I shall be down in a few minutes. Why did you wait for me? You had better go to dinner at once, if you are so hungry."

It took Lois but a short time upstairs, and when she came down she found the three men in the dining-room. Her father was in one of his surly moods, and this she could tell at the first glance. He was a short man, somewhat stout, and pompous both in appearance and manner. Fortunate it was that his only daughter had inherited none of his qualities, but was more like her mother, whose memory she cherished with undying affection. Since her death home had been more of a prison to her than anything else. Neither her father nor her only brother had understood her, and she was forced to depend more and more upon her own reliant self.

"What kept you so late, Lois?" her father asked as soon as she had taken her place at the table. "You know very well that I do not like to wait for dinner."

"I am very sorry, father," was the reply, "but I became so greatly interested in an old man and a girl out on the river that I had no idea how time was passing."

"Who were they, Lois?" her brother enquired.

"What new creatures have you picked up now? You haven't run out of homeless cats and dogs, have you?"

The colour mounted to Lois' temples at these words, for it was not the first time she had been sneered at for her tenderness of heart for all suffering creatures. With difficulty she restrained an angry reply, and went on calmly with her dinner.

"Come, Lois," Sammie urged, "never mind Dick. He must have his little joke, don't you know. He was only in fun."

"A joke with a sharp thorn in it isn't much fun," and Lois looked Sammie full in the eyes. "One might do far worse than take an interest in such people as I met this afternoon out upon the river. They appealed to me very much and I am not ashamed to confess it. The man is a perfect gentleman, while the girl is so pretty, and full of life and fun."

"What's her name?" Dick asked. "I'm getting quite excited over her."

"She's Betty Bean, so she told me, and the old man is David Findley."

"What, Crazy David, that miserable pauper?" Mr. Sinclair asked. "And you call such a creature a gentleman?"

"Certainly, and why not? His face is so beautiful, and his whole manner shows that he has moved much in refined society."

"Ho, ho, that's a good one," and Dick leaned back in his chair and laughed aloud. "Crazy David a gentleman, with a beautiful face, and refined manners! Think of that, dad."

"Lois evidently doesn't know that Crazy David is a pauper, the Devil's Poor, and was sold to Jim Goban to board and lodge for a year. He went pretty low, so I understand."

At these words an expression of surprise came into Lois' eyes, mingled with indignation. She looked keenly into her father's face, thinking that he must be merely joking.

"I can hardly believe that what you say is true," she at length remarked. "I did not know that such things were carried on in a Christian community. Is it possible that an old man such as that was sold like a cow or a horse to the lowest bidder!"

"Well, what else could have been done with him, then?"

"Wasn't there any one in the whole parish, willing to take care of him?"

"H'm, I guess people have all they can do to look after themselves without being burdened with a half-cracked creature such as that. It was the best thing they could do. It would not be fair for one person to have the entire expense of keeping him, so by this method all have a share in his support."

"But I call it degrading," Lois insisted, "not only to the old man himself, but to the people living here. He seems such a gentleman, that I was drawn to him this afternoon."

"Going to take him under your wing, eh?" Dick bantered. "He'll be as interesting as your other protege, I assure you. By the way, I saw him this afternoon, and he looked his part all right, ho, ho," and Dick laughed as he gulped down his tea.

"Who's that, Dick?" Mr. Sinclair inquired.

"Oh, Lois knows," was the reply. "She can tell you all about 'Spuds' as well as I can, and maybe better."

"Why should I know?" his sister asked, somewhat sharply. "I only met him once, and that was years ago."

"But you always take his part, though, so he seems to be somewhat under your care."

"And why shouldn't I? He deserves great credit for what he has done, and it is very unbecoming of you to make fun of him."

"I wish you could have seen him this afternoon, though," and Dick glanced across the table at Sammie. "We were speeding along in the car when we saw him hoeing potatoes in a field by the road. His clothes were all soiled, his sleeves rolled up, and he looked like a regular bushman. I called out to him as we sped past, and you should have seen the expression on his face when he saw us. It was like a thunder cloud. I guess he felt pretty well cut up at being caught at such work, ha, ha."

"Whom are you talking about, anyway?" Mr. Sinclair demanded. "What's all this about 'Spuds,' I'd like to know?"

"Oh, it's only that country chap we met several years ago, don't you remember?" Dick explained. "His real name, I believe, is Jasper Randall, though we have always called him Spuds, because he was digging potatoes when we first met him."

"You don't mean that big overgrown boy who helped us to carry Lois home the day she sprained her ankle at Daltan Creek?"

"The very same, dad. And you remember what fun we had at the way he sat and drank his tea out of the saucer?"

"But I didn't." Lois spoke sharply, while a flush mantled her cheeks.

"Oh, no, you didn't make fun," Dick laughed. "You were mad through and through, and gave us a good solid lecture afterwards."

Lois made no reply, so while the men talked, she let her mind dwell upon that scene of years ago. She saw again the lank awkward lad who was so concerned about her accident. While helping to carry her home, he had been much at his ease, and his eyes glowed with a sympathetic light. But when once in the house, his natural shyness had come upon him, and he did not know what to do with himself in the presence of strangers. One thing stood out above everything else, and that was his look of indignant defiance when Dick laughed because he drank his tea out of the saucer. She liked the way he had straightened himself suddenly up, while his eyes flashed with a peculiar light. The next that she heard of him was several years later when he entered college in Dick's year. Then every time her brother had come home he had such stories to tell her about Spuds. And so he was now living near working on a farm. Why did he not go home? she asked herself. She wondered also what he looked like now. Was he lank and awkward as when she saw him? She longed to ask Dick several questions, but desisted, knowing that it would be to little purpose. Her brother would only make fun of him, and she would be sure to get angry.

When supper was over, the men sauntered out upon the verandah for a smoke. Lois went, too, but sat somewhat apart with a piece of needlework in her hands. She preferred to be alone that she might think. She thought first of old David, and his pitiable condition. What could she do to help him? she asked herself. It was not right that he should be kept as a pauper while there were several people in the parish who could provide for him without the least trouble. Her father was one of them, and she was determined to speak to him just as soon as she could.

From old David it was only natural that her mind should turn to Jasper Randall. She recalled his animated face the day her ankle had been sprained. He was but a big overgrown boy then, and she had just graduated from school. She had never forgotten him, and had followed his career while at college as well as she could from what her brother told her. And so he was now working on a farm nearby. A longing came upon her to see him, and to learn if he had changed much since that day years ago. As she glanced toward her brother and Sammie, so effeminate in their manner, and dressed with such scrupulous care, a feeling of contempt smote her. They disdained honest toil, and would scorn to soil their soft white hands with manual labor. But over there was a young man toil-worn, and no doubt sunburnt, clad in rough clothes earning his living by the sweat of his brow. Such a person appealed to her. He would form an interesting study, if nothing else. There must be some connection between that potato patch and the college, she told herself, and she was determined to find out what it was.

As she thus sat and worked, her thoughts keeping time to her fingers, Sammie came and took a seat by her side. She glanced quickly up, with a shade of annoyance on her face. They were alone on the verandah, for her father and Dick were nowhere to be seen.

"You are very quiet this evening, Lois," the young man began. "I have been watching you for the last half hour, and you never looked our way once, nor took any interest in what we were saying. You are not offended, are you?"

"Offended! At what?" Lois asked as she let her needlework fall upon her lap.

"At me. Have I done anything to annoy you?"

"I wasn't thinking about you at all, Sammie," and Lois looked him full in the eyes. "My mind was upon more important things."

"And you don't consider me important?" the young man demanded, visibly embarrassed.

"Why should I? What have you done that you should be considered important?"

"But my father is rich, and we belong to a good old family. I am a gentleman, and that should count for much."

"So you seem to think," was the somewhat sarcastic reply. "I do not for a moment deny that such things are valuable, but they count for very little in my estimation of a true man. He must prove his worth in the battle of life, and show to the world that he is something apart from how much money his father may have or his family history. Now what have you done that I should consider you important?"

"Nothing at present, Lois, for I am not through college yet. But I am going to do great things some day, and then you will change your opinion of me."

"I hope so," and Lois gave a sigh as she picked up her work.

"You don't believe what I say?" and Sammie reddened.

"Not until I see you settle down to something definite. You do not know how to work, and how, then, can you expect to succeed?"

"But you would not want to see me working like Spuds, for instance, would you?"

"And why not? He is not afraid to soil his hands at honest labor. Why he is doing so I do not know, but there must be some good reason."

"Oh, I know. He wants money to help him to finish his college course. He left very suddenly, so I understand. Of course, he was not in our set, and so I know very little about him. He studied hard, and kept much to himself, so he has always been somewhat of a mystery. But say, Lois, never mind talking about him. I want to ask you something, for I am going away to-morrow."

"What is it, Sammie?" and again Lois laid down her work. She had an idea what he wanted to say, though it did not affect her in the least.

"I — I want to s-say," the young man stammered, "that you are the o-only —"

Sammie was suddenly arrested in his protestation of love by Dick's voice at the door.

"Say, come inside," he called. "It's beginning to rain, and it's spoiled my ride this evening. It's going to be confounded dull to-night, so give us some music, Lois, to liven things up a bit."

With an amused smile, his sister willingly obeyed. Sammie followed her into the house, mentally cursing Dick for his untimely interruption.

CHAPTER IV

A LITTLE CABIN

Betty and old David had a great afternoon out upon the water in the small row-boat. They were delighted with Lois, and after she had left them they watched her until she disappeared within the house.

"Isn't she wonderful!" Betty exclaimed, as she at length picked up the oars which had been lying unused in the bottom of the boat.

"Who is she, anyway?" her companion asked, for it was evident that he was as much lost in admiration as was the girl.

"Oh, she's Miss Sinclair, Lois, they call her, and her father is very rich. He is president, or something like that, of the street railway and the electric light company in the city. Ma knows all about him, and she has told me a whole lot. He was very poor once, so she says. He's awful mean and stuck up and won't have anything to do with the people he knew when he was young. But his daughter isn't a bit like him. She takes after her mother, so I understand, who was a very fine woman."

"Does Mr. Sinclair live here all the time?" David inquired. "I never heard of him before."

"Oh, no. He has a big house in the city. He only bought this place last summer. Lois has never been here before. She came two weeks ago and I think she is going to stay till fall. I hope she does, anyway. Won't it be great to have her here, so we can meet her and talk to her every Saturday afternoon?"

"She seems to be a very fine young woman," David assented.

"Indeed she is, and she's a nurse, too. She's been away training in some hospital for several years, and has just got through."

"Why should she want to be a nurse?" David asked. "If her father has plenty of money why should his daughter want to earn her own living?"

"It's because she's so independent, that's why. She believes every one should earn her own living, and I guess she's right."

A pained expression suddenly overspread the old man's face at these words. But so engrossed was Betty with her own thoughts that she noticed nothing amiss.

"I am going to be a nurse some day," the girl continued. "Just as soon as I am old enough I am going to enter a hospital. Then when I get through I can earn so much money and be such a help at home. And I'm going to help you, too," she added as an afterthought.

"No, child, that will not be necessary then," David replied. "I shall have plenty of money of my own by the time you are a nurse. I shall be manager of the biggest company the country has ever known, for it cannot be long now before people realise how wonderful is the scheme I have worked out. They have been very slow to see, but I am sure that a great change is soon to take place."

"But you might be sick, though," the girl insisted, "and will need me to nurse you. I won't charge you anything, for I shall gladly do it for nothing because it will be you."

"Oh, I wouldn't let you do it for nothing," was the reply. "I shall pay you well and make up for all your kindness to me now when I am so poor."

In this manner the two sat and talked. Happy were they for the time, thinking and planning of the future which looked so bright in their eyes. Neither did they notice for a while where they had drifted, for a stiff wind had risen and was drawing down the creek. It was Betty who first realised their situation. "Oh, look where we are!" she cried, seizing the oars, and placing them in the row-locks. "We can never get back against this wind, and the water is getting rougher all the time. I believe it is going to rain."

"Let me row," David suggested. "I should be stronger than you."

"Did you ever row?" the girl asked.

"Only once. But I think I could do it, though."

"Well, I don't think you could. You're not nearly as strong as I am."

With that she settled herself to the task of pulling back into the creek against the wind which was dead ahead. For some time there was silence as she toiled steadily at the oars. Gradually, however, her strokes became weaker, and she was forced to rest.

"I can't do it," she gasped. "The wind is too strong."

"What are we to do, then?" David asked.

"Land on that shore over there. I guess we can reach it all right."

Again seizing the oars, she swung the boat partly around and pointed for the shore. It was much easier now, and she made considerable progress. The wind increased in strength, and at times the water dashed over the side of the boat. To add to their discomfort the rain began to fall, and by the time the shore was reached their clothes were wet, and David felt cold.

"Help me pull up the boat," Betty ordered. "We'll tie it to that tree, and then we'll look around for some shelter. There's a raftsman's cabin not far away, and maybe we can stay there."

With the boat securely fastened, they made their way along the shore until they came to a path leading up from the water. Following this through the bushes, they soon reached an open space, and there before them appeared a small building covered with tarred paper.

"That's the place," Betty exclaimed, "and I know there is a stove there for I was in it once. The raftsmen used it this last spring. We can build a fire and dry our clothes before we go home."

Betty was the first to reach the cabin, and as she pushed open the door she gave a cry of surprise.

"What's the matter?" David inquired, thinking that she had been frightened.

But Betty did not at once reply. She stood in the middle of the room, looking around in a bewildered manner.

"Well I never!" she at length declared. "Why the place is all fixed up, and somebody must surely be living here. Who can it be, for I never heard a word about it, and I thought that I knew everything that was going on in this parish. Just look at that table now, with the dishes all washed so clean. And there are books, too," she added, "and pictures on the wall. I never knew a man could keep a room so neat."

"How do you know that it is a man?" David asked. "Perhaps it is a woman."

"Why, that's easy enough," and Betty looked around the room. "Don't you see a man's boots there, his clothes hanging up by the stove, and a package of tobacco on the window-sill? I guess it's a man all right."

"Perhaps you are right," David assented. "You know more about such things than I do. Anyway, it's nice to be here out of the storm. But do you think the man will mind when he comes back and finds us here? He might be very angry with us."

"Let him get angry, then," and Betty gave her head a slight toss. "I don't care for angry men. If I can match Jim Goban, I guess I can handle any man who comes here. Leave that to me, and don't you worry. I'm going to do a little exploring, anyway. I want to see what's in that other room. Ah, just what I thought," she continued, when she had opened the door and entered. "It's the bed-room, and the bed is not made. That shows all right that a man lives here. A woman would never think of going away and leaving the bed like that. I'm going to open the window and air the room. Men always keep the windows shut tight, and the house gets so stuffy. There, that's better," she panted, as after some difficulty she forced the window up. "I'm going to make up that bed just as soon as I get the fire going."

There was a box full of dry wood behind the stove, and soon she had a fire burning brightly. She next partly filled a small kettle with water and set it upon the stove.

"You had better take off your wet coat," she suggested to David. "You'll get your death of cold if you keep it on much longer."

"Can't I help you?" the old man inquired, as he stood watching with admiration the girl's light step and the skilful way she did everything. There was a longing in his eyes as well, for he wanted to be of some use but did not know how.

"Yes, you can help me," and Betty smiled upon him, "by taking that coat off and sitting down upon that nice cosy place near the stove. It was certainly made for comfort, and the man who owns this building must spend his evenings there. What a lot of books he has. He must read a great deal."

David was only too glad to obey, so after he had taken off his coat and hung it up back of the stove to dry, he stretched himself at full length upon the settle.

"This does feel good," and he gave a sigh of relief.

"You're tired, that's what's the trouble with you," Betty replied. "You shouldn't have a bit of work to do. You're too old, and you should have some one to look after you all the time."

"How nice it would be if we could live in a place like this, and not go back to Jim Goban's. Would you be willing to take care of me?" David asked.

"Sure, I would like nothing better. But, then, there are some things in the way."

"What are they?"

"Well, you see, there's the question of money. We haven't any ourselves, and I don't think any one is likely to drop it at our feet in a hurry. And besides, Jim's got you for a year and he wouldn't want to give you up; he's going to get a lot of work out of you, so he plans."

"I know that only too well, Betty. But when I get rich, I mean. If I had a little place like this you would look after me, would you not? I would pay you well, and we could be so happy."

"Indeed we could. But you haven't the money yet and we must try to be as happy as we can in the meantime. That's what ma says, and she really does practise it. So I've got to look after you now when you can't pay me. I'm going to see if I can't find something to eat. The man who lives here surely doesn't live on air. He must have some food in the house."

It did not take Betty long to find the cupboard. This was nothing more than a box nailed to the wall, on which a rude door had been fastened. There were three shelves and on these were a loaf of bread, some cold meat, potatoes, eggs and cheese.

"Isn't this great!" she exclaimed, as she brought forth what she needed. "I can warm up these potatoes, and we shall have a grand supper."

"I am worrying about the man who owns those things," David remarked. "He might not mind our using his house, but when it comes to making free with his provisions, it might be a different matter. Do you think it is right for us to touch them?"

"We won't take all," and Betty stood before the table eying the meat and potatoes. "We can leave enough for him. If he is a kind man he will not mind our taking some of his supper.

How dark it is getting," she added. "I shall light that lamp. Now, isn't that better," she continued when this had been accomplished. "We shall have supper in a short time."

While Betty busied herself about the stove, David remained stretched out upon the settle. Outside, the storm increased in fury, and the rain heat against the window. Within, all was snug and warm. The girl even hummed softly to herself as she went on with her work.

When supper was ready, Betty spoke to David. As he made no reply, she went to his side and, to her surprise, found that he was asleep. An expression of tender compassion came into the girl's eyes as she watched him. She knew how tired he was and she would not wake him. It was better, so she thought, that he should sleep. Drawing up a chair, she sat down by his side. A feeling came to her that it was her duty to care for this old man who was so helpless. She could not do much, but when Betty Bean had once made up her mind it was seldom that she could be turned from her purpose.

CHAPTER V

UNMASKED

All the morning Jasper Randall was busy hoeing potatoes in the large field near the main highway. He liked the work, for he was alone and could give himself up to thought as he drove the hoe into the yielding earth. His task suited him well, and as he tore out innumerable weeds, slashing down a big one here and another there, he was in reality overcoming and defeating opponents of the brain. They were all there between the rows, and he could see them so plainly. The lesser ones he could sweep away at one stroke, but that quitch grass was more difficult to conquer. He could cut it off, but its roots would remain firmly embedded in the ground and would spring forth again. It was a nasty, persistent weed. Little wonder that he attacked it most fiercely, for it reminded him of the weed of injustice with which he had been contending for years. Other enemies, like the smaller weeds, he could overcome, but injustice, that quitch grass of life, was what stung him to fury. Little did Simon Squabbles, the tight old skin-flint, realise that the lone man working in his potato field was doing the work of two men that morning, and at the same time slaying a whole battalion of bitter enemies. The contest was continued during the afternoon. The quitch grass was thicker now, and the struggle harder. With savage delight Jasper had just torn out a whole handful and had shaken it free from its earth as a dog would shake a rat, when the honk of an auto caused him to look toward the road. As he did so, his face underwent a marvellous transformation. The car was only a few seconds in passing, but it was sufficient for him to recognise the occupants, see the amused expression upon their faces, and hear their salutation of "Spuds," as they sped by. His strong, supple body trembled as he leaned for a while upon his hoe and gazed down the road after the rapidly disappearing car. He must have remained thus for several minutes oblivious to everything else. Neither did he see his hard taskmaster watching him in the distance. But when he again resumed his hoeing he worked more fiercely than ever, and there was danger at times lest the frail hoe should break beneath his tremendous strokes. Up one row and down another he moved all the afternoon. He seemed like a giant tearing up the earth, rather than a man performing a prosaic task. When toward evening the sky darkened, the wind began to blow and the rain to fall, he hardly noticed it at first. Only when the earth became mucky and stuck constantly to his hoe, did he leave his work and go across the field toward the barn. It was time, anyway, to help with the chores. He was anxious to get through that he might go home. He was glad that it was Saturday, for he would have the next day free.

It was dark by the time his tasks were done, and then he went to the house for his week's pay. He had agreed to work for a dollar and a half a day, and get his own breakfast and supper at home. Thus he had nine dollars coming to him for his week's work. He was surprised, therefore, when Simon Squabbles handed him out only eight dollars and fifty cents.

"There is some mistake here," Jasper remarked as he counted over the money. "I want fifty cents more."

"That's all you're goin' to get," Simon replied. "I saw ye loafin' this afternoon when ye should have been workin', an' 'no work, no pay' is my motto."

"Loafing, do you say?" Jasper asked, thinking that he had not heard aright.

"Sure. Didn't I see ye leanin' on yer hoe watchin' that car which went down the road? An' ye stood there a long time, too."

Into Jasper's eyes leaped an angry fire. He understood now the man he had to deal with. So he had been watching him, and he had taken no account of the work he had done all day.

"You were spying upon me, eh?" he retorted. "Didn't you see how I did the work of two men to-day?"

"All I know is that you were loafin' when I saw ye, an' that was enough."

"Look here, Simon Squabbles," and Jasper stepped close to his employer, "if you were not as old as you are, I'd tie you into a bowknot in the twinkling of an eye. You're not fit to be called a man, and not another stroke of work do you get from me. Keep the fifty cents, if it will do you any good. I am trying to make an honest living, but creatures such as you are the ones who make it almost impossible."

The blood surged through Jasper's veins as he plodded along the muddy road towards his humble cabin. The rain beat upon him and soaked his clothes, but he did not seem to heed it, so filled was his mind with the contemptible meanness of old Squabbles. He was in no pleasant mood, and his hands often clenched hard together as he moved through the darkness. What he was to do in the future, he did not know. Neither did he much care. A reckless spirit was upon him. The whole world was seething with injustice, so he believed. He had tried to be honest, to make his way, but he had been foiled at every step. Why should he try any longer? Simon Squabbles prospered through injustice; Dick Sinclair could ride along in his car, dressed in the height of fashion, while he had to eke out a precarious living by hoeing potatoes. Dick's father had made his money in an unscrupulous manner, and was held up as a shrewd business man. Would it not be as well for him to hurl himself into the game and win out, no matter how? Thinking thus, he came near his cabin, when a light arrested his attention. He stopped short in his tracks and peered through the darkness. At first he believed that he must be mistaken. But no, it shone steadily before him, and he knew that some one was there. The thought made him angry, and he hurried forward, determined to make an example of the one who had dared to meddle with his property. Reaching the building, he peered cautiously through the uncurtained window. As he did so, his anger suddenly ceased when he beheld the pathetic scene within, of an old man lying asleep upon the couch and a young girl patiently watching by his side. Why they were there he did not know, though he felt certain that great necessity must have driven them to take refuge in a strange cabin. He recognised old David as the man he had met that night on the road listening to the voice of Break Neck Falls. He knew that he had been sold to Jim Goban for one year, and the transaction had rankled in his soul for days. The girl he did not know, but she seemed to him like a ministering angel watching over the slumber of the sleeping man. This thought caused him to study her more intently, for notwithstanding his strength and independence of mind, he could not forget the pictures he had seen and the stories he had heard as a child of angels coming to earth on special deeds of mercy. He banished this idea, however, in an instant, and even smiled at his own foolishness as he turned away from the window and moved around the corner of the cabin.

He was about to push open the door and enter when a sudden notion came into his mind which caused him to pause. He stood there with the rain beating upon him as he thought over the idea. Then he stepped toward the door and gave a gentle tap. In a few seconds Betty stood before him, peering into the darkness. The sight of the large man stand-ing there caused her to start and draw somewhat back.

"Excuse me," Jasper began, "but could you give me shelter? It is a rough night and I am wet and hungry. I am sorry to disturb you, but I saw the light from the road and knew that some one was living here."

"Come in," the girl at once replied. "We have a good fire and supper is all ready, such as it is," and she gave a little laugh as she moved back into the room. "We are strangers, too, and I do not know what the owner will say when he comes back and finds us here."

"Oh, I shall take care of you," Jasper returned. "He won't make a fuss when he sees me. If he does, we'll pitch him out of the door, eh?"

"I guess you could do it all right," and Betty smiled as she looked at him. "Mr. David will be so pleased to see you when he wakes. He likes good company."

"How do you know I am good company?" Jasper asked. "Maybe I'm as cross as two sticks."

"Well, then, you can't stay if you are."

"You couldn't put me out, could you?"

"Couldn't I, though? I guess you don't know me. Jim Goban once said that I could beat the devil with my tongue alone, and I guess Jim ought to know by this time what I'm like when I get my ginger up. But you're not that kind of a man. I can tell by your eyes that you're all right. If you're a little cranky now, it's because you're hungry. As soon as you get something to eat you'll be as sweet as molasses candy. Most men are that way."

The sound of voices woke old David, and sitting suddenly up he looked inquiringly around the room as if uncertain where he was.

"Don't be afraid, Mr. David," Betty assured him. "Supper's all ready, and we have a visitor as hard up as we are to share it with us. So come at once and let us get through."

Jasper was greatly amused at the way Betty took full possession of everything in the place. There was nothing forward about her, for she seemed more like a grown-up woman than a girl. He admired her confident and buoyant manner, as well as the thoughtful and deferential way she looked after the old man. The best on the table was for him and he had to be served first. She treated him sometimes as a child, but more often as a superior being. He noted the look of reverential respect in her eyes as she turned them upon him, and he wondered.

During the meal David acted the part of a perfect gentleman. His manners could not have been better had he been at a royal banquet instead of a most humble repast in a rude cabin. He asked Jasper no questions but talked merely about his experience upon the river that afternoon. He was somewhat anxious lest the owner of the cabin should return and resent their intrusion. Jasper endeavoured to allay his fears, reminding him that no one in his senses would be angry at people seeking refuge on such a night.

During the meal Betty had been observing Jasper quite closely, and once the semblance of a twinkle might have been detected in her eyes. She made no remark, however, as to what she was thinking, but while the men smoked when supper was over, she busied herself washing up the few dishes.

Under the soothing influence of the tobacco David became talkative. He was pleased to have so attentive a listener as Jasper, and unfolded to him his wonderful secret.

"Mr. David is going to be a very rich man some day," Betty remarked, as she paused in wiping the dishes.

"I am pleased to hear that," Jasper replied. "Money is the only thing that counts these days."

"Yes," the girl continued, "he is going to be very rich, and I am going to look after him. We shall have such a nice little house and be so very, very happy."

While Betty was talking, the old man fumbled in an inside pocket and brought forth several papers.

"See," and he held one of them up so the light of the lamp would fall upon it, "it is all here. You can understand my plan much better from this. Here is Break Neck Falls, and just below it the plant will be placed. From there power will radiate throughout the entire country. The whole thing is so simple that it is a wonder to me that it has not been thought of before."

"Isn't it great!" Betty exclaimed, looking over the old man's shoulder. "And to think that Mr. David worked it all out himself."

As Jasper sat and watched the two animated faces before him, he had not the heart to say a word that would in any way dampen their enthusiasm. Nevertheless, it seemed to him so ridiculous that old David's scheme could ever meet with any success. How was he to interest people who had the means to carry his plan into effect? But if the thought of doing great things would give him any happiness, he would be the last one to remove such a hope.

The storm raged outside and the wind beat against the window as the three sat and talked. The room was warm and cosy, and Jasper was pleased to have these two visitors on such a lonely night. Simon Squabbles and his meanness he forgot for awhile as he listened to Betty as she told him of her home life. It was just what he needed to take him out of himself, and to make him think of others. But when the girl spoke of Lois and how she had been with them that afternoon on the river, he became doubly interested.

"Oh, you must see her," Betty exclaimed. "She is the most wonderful person I ever saw. Isn't it strange that you have never met her!"

"Why, what chance have I had?" Jasper asked. "Anyway, she wouldn't want anything to do with such a rough fellow as I am."

"Indeed she would. She's not that kind; there's nothing stuckup about her. Maybe you'll see her passing some day. She might call, too, for she is so friendly."

"Call! What do you mean? How could she call upon me if I am miles away from this place?"

"Oh, but you won't be. You'll be right here where you have been for some time."

Into Jasper's eyes came a look of surprise, and he felt his face flush under the girl's keen scrutiny.

"There, I knew I was right," she laughed in glee.

"You thought you could deceive me, did you?"

"Why, how in the world did you know that I live here?" Jasper asked. "Did anybody tell you?"

"No, certainly not. But the Lord didn't give Betty Bean eyes and a mind for nothing. Who else would be poking around this place on a night like this but the owner? And didn't you know where your dry coat was when you came in? And your slippers? And your pipe and tobacco? And —"

"There, there, you have produced evidence enough, and I plead guilty," Jasper laughed. He was greatly amused at the girl's quickness. "You are not offended, are you, at the little joke I played upon you?"

"Oh, no, not all. But next time you do anything like that try it upon a man. A woman's eyes are pretty sharp, and it's hard to deceive her. Mine are, anyway."

David had listened to this conversation and slowly the truth dawned upon him that the owner of the cabin was before him.

"I wish to apologise, sir," he began, "for our rudeness in entering your house. It was only necessity which compelled us to do so, I assure you, and when I am in a position, I shall recompense you handsomely for the entertainment to-night."

"Please do not say a word about it," Jasper replied. "I am very thankful that you have been able to make use of my humble abode. I have enjoyed your company very much. But I think it is time for us to retire, as you need rest. The girl can use that room there, while you can sleep upon that cot."

"But what about yourself?" David inquired.

"Oh, I shall make a place for myself right by the stove. I shall be very comfortable there."

David at first refused to listen to such an arrangement, but Jasper was determined and claimed a host's privilege of making his guests as comfortable as possible. He sat for some time at the little table after David and Betty had gone to sleep. He dwelt long and carefully upon the rude plan the old man had shown him. The more he studied it, the more convinced he became that there was a great deal in it after all. But it would mean much money, and he sighed as he at length blew out the light, stretched himself upon the floor, and drew a great coat over his body.

CHAPTER VI

OUT OF BONDAGE

During the night the storm broke, and the morning was fine and warm. After breakfast Jasper and David sat on a log outside and smoked. Betty was busy in the house, washing the dishes and tidying up the rooms. She hummed softly to herself as she moved lightly across the floor. She was anxious to get through as quickly as possible that she might take David back to Jim Goban's. She felt a little uneasy for his sake as she knew how angry his taskmaster would be with him. For herself she did not care. If Jim said too much, she could leave him at once. And yet she did not wish to go, for she felt that she must look after this old man who was so helpless and depended so much upon her for protection.

When her work was finished, she joined the men outside.

"It's time we were going, Mr. David," she began. "The river is calm now, and it will not be hard rowing back."

"I wish you could stay here all day," Jasper replied. "I shall feel very lonely when you go."

"But we shall come to see you again, sir. It has been so good of you to keep us. But Jim Goban will be angry if we do not hurry home. I know how he will rage as it is. The longer we stay the harder it will be for him," and she pointed to David.

Scarcely had she finished speaking ere a team was heard driving furiously along the road.

"Oh, it's Jim now!" the girl cried, "and I know he is mad by the way he is driving. He's stopping at the gate, too!"

Jim had seen them from the road, and having tied his horse to a tree, he made his way swiftly along the little path leading to the cabin. He was certainly in no pleasant frame of mind, and when he came near he gave vent to his feelings in coarse, brutal language.

David, rose and advanced to meet the angry man, hoping in some way to appease his rage, but in this he was mistaken.

"Ye old cuss," Jim shouted, "what do ye mean by runnin' away with that girl? Ye look as meek as a lamb but I guess ye're about as near a devil as they make 'em."

"He didn't run away with me," Betty sharply replied. "I ran away with him, that's the way it was, and you needn't get on your high horse, Jim Goban. You, yourself, would be the first one to run away with a girl if you could find one crazy enough to run with you."

"Shet up, ye fool," Jim shouted. "I didn't ask you to speak."

"I know you didn't," the girl calmly returned, "but that doesn't make any difference. This is a free country, isn't it? We didn't ask you to come here and make such a fuss, so you can go if you are not satisfied with our company. We're quite happy where we are."

"But I'm not goin' without that cuss," and Jim looked savagely at the old man. "You kin stay if ye want to with the guy who owns this cabin. There'll be a nice little story fer the gossips before long, ha, ha."

At these words Jasper started, while his face went white and his hands clenched together. He had listened in silence to Jim's tirade, and was only waiting an opportunity to explain how the old man and the girl happened to be at his place. But this pointed reference to him was more than he could endure.

"What do you mean by that statement?" he asked, taking a quick step forward. "Please explain yourself."

"There's nothin' to explain," and Jim gave a coarse laugh.

"The neighbours will do all the explainin' that is necessary."

"No, that's not the thing. You made an insinuation, and it's up to you to explain before you leave. I have nothing to do with the neighbours; it's you I am dealing with now. Yon have insulted this feeble old man, and uttered words in reference to me and this girl. I want to know what you mean."

"I don't have to explain anything," Jim retorted. "You mind yer own business, and go to —"

The oath had hardly left his lips ere Jasper with one lightning blow hit him squarely between the eyes. Jim reeled back, and then with a frightful oath leaped forward. But he was powerless before Jasper's superior training and soon he was sprawling upon the ground while his opponent stood bending over him.

"Had enough, eh?" Jasper asked. "If you want some more, get up. I haven't had half enough yet."

"Leave me alone," Jim mumbled. "You'll pay up for this. I'll fix ye."

"What's that you say?" and Jasper stooped lower, "You're going to pay me back? Well, then, I might as well fix you now, so you won't be able to do anything in the future. I might as well have my satisfaction when I can get it. So get up, or I'll knock the life out of your measley carcass."

Seeing that Jasper was in earnest, Jim scrambled to his feet and barely dodged the blow rained at his head.

"Fer God's sake, stop!" he yelled. "I won't do anything to ye. I promise on me word of honour."

"And, you'll be good to this old man?" Jasper demanded.

"Yes, yes," and Jim trembled in every limb. "I'll be good to him if ye don't hit me again."

For a few seconds Jasper looked contemptuously upon the creature cowering before film. He felt that he was lying, and just as soon as he was out of his sight he would treat old David in a shameful manner, and he himself would be helpless to interfere. What could he do? he asked himself. A sudden idea came into his mind.

"What do you get for the keep of this old man?" he asked.

"Only a hundred," was the surly reply. "Not half enough."

"Well, look here, will you give him to me? I will take care of him for nothing."

Into Jim Goban's eyes came a look of surprise mingled with doubt. The man must surely be making sport of him, he thought. Then his natural cupidity overcame him. Here was a chance to get clear of the pauper and at the same time receive money for his keep. But how would the overseers of the poor regard such a transaction?

"Will you let me have him?" Jasper again asked.

"Give me twenty-five dollars and he is yours," Jim replied.

"Twenty-five dollars! No, not a cent. You will make out of it as it is; far more than you deserve."

"I can't do it, then," and Jim made as though to go. "Come on," he ordered David and Betty. "Let's git away from here."

"Hold on," and Jasper stepped, up close to him; "if you do not let me have the old man, I'll lay a charge against you for ill treating him, I saw enough this morning to satisfy any one. Let me have him, and you need have no more worry. Refuse, and you will regret it."

"But what will the overseers say if I give him up?" Jim whined.

"Oh, that can be easily settled. If they make a fuss, send them to me. But I guess they won't bother their heads."

Jim still hesitated. He longed to get more out of this bargain.

"Hurry up," Jasper demanded. "What do you say?"

"Oh, take the cuss, then. I wish ye joy of him. I'm off now. Come, girl, let's git home."

During the whole of this affair Betty had been a most

interested and excited witness. She was delighted at the thought of David's freedom, and when Jim at last agreed to part with him she could hardly repress a cry of joy. It took her but a second to make up her mind, and she was ready when Jim spoke to her.

"I'm not going with you," she told him.

"Not goin'! Why, what d'ye mean?" and Jim looked his astonishment.

"I'm going to stay with Mr. David. He needs me more than you do. I'm going to take him to my own home. He will be happy there and treated like a gentleman."

"Ho, ho! so that's the game, eh? Treat him like a gentleman! Well, do as ye like; it's nothin' to me, so I'm off."

They watched him as he strode across the field, unhitched his horse and drove away.

"There, we're rid of him at last," and Jasper gave a sigh of relief.

"Isn't it great!" Betty exclaimed turning to David. "To think that you are going home with me!"

But the old man was looking at Jasper and did not hear the girl's cry of delight. In his eyes was an expression of gratitude. He tried to speak but words failed him, and tears flowed down his cheeks. Jasper was visibly moved, and turned suddenly to Betty.

"You are willing to keep him for awhile?" he asked.

"Yes. Mother will be so pleased to have him, and I will work hard to help her."

"Where will you work? At Jim Goban's?"

"No, I am through there. But I will get work somewhere. I will talk it over with mother. I think we had better be going now."

Thrusting his hand into his pocket Jasper brought forth several bills.

"Take these," he said, "they are all I can give you now, but you shall have more later."

"But you need the money yourself," the girl replied.

"Not as much as you will need it. So say nothing more about it. Good-bye. I hope to see you again."

Jasper watched the two as they moved slowly across the field and then disappeared down the road. He felt lonely when they were gone, and he sat for some time in front of the cabin lost in thought. At times he called himself a fool for what he had done. Why should he be burdened with that old man when he could hardly make his own living? And besides, he had no work to do, and had given away his last dollar. But notwithstanding all this, a secret feeling of satisfaction stole into his heart that he had helped old David and had taken him out of Jim Goban's clutches.

As he sat there the bell of the nearby church rang forth, and he realised for the first time that it was Sunday morning. He did not feel in a mood for attending service. He needed a long walk to think, and shake off the spirit of depression that was stealing over him.

Entering the cabin, he prepared a small lunch, and then closing the door he struck out across the field in the direction of Break Neck Falls. He wished to go there to view the scene where David planned to erect his plant and do such wonderful things. He smiled grimly to himself as he thought of the old man's delusion. Reaching the brow of the hill just where the trail started from the main road, he paused and looked down to his left. He could see clearly Peter Sinclair's house with the tall trees surrounding it. Bitter feelings came into his heart as he stood there. Over yonder lived a man who had the power to do so much good in the world. He could help old David and give him a comfortable home for the rest of his life. Why should some men have so much of this world's goods and others so little? he asked himself. Then he thought of Dick, and a contemptuous smile curled his lips. He recalled his feelings the previous day when he had watched the car go by and listened to the salutation of "Spuds."

And standing there his feelings suddenly underwent a marvellous change, for walking slowly across the field was Lois on her way to church. She was some distance away so Jasper was sure that she could not see him. As in the past so now he was forced to worship her afar off. It was not for him, poor and unknown, to draw any closer. The trees along the path she walked could bend above her and the bright flowers could smile up into her face. But for him there could be no such favours. He was half tempted to hasten back to church. There he could be quite near and watch her. He banished this thought, however, as he glanced down at his own rough clothes and coarse boots.

Jasper watched Lois until she disappeared from view behind a clump of birch trees. Then leaving the highway he walked slowly along the trail leading to the falls.

CHAPTER VII

AT THE CLOSE OF A DAY

High up on the bank of the brook which flows down from Break Neck Falls Jasper sat leaning against the bole of a large tree. It was drawing toward evening and long slanting shadows were falling athwart the landscape. It was a hot afternoon and the shade of the old spruce was refreshing. By his side was a rough birch fishing rod, and nearby wrapped up in cool, moist leaves were several fair-sized trout. Jasper had not been fishing for pleasure, but merely for food, as his scanty supply was almost gone. The fish would serve him for supper and breakfast. Beyond that he could not see, for he had not the least idea what he was to do to earn a living, and at the same time assist old David.

Though the day was exceptionally fine, Jasper did not enjoy it as at other times. His mind was too much occupied with other matters. All things seemed to be against him in his struggle to advance. It had been the same for years, and now the climax had been reached. What was he to do? he had asked himself over and over again during the afternoon. Should he give up in despair? What was the use of trying any longer? He had seen young men succeeding in life who had not made any efforts. Money and influence had pushed them along. Dick Sinclair would soon join their ranks. He had lived, a life of indolence, and yet it would be only a short time ere he would be looked upon as a prominent citizen. The papers would speak of his ability and write glowing articles about whatever he did. Where was the justice of it all? he questioned. Did not real worth and effort amount to anything in life's struggle?

At length, tired with such thoughts, he drew forth from an inside pocket a small book. It was well marked and showed constant usage. It was a volume of Emerson's Essays, a number of which he knew almost by heart. It was only natural that the book should open at the essay on Self-reliance, for there the pages were most thumb-marked. His eyes rested upon the words: "There is a time in every man's education when he arrives at the conviction that envy is ignorance." He read on to the beginning of the next paragraph, "Trust thyself: every heart vibrates to that iron string."

The book dropped from Jasper's hand and once more he gave himself up to thought. He knew how true were those words. He realised that envy is ignorance, and it was his duty to rise above it. Why should he spend his strength in envying others? He would conquer and make them envy him. Ah, that idea brought a flush to his face. He would trust himself, as Emerson said, and some day the very ones who looked down upon him and spurned him would come to him. How he was to accomplish this Jasper had no idea. But there was comfort in thinking about it, anyway, and he felt sure that a way would be opened whereby he could succeed.

He was aroused from his musing by the sound of voices. Looking quickly down toward the brook, he saw three people walking along the bank. He recognised them at once as Lois, Dick and Sammie. At first he was tempted to withdraw farther back among the trees lest he should be seen. He abandoned this idea, however, feeling quite certain that he would not be noticed where he was. Lois and Sammie were walking together, while Dick was a short distance ahead. What they were saying he could not make out, neither did he care. He had eyes only for the young woman, and he noted how beautiful she appeared as she walked with such an upright graceful swing. Was she happy in Sammie's company? he wondered. She was laughing now, and seemed to be greatly amused at something her companion was saying. Jasper noted all this, and then called himself a fool for imagining that she could ever think of him. No doubt she had already given her heart to the young man by her side, so he might as well banish her from his mind at once. He would go away and never see her again.

Acting upon this impulse, he was about to move softly among the trees and disappear. He had placed his book in his pocket and had reached for his fish when a cry of terror fell upon his ears. In an instant he was on his feet, peering keenly down to see what was the matter. In a twinkling he grasped the whole situation. Just across the brook a wall of rough rocks shelved upwards to the height of about twenty feet. Below, the water swirled and dashed over jagged boulders, receiving its impetus from the falls farther up stream. The path led along the top, and in some unaccountable manner Lois had slipped and fallen over the edge, and had gone swiftly down toward the rushing current below. She grasped frantically at everything on which she could lay her hands, and was only able to arrest her downward descent when a few feet from the water. And there she clung with the desperation of despair, while her two companions stood above half-paralysed with fear, and unable to assist her.

When Jasper saw Lois go down to what seemed certain destruction, he sprang forward and leaped down the bank as if shot from a catapult. Into the brook he recklessly dashed and like a giant forced his way across the current and around hidden boulders. At times it seemed as if he could not keep his feet and that he must be swept away. But that picture of the clinging woman nerved him to superhuman efforts, and slowly but surely he edged his way toward her. When a few feet from the base of the rock, he saw Lois relax and slip downward. Barely had she touched the water ere Jasper with a mighty effort leaped forward and caught her in his arms. Then in an instant they were both swept away. Fortunately, Jasper was a strong swimmer, and as they shot forward he was able to keep Lois' head above water, and work steadily toward the shore.

By this time Dick and Sammie had so far recovered from their fright that they were able to hurry down stream, and stand on the edge of the stream where the bank sloped gently to the water. Here they stood for several fearful seconds watching Jasper as he struggled toward them. They took special care not to wet their feet, but merely reached out and helped to pull Lois ashore and lay her upon the dry ground. More than that they were unable to do, and naturally turned toward Jasper for help.

"We must get her home at once," the latter remarked, kneeling by the side of the prostrate woman. "I am afraid she has been injured by the fall."

Fortunately, at that instant Lois opened her eyes and fixed them upon him in a dazed manner. Then she remembered what had happened, and sat suddenly up and looked around.

"My, I have given you a great fright," she said. "It was stupid of me to trip over that root."

"Are you hurt, Lois?" Dick inquired.

"I am somewhat bruised, that is all. I think I must have fainted and let go of the rock. How did I get here?"

"Oh, Spuds got hold of you and brought you out," Dick explained.

Lois at once turned her eyes upon Jasper who was now standing a few feet away. She noticed his drenched clothes, and also that there was blood upon his forehead.

"You are hurt," she cried. "You have struck your head."

"It's nothing, I assure you," and Jasper gave a slight laugh. "I must have hit it against a rock when we went down, that was all. It will soon get better. Never mind me, I am all right. But you must get home at once."

"Yes, come, Lois," and Sammie, speaking for the first time

since the accident, stepped forward. "We must get you home
at once. Never mind this fellow; he doesn't matter."

"Indeed he does," Lois emphatically replied. "He saved my
life, and I can never thank him enough."

"But I would have saved you, Lois. I was just coming to rescue you when this fellow, who was spying upon us from the
bushes, got to you first."

Lois never forgot the look on Jasper's face as the jealous
Sammie uttered this insinuation. He drew himself up to his
full height, and his eyes glowed with a sudden light of anger.
She saw his lips move as if about to utter words of protest.
Instead, however, he quickly turned, left them, and walking
along the bank for a short distance reached a fordable place in
the brook. He plunged into the water and after a brief struggle
reached the opposite bank and disappeared among the trees.

Lois stood and watched him until he was out of sight. She
was faint and greatly annoyed at Sammie's words. She knew
now what a cad and a coward he really was, and was not even
man enough to give credit to the one who had rescued her.

"Come, Dick," and she turned to her brother, "let's go
home," was the only remark she made, as she took his arm
and walked slowly along the path leading from the brook. She
took no notice of the crestfallen Sammie, who trudged along
behind wondering what had come over the young woman that
she should act in such a strange manner.

Jasper could not fully understand the strange feeling that had
come over him at Sammie's unjust insinuation. His first lightning thought was to knock the fellow down. Then he wanted
to explain, to say that he had not been spying. But he knew
that if he spoke he might get excited. No, it was better for him
to leave at once, and let Lois think whatever she liked. He
had saved her and that was all he cared for. But as he moved
along through the woods, the few words she had said and the

expression in her eyes acted as balm to his wounded feelings. He made up his mind, however, not to be caught in such a way again. He would take good care to keep away from the Sinclairs after that.

Going back to the place where he had left his fish, he picked them up and started down along the brook. He wished to get back to his cabin as quickly as possible that he might change his wet clothes. He was hungry as well, and he longed for a couple of the trout he had caught. He thought much of Lois, and wondered how she was getting along. He hoped that she had not been seriously injured and that she would not catch cold from her plunge into the water. He could not forget the feeling that had come over him as he had sprung forward and caught her as she was falling. He should remember that sensation for the rest of his life, no matter what happened.

Having reached the end of the trail, he moved swiftly along the main highway. He was almost to his cabin when he saw an auto by the side of the road. Something had evidently gone wrong, for two men were anxiously examining it. Jasper was about to pass when one of the men accosted him.

"Excuse me," he began, "but could you tell me if there is a hotel or any place where we can get supper? We have been stalled here for some time, and my chauffeur can't find what is the matter with the car."

"There is no hotel," Jasper replied, "and I know of no people who serve meals. But I have a place right near, and you are welcome to such accommodation as I have. It is very humble, and I warn you not to expect much. I have merely bachelor's quarters, and so am my own housekeeper."

"Thank you kindly," the man returned, "I am very grateful to you, and we shall be delighted to go with you, though we do not wish to trouble you too much. The trout you have make my mouth water. You evidently went in head-first after them," and he smiled as he observed the young man's wet clothes.

Jasper liked this man, and this impression was increased as they walked toward the cabin. He was well spoken, and so gentlemanly in manner that he found it quite easy to converse with him. Everything seemed to interest and please him, especially the cabin. He called Jasper a lucky fellow for having such a place where he could live so quietly away from all bustle and stress of the great outside world.

"It is quiet enough as a rule," Jasper remarked with a laugh, as he lighted the fire in his little stove after he had changed his wet clothes for dry ones.

"Have you lived here long?" the stranger inquired, as he stretched himself out upon the cot.

"Since the middle of May," was the reply. "But I expect to leave shortly. I'm out of a job now, and so must look elsewhere."

"What have you been working at?"

"Oh, anything that turns up."

The stranger was quick to note the almost hopeless tone in Jasper's voice as he uttered these words, and he studied the young man more closely.

"Where did you live before you came here?" he asked.

"At college. I was almost through when reverses came, and so I had to get out. I have been trying to earn enough to finish my course, but everything seems to be against me. I understand farming and naturally took to the land in preference to other work."

"What were you studying at college?" the man asked.

"Electrical engineering."

"I see. But was there not something you could have obtained along that line? Surely there must have been some opening."

Jasper made no reply. There was a reason, but he did not feel inclined to reveal his secret to a complete stranger, upon such a brief acquaintance.

CHAPTER VIII

THE SHADOW OF MYSTERY

When supper was over, the stranger lighted a cigar and stretched himself out upon the cot.

"This is certainly comfort," he remarked, as he watched Jasper clear away the dishes. "It is fortunate that we have found such hospitality. You do not have many such visitors, I suppose. It must be rather lonely for you here."

"Not as a rule, though I have been much favoured lately," Jasper replied with a laugh, and he told how his cabin had been taken possession of the previous night.

"Well, that was cool, I should say," and the stranger smiled. "Walked right in, did they?"

"But I didn't mind, for they were such a queer couple; a feeble old man, and a bright, smart girl of about sixteen. It was nice for me to have them here on such a stormy night. I would have been very lonely, otherwise."

"Where are they now?"

"They left this morning. It is a sad story. But as they are strangers to you, it would hardly interest you."

"Indeed it would," was the emphatic reply. "I am somewhat new to this country, and would like to find out all I can about the life of the people, especially in the country districts."

When Jasper had finished washing the dishes, he sat down upon a chair by the side of the cot, and lighted the cigar his visitor had given him. He then related the story of old David and Betty, taking care to say as little as possible about his own part in the affair.

"And so the old man is at the girl's home now, is he?" the stranger asked.

"Yes, for a time."

"But what will become of him?"

"I do not know for certain. I shall try to assist him all I can. But he will not go back to Jim Goban's if I can help it. It is the height of cruelty for such a refined man to live at a place like that. I do not know what the people of this parish were thinking about to allow him to be put there."

"Has he any relatives?"

"It seems not. He has been a puzzle to every one since the day he came here. He has been the laughing-stock of all the people because of a peculiar notion of his."

"And what is that?"

"He is in love with Break Neck Falls over there, and talks to it as if it were a human being. He believes that the time will come when people will obtain power and light from the falls, and the entire country will be greatly benefited."

"So that is why he is called crazy, eh?"

"Yes."

"Is there really a good reason for his idea? Is there a large waterfall?"

"Yes. I have been there several times, and consider it a good place for a plant. The old man has curious drawings of his entire plans, which I shall show you as he left them with me this morning. He must have forgotten them in his excitement, as I understand he guards them very carefully. People laugh at Crazy David for the jealous way he protects his treasure."

"Did you say his name is David?" the stranger asked.

"Yes. David Findley, so I believe. But he is only known as 'Crazy David' in this parish."

As Jasper uttered these words, the man lying on the cot rose suddenly to a sitting position, and looked keenly into the face of the young man before him as if he would read his innermost thoughts. With an apparent effort he checked himself, and with a slight laugh resumed his former position.

"I got worked up over the hard luck of that old man," he remarked. "It is a downright shame that he should be called crazy, and misunderstood. But, then, that has always been the way. Men who have done most for their fellow men have been looked upon with suspicion, and termed fools or madmen. May I see his drawings?"

For some time the stranger studied the rude lines old David had made upon the paper. Not the slightest mark escaped his notice, and he plied Jasper with numerous questions most of which the latter was unable to answer.

"I am fond of studying human nature," the visitor at length volunteered, as if to explain his remarkable interest in the old man, "and I must say that this is one of the most interesting cases I have ever come across. Here we have an old, poverty-stricken man, somewhat weak-minded, who has the vision and the enthusiasm of youth, combined with a child's simplicity. And he really believes that people of capital will carry out his ideas, does he?"

"Yes, he is sure of it."

"And he has no doubts as to the final outcome?"

"No."

"This scheme gives him considerable pleasure, I suppose."

"Yes, it is his very life. It cheers him and buoys him up, and makes him treat all discomforts as of the present, which will vanish when once he comes into his own."

"So he expects to get very rich, does he?"

"Oh, yes. He talks about what he will do when he has money. It certainly would be a great pity to take such a hope from him. I believe it would kill him at once."

For a long time they talked, and it was late when they went to bed, the stranger with the chauffeur in the adjoining room, and Jasper upon the cot. The latter found it hard to get to sleep, as many thoughts kept surging through his mind. He wondered why his visitor should take such a keen interest in the welfare of old David. He recalled, too, his sudden start when David's name was mentioned, and the excuse which had been given did not altogether satisfy him.

Jasper was awake early next morning, and had the frugal breakfast ready by the time his two visitors came from their room. As soon as breakfast was over, the chauffeur left to look after the car. The stranger then pushed back his chair, lighted a cigar, and handed one to Jasper.

"Please do not trouble about the dishes now," he began in a tone which somewhat surprised the young man.

"I have been thinking over what you told me last night, and am greatly impressed by the sad condition of that old man. You have no work in view, so I understand?"

"You are right," Jasper replied.

"Well, then," the other continued, "I wish to make a definite proposition to you on several conditions. I wish to employ you for one month, and will give you one hundred and fifty dollars, if that will be satisfactory."

It was Jasper's turn now to start, and look with astonishment at the man before him. Was he in earnest? he asked himself, or was he merely joking?

"Ah, I see you are astonished," and the stranger smiled, "but I assure you that I mean what I say, and to prove it, I shall pay you in advance."

"But what are the conditions?" Jasper stammered.

"They are three," the stranger replied after a slight pause. "First, that you are to take special care of that old man. How you are to do it I shall explain later. In the next place you are to ask no questions as to why I am doing this. And last of all, you are not to say who is doing this, neither to the old man nor, in fact, to any one."

For a few seconds Jasper looked at the stranger in a quizzical manner. He was wondering whether the man was really in his right mind.

"Isn't that a strange proposition to put to one you know so little about?" he asked.

"In most cases it might be," was the quiet reply. "But I have good reasons for what I am doing, and do not think that there will be any mistake. Are you willing to enter my employment for a month?"

"Now, that all depends. I need the money, God knows, but I must understand more about what is expected of me in connection with the care of the old man."

"I can easily settle that. You are first of all to get a good place for him to live, and, if possible, secure some dependable person to be his companion who will take a special interest in his welfare. You are to keep a detailed account of all expenses, and send the bill to me at the end of the month. This address will find me," and he drew forth a card and handed it to the young man.

There was nothing on the card to reveal to Jasper the identity of the man who was taking such a remarkable interest in old David. It simply told that the stranger's name was Robert Westcote, of 22 Princess Street, Woldun.

"I think everything is satisfactory now," and Jasper lifted his eyes to the stranger's face. "I am not likely to ask any questions, and as to telling people who you are, there will be no trouble about that. In fact, I am not intimate enough with any one here to wish to tell, even if I desired to do so."

"That is good," Mr. Westcote replied. "I could not have chosen a better person for my purpose."

"When do you want me to begin my work?" Jasper asked,

"At once, that is, if you can see your way to do so. But first of all, I should like to visit this old man. I am somewhat curious about him now that he is under my protection. How far is he from here?"

"About five miles, I should judge, though I have never been there myself. He is at Mrs. Bean's, and she lives on a back road."

"Very well, then, we shall go just as soon as the car is ready, and I should like for you to go with me."

It took the chauffeur some time to find out what was the matter with the car, and when the damage was repaired, the three started down the road at a fast rate. This was something new to Jasper, and he leaned back in the comfortable seat and gave himself up to the enjoyment of the moment. He need not worry any more for the present about his living, as he had a cheque for one hundred and fifty dollars safely stowed away in his pocket. As to the mystery connected with it all, he did not feel inclined to bother his head. In fact, he was becoming greatly interested, and was now quite anxious to see what the final outcome would be, and why this stranger had taken such an unusual interest in an old pauper.

It did not take them long to reach Mrs. Bean's house, where they drew up before the gate. It was a small, humble abode, but everything about the place was scrupulously neat and clean. Flowers bloomed in front of the house, while several large trees stood a short distance away. Under one of these they saw old David sitting in a rocking-chair with Betty by his side. She had been reading to him but had laid down her book to look at the car, which was an unusual thing in that settlement. Seeing Jasper, she sprang quickly to her feet with a cry of delight, and hurried toward the road. Her face was aglow with excitement, and Mr. Westcote thought that he had never beheld a more perfect picture of radiant health and beauty. "This is the young woman I was speaking to you about," Jasper remarked, as he stepped from the car. "I am delighted to meet you," and Mr. Westcote held out his hand. "I have heard about you, and have been quite anxious to see you. How are you making out with your new charge?" "Great," and a smile wreathed the girl's face. "He is so happy here, and likes for me to read to him. But he is so funny at times, and interrupts me to ask questions."

"What about?" Mr. Westcote enquired.

"Oh, about Break Neck Falls. He wants to know if I can hear the water speaking, and, of course, I always do," she added with a slight laugh. "He wanted me to go there this morning, but as mother and the boys are away I could not leave, so I am trying to satisfy him by reading."

"Would your mother be willing to keep him for a time, do you think?" Jasper asked, "that is, if she were paid enough?"

"I'm afraid not," and the girl's eyes roamed in a thoughtful manner toward where David was sitting. "You see, our house is too small, and there is hardly room enough as it is. And besides, we are too far away from the Falls. Mr. David needs to be quite near so that he can visit the place whenever he takes the notion, which is quite often. That is the only thing which will make him happy."

"Quite right," Mr. Westcote assented. "He should live as near as possible. But may we see your charge?" he asked.

"Certainly," and Betty at once led the way across the field to the big shady tree.

Old David, seeing them coming, rose to meet them. He stood very erect and dignified as Jasper took his hand, and then introduced Mr. Westcote. He was visibly embarrassed that he did not have chairs for all, and offered his own to the stranger.

"Please keep your seat," Mr. Westcote told him. "I prefer to sit on the ground. What a delightful place you have here, sir," and he looked around upon the scenery.

"It is very beautiful," David assented, "and I can hear the Falls so plainly, especially at night."

An amused twinkle shone in Betty's eyes as she turned them upon Jasper's face. She knew very well that it was impossible to hear the sound of the falling waters, and that it was purely imagination on his part.

The stranger, however, did not smile. In fact, there was an expression of sadness upon his face as he watched David. He said very little, being content to let the others do the talking. But he observed the old man very carefully without apparently doing so. What his thoughts were he kept to himself, and when he arose to go, he took David's hand in almost a reverent manner, and looked searchingly into his eyes as if trying to find something there which he missed. He hardly spoke a word on the way back but seemed lost in deep thought. As Jasper alighted from the car in front of his cabin, Mr. Westcote laid his right hand upon his shoulder.

"Take good care of that old man," he said. "Let nothing interfere with your watchfulness until you hear from me again. Get the best place you can for him, no matter what it costs."

That was all, but the expression upon the stranger's face, and the impressive manner in which he uttered these words gave Jasper cause for deep thought during the remainder of the morning.

CHAPTER IX

UNITED FORCES

Jasper was now in a position to give up his entire time to old David's interests. No longer need he worry about working on the farm, nor how he was to obtain his daily food. He was provided for a month at least, and he was most anxious now to enter upon the odd task which had been assigned to him. Robert Westcote, the stranger, interested him greatly, and he felt sure that he should hear more about him later.

Having eaten his simple lunch, he started down the road. The village of Creekdale was about two miles away, and there he hoped to find a house suitable for David. The only man he knew in the place was the storekeeper, and from him he believed that he could secure some information, and at the same time get his cheque cashed.

It was a beautiful afternoon, and his heart was lighter than it had been for many a day. He walked along with the swing of a man who has a definite purpose in life, and from whose heart all gloomy thoughts have been banished. He did not try to account for this mood. It was sufficient for him that in some way a load had been for a time lifted from his mind. He would let the future look out for itself, and enjoy the present as far as it was possible for him to do so.

Reaching a clump of trees, he sat down by the side of the road to rest. The shade was refreshing, for he was quite warm as he had been walking fast. Birds sang in the branches above him, and fanned the air with their light wings. Butterflies zigzagged past, and honey-laden bees sped by like express trains. He watched them with much interest, and mused upon their activity. Each had a special work to do, and was performing it to the best of its ability. He was glad now that he was alive, and had something definite in view. It was far better than groping around in a haphazard way looking for work. Something seemed to tell him that he was entering upon the trail of a mystery and he was eager to follow the scent wherever it might lead. The spirit of adventure was in his blood, mingled with the nectar of romance. It had always been there, inherited from his ancestors. It was that same spirit which had caused him to leave the farm and enter college several years before. It had always been with him, and was stronger now than ever. He would follow the quest to the end, and see what the outcome would be.

Jasper was about to rise and proceed on his way when, glancing along the road, he saw Lois coming toward him. His heart beat fast when he saw her, and his first impulse was to get away out of sight. Why should he meet her? he asked himself. She had no use for him, and would not consider it worth while to talk to one of whom her brother and Sammie Dingle were always making fun.

As he hesitated, Lois drew nearer. She was walking very slowly as if in deep thought. She wore a simple white dress, and a light, broad-rimmed hat which partly shaded her face. To Jasper she seemed the very embodiment of grace and beauty as she moved toward him. In her all the charm of the glorious day, of bird and flower seemed to be combined. He was lifted out of himself, entranced, and by the time she was opposite the clump of trees he was standing by the side of the road, with hat in his hand, confused and abashed.

His sudden appearance startled Lois for an instant.

But when she saw who it was, she smiled, and held out her hand.

"I didn't notice you," she began, "as I was lost in thought. But I have wanted to see you to thank you for what you did for me yesterday. I shudder to think of what would have been the result if you had not been there. I hope you were not offended at Sammie's words."

"And you feel none the worse for your fall and wetting?" Jasper evasively replied.

"Oh, no, I am all right now. It takes more than that to knock me out. I was going over this morning to thank you, but —"

She paused, and looked thoughtfully across the fields.

"I know," Jasper hastened to explain. "You didn't like to come to my shack. It is only natural. It would have given people something to talk about."

Lois looked at him for an instant and a sudden fire of resentment shone in her eyes, while her face flushed.

"Do you consider me such a weak person as that?" she demanded. "Do you imagine that I care what people might say? I never let the frills and shams of life interfere with me when I am in the way of duty."

"Forgive me," Jasper apologised, "if I have offended you. I spoke without due thought. But one hardly knows how to take people these days, and I am sorry that I judged you wrongly. I am so glad that you are not like others."

"We will forget all about it," Lois replied, with a smile. "Yes, I was going to see you this morning to thank you, no matter what people might say, but I was sent for by Mrs. Peterson who lives just back there, and I have been with her ever since. She is in great trouble, as her husband is an invalid, and she has no way of making a living. She is thinking of taking in summer boarders, and she wanted to talk to me about it."

"And what did you advise?" Jasper questioned.

"Nothing," was the emphatic reply. "It is a difficult problem, and I do not know what can be done. In the first place, the house is too small for more than two or three boarders, and she could not expect to have them for more than a few weeks at the most in the summer time. If she could have them all the year around it would be different. And besides, it would be very hard for Mrs. Peterson to look after them. It takes most of her time caring for her husband, who is quite weak, and not always very considerate, I am afraid."

As Lois was thus talking, Jasper was doing some serious thinking. He was greatly interested in what she told him, not so much about the Petersons as others he had in mind. He believed that here was the very place for old David.

"Do you mind going back with me to see Mrs. Peterson?" he asked.

"Why, no," Lois replied, turning her eyes to his, as if trying to comprehend why he should wish to meet Mrs. Peterson. "It will be better than standing here in the heat."

As they walked slowly along the road Jasper told her about David, how he and the girl had taken refuge in his cabin, where the old man was at present, and that he was looking for a suitable place where he could live. He said as little as possible about his own share in the matter, excepting that he had rescued David from Jim Goban and was going to see that he was well cared for. He did not say anything about Robert Westcote, remembering his obligation of silence.

Lois was much interested in what he told her, and her mind was very busy as she walked along by his side wondering where he was to get the money to carry out his plan.

"It will cost considerable," she remarked when he was through. "Do you think you can manage it?"

"I am quite certain that there will be no trouble," he replied. "Just why I am doing this I cannot explain now, but

I assure you there will be no difficulty. David is to be well provided for, as far as money is concerned, and he is to have some one to look after him all the time."

"What, at Mrs. Peterson's, if she will take him?" Lois asked in surprise.

"Yes, that is my idea. If that girl Betty will come, she will be just the person."

They had paused now and were standing at the entrance of the lane leading up to the Peterson's house. It was a most beautiful spot, with tall trees lining both sides of the drive-way. They were on a gentle elevation with the village of Creekdale on their left but a few rods away. It was an interesting collection of snug country-homes of farmers, river boatmen, and several retired sea captains. All the people in Creekdale knew one another's business, and the women could see what their neighbours were doing, and some could easily talk from door to door about the events of the day.

It was only natural that Mrs. Raymond should leave her washing-tub long enough to watch Lois and Jasper as they stood for a few moments by the side of the road. She wondered what they were doing there, and her curiosity was so much aroused when they at length walked up the drive-way to the Peterson's house that she slipped over next door to discuss it with Mrs. Markham.

The people of Creekdale often talked about the Petersons, calling them stuck-up because they mingled but little in the social life of the place. "I have lived next door to them for nigh on to ten years," Mrs. Raymond once confided to a neighbour, "and only once have they been in my house. I guess Captain Peterson must have some money laid by, for he does nothing but work in his garden and look after his hens, cow and pig."

When, however, the Captain was stricken with partial paralysis and was unable to work, the belief became general that he certainly did have considerable money laid away.

The Petersons' house was as neat and cosy as hands could make it. A spacious verandah swept the front and south end of the building. Over this clambered a luxuriant growth of grape vines. Here Captain Peterson was lying in a large invalid's chair, puffing away at a short-stemmed corn-cob pipe. He was surprised to see Lois back so soon, and he looked with curiosity upon Jasper, wondering where he had come from.

"Couldn't leave us, eh?" he questioned, as he gazed with admiration upon the bright, animated face before him.

"No, I had to come back," Lois laughingly replied. "Your company is so attractive that I could not resist the temptation of bringing another to enjoy it. This is Mr. Jasper Randall, Captain Peterson. He has come to see you on special business."

"Glad to see you, sir," and the captain reached out his hand. "Have a chair; there's one right there. Do ye smoke?"

"Oh, yes," and Jasper thrust his hand at once into his pocket. "Do you mind?" he asked, turning toward Lois.

"Not at all," was the reply. "But you two smoke to your hearts' content while I have a chat with Mrs. Peterson. I suppose she's in the house, Captain?"

"Yes, in the kitchen. At least, I heard her there a short time ago."

Lois was absent for about twenty minutes and when she returned the two men were talking in the most friendly manner.

"This is the first good chat I've had with a man for a long time," the captain told her. "He has made me feel better already."

"I hope he hasn't forgotten the object of his visit in listening to your sea yarns," Lois laughingly replied.

"Tut, tut, girl," and the captain blew a great cloud of smoke into the air. "D'ye think that is all I talk about? We had some-thing just as interesting to discuss to-day, and so I forgot all about the yarns."

"And so you are willing to take old David and Betty into your house, are you?"

"Sure. I'm satisfied if Julia is. She's in charge of the ship now since I've lost my sea-legs."

"Mrs. Peterson is delighted at the thought of having them," Lois replied. "Here she comes now, and can speak for herself."

Mrs. Peterson was a pleasant-faced little woman who appealed to Jasper at once. He felt quite sure that she was just the person to look after David. She appeared so motherly and sympathetic that it was easy for him to talk to her as she showed him the rooms David and Betty could have.

"Why, you will give them half of the house," Jasper exclaimed.

"Only three rooms." was the reply. "The old man can sleep downstairs, and he can have this big room adjoining. The girl can have a comfortable room right at the head of the stairs."

Jasper and Lois were both greatly pleased, and as they walked away from the house they discussed it like two ani-mated children.

"How delighted David will be with the place," Lois remarked. "He will be so comfortable there, I feel sure, and Mrs. Peterson will take such good care of him."

"And he will be able to hear the falls so plainly," Jasper replied. "He can sit on the verandah or at the window of his room and listen to the waters as long as he likes. It is just the place for him."

"How much does Mrs. Peterson want a week for their board?" Lois enquired.

"I never asked her," was the quiet reply. "I shall find that out later, for it is a matter of minor importance."

Lois glanced up quickly into her companion's face. She longed to know where the money was to come from. Surely this man who was working digging potatoes did not intend to pay the entire amount. But Jasper volunteered not the slightest information. He continued to talk about David, and his surprise when he learned of what was being done for him.

"I am so grateful for your assistance this afternoon," Jasper told Lois as they at last paused at the gate leading to the Sinclair house. "I started forth uncertain what to do, and behold, everything has turned out as if by magic."

"I am thankful that I have been of some assistance," was the quiet reply. "My mind is greatly relieved, too, for I was much worried about the Petersons. Two heads are better than one after all, are they not?"

CHAPTER X

WHEN DREAMS COME TRUE

"Isn't this lovely!" Betty exclaimed, as she stood in the middle of the large room which had been assigned to David.

It was the second day since their arrival at the Petersons' house, and their delight at everything was not only amusing to Mrs. Peterson but somewhat pathetic as well. She could not account for the girl's remarkable care of the old man. She would allow nothing to interfere with her attention upon him, and she arranged a cosy spot by the big north window where he could sit and listen to the sound of his beloved falls.

"You will spoil him," Mrs. Peterson told her once when they were alone in the kitchen. "You will make him as helpless as a child. It is not good for men to be waited upon too much."

"Are you not afraid of spoiling your husband, then, Mrs. Peterson?" Betty replied. "You treat him just like a child."

"Oh, but he is an invalid, and can't help himself. That is the reason why I have to wait upon him."

"But Mr. David is a wonder," Betty insisted, "and he must not be neglected."

There was such an expression of admiration in the girl's eyes that Mrs. Peterson had not the heart to smile at her enthusiasm.

"In what way is he a wonder?" was all she asked, as she went on with her work.

"Oh, he has a great thing in his head, which he is thinking about all the time. It has to do with the falls, and he has told me a whole lot about it. He will be very rich some day, and we are going to have such a nice house of our own. You see, I am to be his housekeeper, and nurse him when he is sick."

It was a great pleasure for Captain Peterson to have David and Betty at the house. No longer did he have to sit alone for hours upon the verandah as he had an audience now to listen to his tales of the sea and the places he had visited. David was a good listener and enjoyed hearing the yarns, although he kept one ear open for the sound of the falls. Nothing must interfere with his interest up there.

One afternoon the captain was speaking about England, and mentioned Liverpool. David became unusually interested, and even let his pipe go out as he sat with his eyes fixed intently upon the captain's face.

"You seem to know Liverpool pretty well," he at length remarked, as the captain paused to re-light his pipe.

"Should say so," was the reply. "Guess I know about everything there worth knowing, especially along shipping lines."

"There must be some big firms there, eh?"

"Big! I should say so. Why, I could name a dozen right offhand, which have ships sailing around the world. Now, there's the Dockett concern, for instance. Holy smokes! but they're wealthy. If I told you the business they do you wouldn't believe me."

"No?" David laid his pipe upon the verandah railing. He had to do it because his hand was trembling so violently that he could hold it no longer.

"Indeed you wouldn't," the captain continued, not noticing his companion's agitation. "And you should see old Dockett himself, who owns it all, so I understand."

"What about him?" David asked in a voice scarcely above a whisper. For once he had forgotten his beloved falls.

"Ho, ho, I wish you could see him," and the captain leaned back and laughed as he had not laughed for months. "He certainly is a queer one."

"In what way?" David questioned.

"Well, it is hard to explain. He looks like a bear, and he acts like one, too. My, I've heard him get his tongue on men lots of times, and he is a holy terror. But he's a great business man, so I believe, and has made heaps of money."

"What does he do with it?" David asked.

"Piles it up, I guess. He hasn't a chick to leave it to, so I understand."

"Hasn't he a wife?"

"No, not when I last heard of him, which was five years ago. It isn't likely he's married since then."

David was unusually quiet the rest of the day. There was a far-away look in his eyes and nothing interested him, not even the voice of his falls. Betty was quite anxious, and confided her trouble to Mrs. Peterson.

"Do you think he is going to be sick?" she asked. "Suppose he should die, what will become of that great thing he has in his head?"

"Oh, I guess he is all right," Mrs. Peterson soothed. "Perhaps he is thinking out something else, and will surprise us with some new idea."

"Oh, do you think so?" and the girl's eyes grew big with wonder. "Won't it be great if he does!"

David was much brighter the next morning and sat for some time out upon the verandah. Betty had gone to the office for the mail, as Mrs. Peterson was too busy about the house. She did this nearly every day now, and enjoyed the walk. The captain was always anxious to get his daily paper, and sometimes there would be a letter from an old friend.

It was almost noon when Betty arrived. Her cheeks were flushed more than usual and she was greatly excited.

"What's up now?" the captain enquired. "Haven't been scared, have ye?"

"It's a letter for Mr. David!" she replied. "Just think of that!"

"H'm," and the captain gave a grunt of disgust. "Is that all. I thought maybe ye'd seen a ghost. Why should a letter so upset you?"

"Oh, but he never got a letter before since I've known him, and it must be very important."

While the two were talking David rose from his chair and stepped toward Betty.

"A letter for me?" he asked, in a somewhat doubtful voice.

"Yes, here it is. You had better open it at once."

The old man took it in his hand and stood studying it for a few seconds. Then he slowly opened the envelope, and drew forth the letter. As he scanned the contents, his eyes grew suddenly wide with astonishment and his hands trembled violently.

"Oh, Mr. David, what's the matter?" Betty cried as she observed his intense excitement. "Is it some bad news?"

But the old man did not seem to notice her. He stood there, shaking in every limb, staring upon the letter.

"Tell me what it is," the girl again demanded. "I want to know at once."

This imperious order brought David to his senses, and without a word he handed her the letter. Eagerly seizing it, she began to read. It took her longer than the old man to make out its meaning, and when the truth at last dawned upon her mind she gave a glad cry of joy, and her eyes beamed with delight as she turned them upon his face.

"Oh, isn't it great!" she exclaimed. "Five thousand dollars for that thing in your head, Mr. David. Won't you be rich. Now we can have a house of our very own, and I can be your housekeeper!"

"But that isn't all, Betty," David replied. "I am to be Honorary President of the company, just think of that. And they are to carry out my plans and do just what I wish. Girl, my dreams are to come true at last. I shall live to see my beautiful falls bringing a blessing to the entire country. I wonder if people will laugh at me now, and call me crazy."

It was only natural that intense excitement should reign at the Haven for the next few hours. The captain and his wife were greatly impressed by the good fortune which had come so suddenly to old David. They could hardly believe it possible, and they had the feeling that there had been some mistake. But Betty would not hear of such a thing. She was sure that it was all true, and it was due to the wonderful thing that David had in his head.

Dinner was late that day, and they had just finished when Jasper arrived. Then out upon the verandah he heard the remarkable story. It was Betty who told it, while David and the captain sat smoking near by. He was shown the letter as well, the cause of all the excitement. Jasper read it over several times, and then stepping over to David he grasped his hand.

"Allow me to congratulate you, sir," he began. "Such good luck does not come to many in this country. I am so thankful that your plans are to be carried out after all."

"And they are to consult me, and carry out my every wish," David replied. "It is so stated there," and he pointed to the letter.

The enthusiasm of the old man was so intense and childlike that Jasper had not the heart to say one word that would in any way dampen his joy. To him, however, the whole thing was a great puzzle. Was it a joke, he wondered, which some people were playing upon this simple-minded man? A company was mentioned, but its name was not given. And further, why should any company be willing to pay five thousand dollars for David's idea, which was not new? It had been successfully carried out in other localities. Surely a concern which was able to make such a liberal offer must have full and accurate knowledge about hydro-electric plants and what they had accomplished in the past. And why should David be made

Honorary President of the company? Was Robert Westcote, the stranger, the cause of it all? He had not heard from him since the day of their visit to Mrs. Bean's, and but for the cheque which he had received he would have been inclined to consider the whole thing as a hoax.

Jasper kept his thoughts, however, to himself, and sat for some time on the verandah taking but little part in the conversation. Betty and the captain did most of the talking, while David sat near with a happy expression upon his face.

"When are you thinking of starting housekeeping on your own account?" the captain enquired. "You'll be so mighty important now that you won't want to stay with us any longer."

"Don't you worry, Captain," Betty laughingly replied. "We're not going to leave you just yet. You see, we haven't any house to go to, and it will take the rest of the summer to make arrangements."

When Jasper left the Haven he walked slowly down the road toward the post office thinking over carefully all that he had just heard. Every day he had been expecting news from Mr. Westcote, giving information as to what was expected of him. Hitherto he had been disappointed. But to-day he was rewarded when the postmaster, in addition to his daily paper, handed him out a letter. Jasper felt that this was the one he had been looking for, and he hurried out of the building and carted homeward. Reaching a shady tree by the side of the road, he sat down upon the ground and tore open the letter. A week of thought and inactivity had made him anxious to know something more of what was expected of him, and he was quite certain that now the veil was to be lifted and the mystery partly solved.

The letter was from Robert Westcote, and although it was somewhat brief it brought him considerable satisfaction. His eyes kindled with animation and his pulse quickened as he considered the message he had just received and meditated upon the possibilities of the future.

CHAPTER XI

CURIOSITY AND ANXIETY

Never in the memory of the oldest inhabitant had Creekdale been so greatly excited. How the news first arrived no one could tell. But everybody seemed to have heard the rumor at once, and immediately there was much running to and fro among the villagers. The store was the principal place where the men gathered to discuss the report and to find out what was the latest bit of information. Men would find some excuse for leaving their work in the fields in order to drop into the store during the afternoon lest some choice morsel of news should be missed. Every evening they would gather there such as they had never done before in the summer months. It was always in the winter that they made the store their headquarters when work was not so pressing.

It was Andy Forbes, the storekeeper, who made it a point of keeping abreast of the times. What he didn't know of the events of the parish was not considered of any importance. He had a way of appearing to know more than he really did. But concerning this affair at the falls he was completely blocked.

"The whole thing stumps me," he acknowledged one night, after an animated discussion had taken place as to the purpose of it all. "I can understand about the engineers making the surveys to find out how much power can be obtained from the falls. That Light and Power Company in the city has been playing the hog too long, and robbing the people. It is something fierce what they charge. It is only natural that an opposition company should be formed to force down the prices. But the question is, Who is back of this new movement? and what has Crazy David to do with it?"

"And so you really think he knows something about at?" Ben Logan enquired.

"Sure. I could tell you a number of things but my position as postmaster compels me to be silent." This was merely another of Andy's methods, and it always impressed his hearers in a marked degree.

"But what about that chap who was working for old Squabbles?" Billy Dexter asked. "He seems to be mixed up somehow with the affair. He spends most of his time now at the falls with the engineers. I understand that he was the one who got the Petersons to take in Crazy David and that girl, Betty Bean."

"Oh, he's a queer one," Sandy Morton replied. "I met him the other day on the road and asked him what was going on up at the falls and who were the men back of the work? My, you should have seen the look he gave me. It was 'Mind your own business,' as plain as if he had said it in words. I ought to have knocked him down, for it was a dead insult."

"Better not try anything like that, Sandy," Ben Logan laughingly gibed. "He'd wipe up the dust with you in no time, if I'm not much mistaken. Anyway, he minds his own business, and that's something in his favour."

"I believe he's working for the bunch," the store-keeper volunteered. "I cashed a cheque of his some time ago, and — but, there, I must not let out secrets."

While the people of Creekdale were consumed with curiosity at what was taking place at the falls, Peter Sinclair was becoming filled with anxiety, which increased as the days passed into weeks. Lois found it harder than ever to get along with him, and she always dreaded his home-coming every evening from the city. Occasionally he travelled on the river steamer, but as a rule Dick drove him to the city in the morning in the car and brought him back at night. This was to the young man's liking, as he found it lonely in the country where he missed his boon companions. Lois was glad that this was so as she could have the days free to follow her own inclinations. But she was always careful to have dinner ready when her father and brother arrived, and to make their home-coming as bright and pleasant as possible.

Whether Mr. Sinclair appreciated this attention Lois did not know, as he never made any comment. At times, he treated her as if she were merely a housekeeper, and not his own daughter interested in his welfare. He ate and slept in the house and spent his Sundays there. But apart from paying the bills, which, were always light, he left everything else to his daughter.

The night when the men of Creekdale were talking so earnestly at the store, Mr. Sinclair was late reaching, home. Dinner had been waiting for over an hour, and Lois was reading on the verandah, for it was a beautiful evening, with not a ripple on the surface of the river. She longed to be out there in her little boat where of late she spent so much of her time.

To almost any one else this home-coming would have been a great pleasure, especially if the day in the city had been trying. He would have found the cool, quiet house with such a daughter waiting to receive him most comforting. But with Mr. Sinclair it was altogether different. He did not seem to notice the neatly-set dining-room table, with its snow-white linen and the fragrant flowers so artistically arranged in the centre. Neither did he pay any special attention to Lois, who, clad in a simple white dress, sat at the head of the table.

Lois intuitively realised that there was something out of the ordinary worrying her father. He was more silent than ever, and took no part in the conversation between his son and daughter. Dick related to Lois his experience that afternoon with a party of his friends who had motored over to the Sea Breeze Park, and had luncheon at the Sign of the Maple.

"It's a dandy place," Dick exclaimed, as he passed his plate for another helping of roast lamb. "They certainly do serve things up in style, and it is no wonder that so many city people go there. But you could never guess who came in while we were eating."

"Any one I know?" Lois asked.

"Sure; a special friend of yours," and Dick gave a knowing grin. "He's been under your care for years. I guess you know Spuds all right."

Lois' face flushed at these words, but she looked calmly at her brother.

"What is there remarkable about seeing Mr. Randall at such a place?" she enquired. "Why shouldn't he go there as well as you or any one else?"

"Oh, nothing in that, only I thought maybe you'd be interested."

"So I am in a way, as I thought that Mr. Randall was up at the falls. He seldom goes to the city, so I understand, but attends strictly to business."

"I guess he was doing that all right at the Sign of the Maple. He seemed to be so busy that he forgot to eat."

"Was he alone?"

"Oh, no. There was the prettiest girl I ever set eyes on. I tell you Spuds is a lucky fellow to know such a beauty. He's gone up a peg in my estimation since I saw him with her. You should have seen her eyes, especially when she smiled at something her father was saying."

"Her father, did you say?" Lois asked. It was somewhat of a relief for her to know that there was a father present and that she was not alone with Jasper.

"Well, I suppose he was her father," Dick replied, "though I am not positive. He was a fine looking man, anyway. I'd like to get acquainted with him, for it's worth knowing such a chap who has a daughter like that. I wonder how Spuds happened to meet him. By jingo! I've got it," and Dick brought his fist down upon the table with such a bang that the dishes rattled. "I'll bet you anything that he has something to do with that Break Neck Falls affair, for old Tim Parkin, the big lumber merchant, was along, too. He owns some fine timber tracts up this way, and no doubt there was a deal on. That confounded mysterious company will need a great amount of lumber, if rumours are correct."

As Dick uttered these words his father looked up. His interest had been suddenly aroused, and for the first time he joined in the conversation.

"Did you say that Tim Parkin was at the Sign of the Maple?" he growled.

"Yes, Dad," the young man replied. "He was looking bigger and more prosperous than ever. He seemed mighty pleased over something."

"Did you near what they were talking about?"

"No, I couldn't make out anything as we were on the opposite side of the room." "But you could see the girl, though. If your ears had been half as good as your eyes you would have heard what was being said."

"But any one can see much farther than he can hear," Dick protested. "You surely don't expect the impossible from me, do you?"

"I don't expect anything from you, sir," and Mr. Sinclair glared at his son. "I have long since given up expecting. All you care for is to have a good time riding around in the car, attending parties, and looking for the prettiest girls. If you were as much interested in business as you are in pleasure you would be of some use to me. But I guess you'll have to get a hustle on mighty goon, though, from the look of things. I won't be able to indulge you in your idleness much longer."

"Why, Dad, what do you mean?" Dick enquired. "You're not going to throw me overboard, are you?"

"Oh, no, I won't do it. But there are others who will, or I'm very much mistaken."

"Who — why?" the young man stammered. "I don't understand you, Dad."

"I mean that new Light and Power Company which has been formed. That is what will do it."

"Oh, is that all?" and Dick breathed a sigh of relief. "You certainly did give me a jolt. I thought you were speaking of something real. But that company's all a hoax, isn't it? Tommy Flowers said it was nothing but a scare to force you to cut your rates. The whole thing is so mysterious, so people say, that they consider it a put up job to force your hand. Why, the names of the men who form the company are not even known."

"H'm, that's all that people know about what is going on," Mr. Sinclair retorted. "That company is no hoax, mark my word. It means business of a most serious nature, and it is getting to work, too. Don't you live in a fool's paradise, boy. If you do, there will be a rude awakening, and sooner perhaps than you expect."

"What, have you heard anything of late, Dad?" Dick asked.

"Well, I have heard enough, and it is more than hear-say at that. A strong company has been formed to utilise the water of Break Neck Falls for light and power to supply not only the city but the entire country. The scheme is a big one, almost gigantic, I should say. And there seems to be plenty of money back of it, too. It is an English concern which has recently opened an office in the city.

"What is the purpose of such a company working here?" Dick questioned. "One would naturally think that a city much larger than ours would offer more inducements."

Mr. Sinclair pushed back his chair from the table, and lighted a cigar. "That is one of the things which puzzles me," he at length replied. "Why a company with large capital should build a big plant at the falls to supply light and power in such a limited locality, is more than I can understand. I cannot see how it will pay even if it gets full control."

"Who is in charge of the city office?" Dick asked.

"A man by the name of Westcote. He is an Englishman, so I believe. He seems to have full charge of everything. He must have been the man you saw at the Sign of the Maple with Tim Parkin, for he has a daughter with him, who recently came to the city."

"But what has Spuds to do with the concern, and how did he come to meet this man Westcote?"

"He is evidently in his employ. But where he met him I do not know. Perhaps Lois can tell us," and he glanced around upon his daughter.

Lois suddenly started and looked keenly at her father as if she had not heard aright. This was the first time that he had ever hinted at any interest on her part in Jasper. A feeling of resentment welled up in her heart.

"Why should I know?" she enquired, "and what reason have you for asking me such a question?"

Mr. Sinclair, however, did not deign to make any explanation, but puffed away at his cigar. Lois took this as a direct insult and started to leave the table. She wished to get away by herself that she might think it all over.

"And where does old Crazy David come in?" her father asked. "What interest has he in that concern?"

"I have not the slightest idea," Lois impatiently replied. "Why do you expect me to understand such things?"

"But you should know. You see that old man every day, and are so interested in his welfare. Surely he must have told you something, and if he did not you should have tried to find out. Remember, you are my daughter, and my interest should be your first concern. Both you and Dick think that you have no responsibilities in life, and that I will always provide for you. If we are not careful that new company will put us out of business; so you two must do all you can to help me. Something must be done to cheek that concern and I want you to assist me. As it is, I am working in the dark and do not know what to expect next, or who are the ones working against me. Is it old David who is merely acting the part of a fool, or is it that young man who pretended to be a hired hand, who worked awhile for Simon Squabbles? There is something queer about the whole thing, and I am nearly crazy trying to puzzle it all out."

To these words Lois made no reply. She quietly left the table and made her way out of the house and walked down to the shore. Here she felt more at home, and the stillness which reigned over land and water soothed her, bringing a restful peace to her heart and mind.

CHAPTER XII

PYRAMID ROCK

A good home, plenty of well-cooked food, and proper attention did much for old David. His strength, and health improved, and although he lost nothing of his interest in the falls, he was quite content to listen more to the sound drifting down the valley instead of visiting the place as often as formerly. The spot he liked best of all was the cosy corner on the verandah, just outside the window of his room. Here the vines clambered up over the sides, forming a shelter from the burning sun and a refuge from the wind when the days were cool.

Jasper was a frequent visitor at the Haven, and he was not slow to notice the change that had come over David. Hitherto the old man had been content to listen to the voice of the falls and utter brief and almost mystic words about what the water would do. But latterly he had given greater vent to his thoughts and enlarged upon the plans he had been revolving in his mind.

It was a beautiful evening not long after Jasper had been at the Sign of the Maple, that he was sitting with David and Betty in the accustomed place. The captain had retired, and Mrs. Peterson was busy in the kitchen. Jasper told of the progress that had been made at the falls and how the engineers had finished their preliminary work, and had declared the undertaking most feasible. The definite start of building would not begin until the next spring, though in the meantime necessary preparations would be made so that the work could be pushed forward then as rapidly as possible. Logs would be needed for building purposes, and many large poles suitable for carrying the wires to the city and throughout the country.

"I have been requested to undertake this work," Jasper told them, "and so will be busy all the fall and winter. In a few weeks I hope to have a number of men and teams at work in the woods. It will be a fine thing for Creekdale as it will put so much money in circulation by giving employment to all available men during the winter when as a rule little is going on, so I understand."

"Oh, won't that be nice," Betty exclaimed, while her eyes danced with animation. "My brother will be able to earn money right at home. Jimmy has been planning to go to the city next winter to earn some money to help pay off the mortgage on our place. Mother doesn't want him to go as he is only sixteen, but he thinks he should be earning something."

"You have some fine trees on your place, have you not?" Jasper asked in reply.

"Oh, yes, lots of them. You see, our farm is part of the old Dinsmore Manor, and no logs have been cut on it for years as they have not been worth much. My father said before he died that they would bring a lot of money some day, and they would make us rich. That's why mother has been holding on to the place and trying to pay off the mortgage. But she finds it hard work. Jimmy works for the neighbours, but Steve and Dora can't earn anything yet. I am helping all I can."

"Those trees are very valuable now," Jasper remarked.

"Have you seen them?" Betty asked, in surprise.

"Yes, I have been all over the place, and there are acres

of the finest trees I have ever seen. We shall need many of them, that is, if your mother will sell."

"Won't that be great!" and the girl clapped her hands with delight. "I know she will sell if she can get a fair price for them."

"There should be no trouble about that, Betty. Logs are higher than they have been for years, and those who own them are fortunate. The company wants only the best and is willing to pay a good price, so I believe. But there is something I would advise your mother to do."

"What is that?"

"Keep a sharp look-out upon those trees. The city Light and Power Company, of which Mr. Sinclair is manager and principal owner, has land right next to yours. Most of the best trees have been cut there for poles, and it is only natural that envious eyes should be east upon your mother's valuable property. Mr. Sinclair does quite a lumbering business on his own account, so I understand."

"Oh, do you think that Mr. Sinclair would do anything like that?" Betty asked in surprise.

"I trust not," was the reply. "Nevertheless, it is just as well to be on guard in case something does happen. You might speak to your mother about it when you see her."

The next day David and Betty paid a visit to the falls. They had not been there for over a week, which was a most unusual thing. It was a beautiful afternoon, and a complete harmony seemed to reign everywhere. David was in excellent spirits and he talked much about the wonderful improvements which were to come to the country. He pointed out a number of the stakes the engineers had driven into the ground, and explained where the power house would be built.

"A year from now," he told her, "there will be wires running to the city and all through the country. The city people will have light for their houses and power for their machinery at cheap rates. The farmers will have electric lights right in their homes and barns; they will have power to saw their wood, churn their butter, thresh and grind their grain, besides doing so many other things. It will make a wonderful change in the lives of all. Young people will not want to leave the farms and go to the city. It will be a joy for them to remain, and so much of the drudgery will be taken away."

"Won't that be splendid!" Betty replied. "How did you ever think of all those things? Why, the people didn't know you were thinking so much about their welfare when you were living all alone, and when they said you were crazy."

"No, girl, they did not know," and the old man gazed thoughtfully off into space. "They believed that I was a fool, and perhaps they had reason for so thinking. You see, I was very poor and had no means of carrying out my plans. It has always been the way, and why should I have expected anything different from thousands of others who have tried to help their fellow men? But now things have changed, and they will soon learn that old David was not so crazy after all."

They were seated upon the bank of the stream as they thus talked. On a bough of a near-by tree a squirrel was scolding, and off in the distance several crows were lifting up their raucous voices. Betty picked up a stone and tossed it into the water below, and then watched with interest as it fell with a splash.

"I can throw farther than you, Mr. David," she bantered. "I can throw a stone to that big rock over there."

"I haven't thrown a stone in a long time, my child," was the reply.

"Well, try it then," was the command. "Here is a nice smooth one."

Rising to his feet, David took the stone and with a wide sweep of his long arm hurled it far down the stream almost to the base of the rock.

"You didn't do it," Betty shouted with delight. "I can beat that, see if I can't."

She half turned to pick up another stone when she suddenly paused as her eyes rested upon a man coming toward them. It was Peter Sinclair, and as he drew near and spoke to them, it seemed to Betty that the atmosphere had changed, and the day was not as fine as it had been but a few seconds before. She wanted to get away, for this man's presence seemed to weigh upon her in an ominous manner. The reason why she could not explain.

"Having a nice time here, eh?" Mr. Sinclair remarked, as he sat down upon the bank. "That walk has puffed me. Do you come up here often?" he asked, turning toward Betty.

"Whenever Mr. David takes the notion," was her reply. "I always come with him, and we have such a pleasant time."

"And do you always stop here and spend your time in throwing stones at that rock? Are you not wasting your time?"

"We might be doing worse, though," Betty replied, somewhat nettled at the man's words. "We might be throwing stones at you or somebody else."

"At me!" and Mr. Sinclair looked surprised.

"Yes, at you. But perhaps it's safer to throw them at that rock over there. It doesn't mind for it knows we're only in fun. It's a special friend of mine, and that's why I like to be near it. You would never believe that it saved half my father's farm several years ago."

"What, that rock?"

"It certainly did, and I shall never forget what it did for us."

"Tell me about it," and Mr. Sinclair sat down upon the ground. The mention of the Bean farm had suddenly aroused his interest, and made him willing to listen to this country girl's story.

"It was a long time ago," Betty began, "just after my father was married. He had bought a piece of land off of the

Dinsmore Manor, about one hundred acres, I think it was. After he had paid for the place there was some trouble about the line between him and the man who had bought another piece of the manor next to him. They agreed to have the line run over again. I don't understand all about it, but, anyway, when the line was run it cut my father's place almost in two, and he was afraid he was going to lose all that land where those fine logs are now. It was a funny mistake, but it was soon settled."

"What had that rock to do with it?" Mr. Sinclair enquired.

"Oh," and the girl gave a slight laugh. "I forgot that part. You see, the surveyor was to start running the line from the big pyramid rock on this brook. It is called that because of its shape. Father happened to be away from home the day the line was run and the surveyor started from another rock farther down the brook, which looks something like that one over there. Wasn't it funny? So you see that is why I am so fond of that big rock and come here as often as I can to be near my good friend."

As Betty finished, a peculiar expression might have been detected in Peter Sinclair's eyes, and for a few seconds he gazed steadily at the rock before him. It seemed that the girl's story had greatly interested him and started him off on a new line of thought. Just what it was he kept to himself and with an apparent effort turned his attention once more to Betty.

"You will not come here as often, I suppose, when the company gets to work," he remarked. "Things will be much changed along this brook, and perhaps your old friend, the rock, may be disturbed."

"You are right, sir," David replied, speaking for the first time. "There will certainly be marvellous changes all over this country in a year or two. You will hardly know the place then."

"That is interesting. And can you tell me who will perform these wonders of which you speak so confidently?"

"The falls will do it," and David stretched out his right arm. "Light and power will come from there to transform city and country. Living will be made far more tolerable in both."

"But who are the men back of all this?" Mr. Sinclair asked. He felt sure now that he was on the verge of a new discovery.

"I am the man," and David stood proudly erect. "It was my plan which suggested the movement."

"I know all that," and Mr. Sinclair rose impatiently to his feet. "But where does the money come from? and, who are the men who form the company? That is what I want to know."

"That I cannot tell you, sir. And why should it matter? I am concerned about the improvements and not where the money comes from."

"H'm, that's a queer way to do business," was the disgusted reply. "Well, I must be off up the brook. I've wasted too much time already. Look out for your big rock, little girl, and see that no one disturbs it."

"Oh, I guess it'll stay there all right," Betty replied with a laugh. "My friends never leave me."

They stood and watched Mr. Sinclair until the tree hid him from view.

"I don't like that man," and Betty stamped her small foot upon the ground. "He makes me feel creepy all over just like I always do when I see a snake or a rat. Let's go home."

About an hour after they had left the place, Peter Sinclair drew near, and stood looking at the big rock across the brook. Then he walked along the bank until he came to the smaller rock of which Betty had spoken. He next turned his eyes northward and pointed with the forefinger of his right hand as if tracing an imaginary boundary line. As he did so a smile of satisfaction lighted his face, and when he left the brook and started homeward, his step was quicker and more elastic than it had been for many a day.

CHAPTER XIII

THE DISTURBING LETTER

It took Jasper longer than he had expected to get everything ready for his fall and winter lumbering operations. He found it hard to obtain as many teams as he needed, and greater difficulty still to procure the right kind of men. He offered good wages, but the choppers held out for more. Although such matters had been left to Jasper, yet he did not feel inclined to pay such wages as were demanded. At length, however, he succeeded in rounding together a band of men upon whom he felt he could depend, and he hoped in a few days to begin work upon the building of the cabins for the men and the stables for the horses.

Jasper often mused upon the peculiar situation in which he was placed. Everything seemed to depend upon him. The engineers, having made their surveys, had departed, leaving him in charge. The buying of the food supplies devolved upon him, though the bills were sent to the city office for payment. He had not seen Robert Westcote since the day he had luncheon with him at the Sign of the Maple. He had merely received specific information as to the various kinds of logs required, their length and size, as well as the places where they were to be hauled near the falls.

During these busy days Jasper had seen nothing of Lois. He knew that she visited the Haven regularly, and Betty always had a great deal to tell him about her. But somehow he had missed meeting her, and every time he left he felt disappointed, and made his way back to his lonely cabin which seemed to become more lonely as the days passed. Sometimes he would stand on the hill and look down upon the Sinclair house, hoping that he might catch a glimpse of her who was so much in his mind. He would scan the river, thinking he might see her out there. At length a great longing came upon him to see her before he should go into the woods. He knew that in a few weeks at the most she would be leaving for the city with her father, and then all hope of meeting her again for months would have to be abandoned. Somehow he could not bear the thought of her going. As long as she was near he could work better, and her presence in the place was like an inspiration. He felt that she knew what he was doing, and took an interest in his welfare. But in the city she would be far away, and taken up with so many interests she would have no time to give any thought to him.

All preparations had now been made for the lumbering operations and work would begin on Monday morning. Saturday found Jasper with nothing to do. He spent the forenoon in packing up his belongings to take with him into the woods. They were very few, and one small grip would contain his scanty library which he could not bear to leave behind. The next time he went to the city he intended to purchase a number of books upon which he had set his heart. He would have the long winter evenings for reading in the little cabin he was to erect for his own special use.

About the middle of the afternoon he decided to pay a visit to the Haven. He wished to see David and Betty before going away, and learn how they were making out. But the hope that he might see Lois was the real reason why he decided to go. Several times he had thought of visiting her at her own home. But as he had never been there and had received no invitation, he did not feel inclined to go where perhaps he was not wanted, and where his presence might be looked upon as an intrusion. He often upbraided himself for thinking about her at all. What hope had he that she would ever deign to look upon him with favour? What had he to offer her? He was poor, and he had no guarantee that his employment with this mysterious company would be permanent. In a few months he might again be seeking for work.

But no matter what resolutions Jasper made he could not banish Lois from his mind. It was she who several years before had unconsciously inspired him to launch out into the world and make something of himself. The thought of her had always urged him on when most depressed and discouraged. In his darkest hours of gloom he had seen her eyes filled with sympathy fixed upon him as on that day he had first met her and had fled disgraced from her father's house.

Such impressions were not easy to banish in an instant, and so as he knocked at the door of the haven he fervently hoped that Lois might be there. But as he entered David's room other interests engaged his attention. Hitherto all had been peace there. The old man was generally seated by the open window listening to the voice of his beloved falls. But now there was a distinct atmosphere of excitement. Mrs. Bean was there, and her face had a most worried expression. Betty had been crying, but seeing Jasper she brushed away her tears and sprang to her feet.

"Oh, Mr. Jasper," she cried, "isn't it awful! Have you heard the news?"

"What news?" Jasper asked in surprise, as he took a chair by David's side. "I haven't heard anything of special importance."

"It's about Mr. Sinclair, that's who it is. Just think, he wants to take all of our logs!"

"Take your logs!"

"Yes, that's what he's going to do. Mother got a letter from him and she has just read it to us. He says there is a mistake about the line between his place and ours, and that all those fine logs belong to him. He says he had a new line run last week and that the old line is wrong. He warns mother not to touch or sell a log there, for if she does he will sue her."

Betty was excited, and her words rushed forth like a torrent. For a few minutes Jasper could hardly believe that he had heard aright.

"Do you mean to tell me," and he turned to Mrs. Bean, "that what your daughter says is true? Surely there must be some serious mistake."

"I'm afraid not," was the reply. "There is the letter, which you can read for yourself."

It took Jasper but a few seconds to scan the brief note, and when he was through he sat staring at it as if he had not seen aright. Was it possible, he asked himself, that Peter Sinclair was stooping to such a contemptible piece of business? And to do it to a widow at that added to his meanness. What justification did he have for doing such a thing? he wondered.

"Was there ever any dispute about the line?" Jasper asked.

"None at all," Mrs. Bean replied. "A mistake was made years ago just after we were married. The surveyor started from the wrong rock up the brook, and the line then run cut off that part which Mr. Sinclair is now claiming. But it was rectified just as soon as my husband came home, and there has been no trouble since until now."

"Did Mr. Sinclair notify you that he was going to have a new line run?" Jasper enquired.

"No, I knew nothing about what was taking place until I received that letter."

"I wonder what suggested such a thing to him?" Jasper mused as if to himself. "There must have been something."

"Why, I think I know." Betty exclaimed. "I do not believe he ever thought about it until that day he was talking to Mr. David and me up the brook. We were near Pyramid Rock, and I told him about the mistake the surveyor had made years ago in running the line. He seemed to be very much interested then. Maybe that was what started it. Just think, it was all my fault. Oh, if I could only hold my tongue once in a while how much good it would do."

At that instant a knock sounded upon the door, and when Betty had opened it Lois entered. She looked surprised when she saw the visitors in the room, and at once noticed the worried expression upon Mrs. Bean's face.

"This must be your special afternoon for receiving company," she remarked with a smile, as she took David's hand. "It isn't often you have Mrs. Bean and Mr. Randall to see you on the same day, is it?"

"Mr. Randall has been here before," was the reply, "but this is the first time that Mrs. Bean has favoured me with a call. It was special business which brought her here to-day."

"You're not going to take Betty away from Mr. David, are you?" Lois asked, turning to Mrs. Bean.

"Oh, no; it is something far different from that. It is a very serious matter, I assure you."

"What, no one ill at home, I hope?"

"No. The boys were well when I left."

An awkward silence followed, and Lois felt that there was something of a private nature which these people were discussing, and that she had interrupted their conversation.

Jasper, who had risen to his feet as Lois entered the room, divined the thoughts which were passing through her mind, and came to her assistance.

"Let Miss Sinclair see the letter, Mrs. Bean," he suggested. "Perhaps it will explain matters better than we can."

Without a word Mrs. Bean complied with this request, and then leaned back in her chair with a deep sigh.

Much mystified, Lois ran her eyes over the letter, and as she did so her face underwent a marvellous transformation. The sunny expression departed and the colour faded from her cheeks, leaving them very white. The words seemed to fascinate her, and for a while she stood staring upon them. Then a tremor shook her body, and her right hand closed, crushing the letter within it. With a strong effort she regained her composure and turned toward the widow.

"I cannot understand this," she began. "I had no idea that my father would do such a thing. There must be some mistake. I shall go now and think it all over. Will you come with me, Mr. Randall? I would like to speak with you."

Without another word the two left the house and walked slowly down the lane leading to the road. Presently Lois stopped and turned to her companion.

"I am almost heartbroken over what my father has done," she began. "I have stood by him, and have tried to shield him all I could, but what is the use of doing so any longer?"

"Could you not speak to him, and induce him to change his mind?" Jasper asked.

"I can do nothing. He has even turned against me. He believes that I am his enemy, and that I know more about the affairs of the new company than I am willing to tell him. He is becoming more unbearable every day. Only last night he told me that I could leave him whenever I wanted to as he could get along better without me. He said that he did not want a traitor in his house. Oh, it is terrible! I cannot understand what has come over him. He was always hard and unsympathetic, but never like this."

"And will you go?" Jasper enquired.

"At first I thought I would. But after thinking it all over very carefully I have decided to remain with him. He needs me now more than ever. You have no idea what a helpless man he is. I shudder to think what would become of him should I leave him at the present time."

"But it might teach him a lesson if you should leave him for a while," Jasper urged. "It is not right that your life should be made so miserable."

He was looking into her downcast face as he said this. Her hands were clasped before her, and how he longed to seize them in his, and tell her all that was in his heart; how he would look after her and bestow upon her that love which her father denied her.

"I must not forsake him," was her low reply. "He is my father, and I must remain by his side. I promised my mother that I would. We shall leave for the city next week, and I dread the thought of going."

"But you will be able to forget much of your trouble there, will you not? Your social life will be so different, and —"

"Don't speak of such a thing," she interrupted. "You little realise how I despise so many of the social gatherings held there. What do they amount to? What good do they do? I enjoy amusements, but I think people should not make them the sole object in life. But that seems to me to be just what so many do. I want to be of some use in the world, and I believe the best way to be happy is to help others."

They were walking slowly along as Lois uttered these words. She spoke deliberately as if she had considered them carefully, and was not speaking under the influence of the moment.

"You are right, Miss Sinclair," Jasper replied. "I, too, have come to realise that he who thinks only of self finds unhappiness, while he who forgets self in seeking to help and uplift others will find the greatest joy."

The tone of certainty in his voice caused Lois to glance up into his face. She liked his words, especially as she felt they were real.

"And you were not always like that?" Lois asked.

"Oh, no. Only recently have I come to view things in a different light."

"What caused the change?"

"It was old David."

"Old David! I am surprised to hear you say that. I had no idea that he was able to influence any one except Betty Bean."

"He has influenced me as well, though it was all done unconsciously. I have been watching him closely for some time, and ever since I have known him he has been so happy. Even when he had not a cent and was sold to the lowest bidder, he did not lose heart. And why? Because he was thinking of others, and what his plans would do for the people both in the city and in the country. He was willing to endure poverty and taunts that those around him might be benefited. He was misunderstood, but it made little or no difference to him. He was happy in the thought that he was going to do good. To me he is a wonder, and I believe I can do no better than endeavour to follow his example and think less of myself. When I entered into the employ of this new company I did it merely for the money I was to get out of it, and a certain spirit of curiosity as to the outcome. Now, however, I am working with a far higher motive. I begin to see what a benefit this undertaking will be to the entire community and a blessing to so many, even though at present they may not realise it."

They had reached the gate leading to the Sinclair house by the time Jasper had finished. The colour had returned to Lois' cheeks, and her eyes were now filled with animation.

"Oh, I am so glad to hear you speak as you do," she replied. "It strengthens my own convictions to hear you express yourself that way, and I feel that I shall bear my part more bravely in the city than otherwise I would have done."

Jasper's pulse beat quicker at these words. So she would think of him, then, in the midst of her active city life. There was a great comfort to him in the thought.

"You will return next summer, I suppose," he remarked. "We shall miss you very much in the meantime."

"I hope to do so, and it will be something to look forward to. But you will surely come to see us when you visit the city. I shall be so anxious to hear all the news from Creekdale."

"Nothing would give me greater pleasure," Jasper replied. "But I do not expect to leave the woods before spring. Even if business should take me to the city, I should not feel like making a social call. I should frighten you and your friends who might happen to be with you by my rough clothes and hard hands. Oh, no, it would not be proper, so I had better stay away."

Lois was not slow in detecting the note of bitterness an his voice as he uttered these words. She was aggrieved that he should think that his rough appearance would make any difference to her. And yet she understood his feelings. His sensitiveness would make him most unwilling to go to a place where he would be looked upon with ridicule, and at the same time embarrass the ones he happened to visit.

"You need not worry about your appearance when you visit me, Mr. Randall," and her eyes met his as she spoke. "I shall think all the more of you if your hands are rough and your face weather-beaten. I shall never be ashamed of the marks of honest toil. I must go now, but I shall expect to see you before spring."

To Jasper that was one of the happiest times of his whole life. He believed that she was interested in him, while the look in her eyes and the words she uttered were to him an inspiration during the following days and weeks of weary work in the woods.

CHAPTER XIV

SUBTLE INFLUENCE

Although Lois preferred to remain in the country, yet she did not waste her days in repining over her life in the city. She at once looked about for opportunities of usefulness. These she found in St. Saviour's, the church she attended. Her musical abilities made her a welcomed member of the choir. But she was not satisfied with merely singing. She wished to do more, and she soon found an outlet in assisting the unfortunate ones in the parish. It was through "The Helping Hand Society" that she found she could do the most effective work, and she never tired of going from house to house where her services were most needed.

Dick often upbraided her for giving so much of her time to Church work, and said that she should go with him to dances and whist parties.

"I have no interest in such things," she told him over and over again. "There is too much to be done around us in helping others, to spend all of one's time upon such gaieties."

"But think what people are saying," her brother protested. "They call you unsociable and stuck-up, and it is hard for me to listen to such things."

Lois laughed at Dick's fears and told him not to worry. She said that she was quite able to look after herself, and did not mind what people were saying so long as she was doing what was right.

When Christmas season came around Lois found herself

more busy than ever. There were so many baskets to be provided for the needy, and this year they were going to send a number to poor families out in the country districts. It was just when she was in the midst of this work that Dick asked her to attend a dance with him on Thursday night.

"If you don't go this time I shall never ask you again," he told her. "It's to be at Mrs. Dingle's, and you know how cut up she will feel if you refuse her. Sammie, too, is expecting you, and he will never visit us again if you do not go."

"But how am I to leave my work, Dick?" Lois questioned. "We are so busy every night packing the boxes, which we must get off as soon as possible. I am more interested in them than I am in what Mrs. Dingle and Sammie might think. They surely know by this time that I do not care for them."

"Well, come for my sake, then," Dick pleaded.

"That is a better reason why I should go," and Lois smiled upon her brother.

"And you will go?" Dick was all eagerness now. "There's to be a jolly crowd there. Sammie told me that he has invited a crack-a-jack of an artist he met at the club. He is an English chap and has been out here only a short time. He puts out some great stuff in the way of pictures, so I understand. Then, that Westcote girl is to be there. My, I'm anxious to meet her. She is worth while if what I hear about her is true."

The mention of the Westcote girl gave Lois more interest in the dance than she had hitherto taken. She did want to see her as well as Dick, for she had often thought about her since she had heard that Jasper had luncheon with her and her father at the Sign of the Maple. It was unusual for her to take an interest in a stranger. But this was different, and so she decided to accompany her brother.

Mrs. Dingle was delighted to have Lois at her party, principally on her son's account. She had chosen her for Sammie from all the eligible girls she knew, and the idea that Lois might object to becoming Mrs. Sammie Dingle never once entered her mind. There were financial reasons as well, for was not Peter Sinclair manager and chief owner of the City Light and Power Company?

Lois had not been long in the room, ere she felt herself affected by some unknown influence. She could not account for this feeling as she had never experienced, anything like it before. Even when on the floor in the midst of a dreamy waltz, a sense of dread almost overwhelmed her. A weight seemed suddenly to press upon her heart, as if some terrible disaster were near. Hers was not a mind to be easily disturbed by such things, and she was not naturally of a superstitious nature. She tried to shake off the feeling, but all in vain. What was the cause of it? she asked herself over and over again.

That waltz was the longest she had ever experienced; and most thankful was she when Sammie at last led her off the floor. As she was about to sit down she happened to glance to her right, and as she did so her eyes met those of a man standing not far away. Intuitively she realised that there was the source of her strange agitation. It was only for an instant that their eyes met, but it was long enough for Lois to realise that some subtle influence had come upon her which would affect her whole life.

With as much composure as possible she resumed her seat. She longed to be alone that she might think it all over, and endeavour to cast off the spell which was depressing her. She tried to reason it out, but her thoughts were interrupted by Mrs. Dingle who stood suddenly before her.

"Lois, dear," she heard her say, "I want you to meet my famous guest, Mr. Sydney Bramshaw, the noted English artist, who has favoured us with his presence to-night. I have been waiting this opportunity ever since you arrived, but could not get you and Sammie separated long enough to do so until now."

These closing words annoyed Lois and she longed more than ever to leave the room, especially so when Bramshaw sat down by her side and began to talk to her in a familiar manner.

"I wanted to meet you as soon as I saw you enter the room," he told her, "and I almost despaired of obtaining an opportunity."

"Why should you be so anxious to meet me?" Lois replied. "I am sure that I have done nothing to merit your special attention."

"Oh, but you are so decidedly superior to the rest, don't you know. I am somewhat gifted with a discerning mind, and am able at a glance to tell the gold from the dross."

If Bramshaw imagined that his companion was susceptible to such flattery he was greatly mistaken. His words disgusted Lois, and yet she must remember that he was Mrs. Dingle's guest and that she must be agreeable as far as it was possible.

"You are an artist, so I understand," she replied.

"Yes, in a way. I am fond of observing the beautiful in the common things of Nature, and placing them upon canvas. So many go through life with their eyes shut. They have eyes but do not see. With me it is different, and because of my ability to see and depict the real things of life, I have received considerable recognition."

"That must give you satisfaction," Lois murmured.

She tried to seem interested, but it was a difficult undertaking.

"It does in a way," and Bramshaw assumed an air of careless indifference. He was a little man, and his effort made him seem ridiculous. "But, it is so seldom that one meets with kindred spirits, don't you know. There are so few who are able to discuss the finer points of art. I would not mind in the least enlightening those around me, but they, as a rule, are so unwilling to listen. With you, however, it is different. You have a trained mind, and that makes such a vast difference."

Lois was about to make some half-hearted reply, when her eyes rested upon the face of a girl on the opposite side of the room. It was the most beautiful and perfect face she had ever seen, and she wondered who she was and where she had come from. She tried to listen to what Bramshaw was saying and at the same time watch the girl before her. She was talking to Dick, and she noted the animated expression upon her face as she smiled at something he was saying. It must have been about her for she suddenly turned and their eyes met. For an instant only the girl hesitated, and then with a graceful movement swept swiftly across the room and stood before Lois.

"Pardon me," she began, as she took Lois' hand, "I could not help coming to you as soon as I saw you. Your brother was telling me what a hard time he had to get you away from your Church work to come to the party. When I heard that I wanted to meet you at once. I am Margaret Westcote, and have been in this country but a short time, and everything is so new and interesting to me."

"Ducedly tame, I call it," Bramshaw interposed before Lois had time to say a word. "I can't for the life of me see what you find congenial in a land like this, Miss Westcote."

"It all depends upon what you call tame, Mr. Bramshaw," was the somewhat sarcastic reply. "If you spend your time thinking only about yourself it is no wonder you are bored. I haven't heard of your doing anything worth while since you came to this city."

"Come, come, Miss Westcote," Bramshaw protested, as he stroked his silky moustache with the soft white fingers of his right hand. "Artists, you should realise, are generally misunderstood. You cannot judge us according to ordinary standards. We are often most intensely busy when we seem to be inactive. Our apparent idleness is the time when valuable impressions are being imbibed to be produced later in master-pieces for the benefit and admiration of the whole world. It is utterly impossible for ordinary minds to grasp this, but it is true, nevertheless."

"I beg your pardon, Mr. Bramshaw," and the girl made him a slight graceful bow, "I really forgot that you are an artist. Appearances are so deceptive, you know. I shall leave you now to carry on your imbibing process. Perhaps Miss Sinclair will come with me, so that you can have the imbibing time all to yourself. It would be a pity to spoil your great masterpiece."

Lois was surprised at Miss Westcote's sarcasm, and, she fully expected that Bramshaw would be angry. But he did not appear to mind in the least. On the contrary, he smiled all the time she was speaking, as if her words greatly amused him. Lois was glad of any excuse to leave this man whose very presence depressed her in a remarkable manner. When at last alone with Miss Westcote in an adjoining room, she sank into a comfortable chair in a cosy corner. Her face was unusually pale, and this her companion at once noted.

"You are tired," she sympathetically remarked, taking a seat by her side. "You seem to be greatly upset."

"It is that man," Lois replied with considerable emphasis. "I never had any one to affect me as he does. I cannot under-stand it. I am not superstitious, and I have always prided myself upon my self-confidence, but I cannot account for the feeling that has come over me to-night."

"Oh, that man would upset almost any one," Miss Westcote replied. "I can not endure him."

"You do not evidently mind speaking plainly to him," Lois remarked.

"Certainly not. When I take a dislike to any person I generally say just what I think, especially to such a cad as that."

"You know something about him, then?"

"All I want to. He has been trying to get my father to give him the position of looking after an old man up the river. Mr. Randall has been doing it, and Bramshaw wants to have him discharged so he can get the job. Just think of that."

"Why should he wish to do that?" Lois asked in great surprise. "If he is an artist why should he want to take care of old David?"

"So you know the old man?" Miss Westcote enquired.

"Oh, yes. And I know Mr. Randall, too. He is so good to old David."

"I know he would be. I met him once at the Sign of the Maple with my father, and he seemed to be so different from most men. He was so manly and had such a strong face. I liked him as soon as I saw him."

"He deserves great credit, Miss Westcote. He is a self-made man, and his life has been a hard one. He has had to struggle against many obstacles. But he will win and make a name for himself, I feel quite sure."

It was impossible for these two to be long alone in such a quiet spot. Just when the conversation was becoming interesting, they were sought for by their partners for the next dance, and reluctantly they were forced to forego the many things they wished to say to each other.

CHAPTER XV

THE "CUT-OFF"

The meeting with Margaret Westcote was a great event in Lois' life. Hitherto, her lot had been somewhat of a lonely one, with no special girl friend to share her confidences. Her interests had always been so different from others that she was not looked upon by any as a boon companion. She often reasoned with them and asked why they should make selfish pleasure the principal motive of living when they could have more enjoyment by putting self last and others first.

With Margaret Westcote, however, it was different. She was after Lois' own heart, and the two were as one in their interests. Each supplied what the other lacked; one her vivaciousness, and the other her calmness of mind. Their friendship was not a growth but a fusing at the first meeting. They were now very much together, and Margaret took a keen interest in the work of getting the Christmas supplies ready for needy families.

Dick was delighted that this beautiful girl was so much at the house, and for the first time in his life he found Church work most interesting. He was always ready to help, but was generally in the way. It was quite evident that he was greatly in love with Margaret, though she on her part treated him as a mere boy and not as a lover. He could not seem to realise that she was an excellent judge of character, and preferred men who did things instead of spending their time in idleness. Lois understood the girl's feelings, and the truth began to dawn upon her that Jasper Randall was Margaret's ideal type of a man. One who could battle and overcome was the man who appealed to her. Whenever Jasper's name was mentioned Margaret's eyes would sparkle with animation, and she never tired of talking about him and the struggle he had made in life.

The week before Christmas Lois became more enthusiastic than ever with the work of getting the boxes ready to be sent to the various families. She longed to interest her father, and one morning before he left for his office she asked him if he would not do something for the families of the men who were working for him in the woods on the old Dinsmore Manor. She had never spoken to him about the letter he had written to Mrs. Bean, feeling sure that it would be of no avail. But she had learned through a letter from Betty that the choppers had not yet crossed the line, and for this Lois was thankful. Perhaps he did not intend to take the logs, she reasoned, but had written the letter during one of his cranky moods, with no intention of putting his threat into practice.

"Why should we send anything to country families?" her father asked her. "They earn good money, and why should we help them?"

"But there are some very poor families," Lois replied, "and I know they can hardly make a living. There is Mrs. Bean, for instance. She hasn't the bare necessities of life at times, and a present this Christmas would be a blessing to her."

"I can't help that," Mr. Sinclair angrily retorted. "It's none of my business if she is poor. Where would we be, I'd like to know, if we handed out to such people? Why, there are thousands of them."

It was in no happy frame of mind that Mr. Sinclair left the house and made his way down town. Reaching his office, he seated himself before his desk and spread out a somewhat soiled piece of paper. Over this he ran his finger until it stopped at a certain mark. "Camp Number One," he muttered. "Ha, ha! good timber there, and close to the line, too. Camp Number Two — much nearer the line," and his finger moved over the paper to another mark. "Camp Number Three, and over the border into the enemy's country, ha, ha! Good for five thousand. Pine timber, straight and clean as masts, and thick as hair on a dog's back. How they'll squirm, those country clogs, when they see their good logs floating down the river. But they're mine. The new line is right, for the best surveyor in the Province ran it. Fifty rods inside the old one, ha, ha! I expect they'll make a fuss and put up a big kick. But I'll fight them, and then we'll see what money will do."

A knock sounded upon the door, and three men entered with hats in their hands.

"Mr. Sinclair, I believe," the spokesman began.

"Yes, that's my name, and what can I do for you?" the lumberman replied.

"Well, you see," continued the other, "we've come to the city on purpose to have a talk with you about that line you had run between your land and ours."

"Well, and what about it?" snapped Sinclair.

"We've been appointed a committee to inform you that your men are cutting logs over the line, and are encroaching on the shore lots. They began day before yesterday."

"What, the men of Camp Number Three?"

"Yes."

"But that timber is mine," Sinclair replied. "I sent a surveyor there last summer and he found that the old line was wrong. A new one was run which gives me fifty rods off the rear of your shore lots."

"There must be some mistake, Mr. Sinclair," the countryman calmly returned. "Our forefathers received their lands as grants from the Crown after the Revolutionary War. A line was then run which separated the shore lots from that portion of land known as the 'Dinsmore Manor,' and there has been no dispute over it until now."

"Look here!" and Sinclair sprang to his feet. "I know my business and attend to it. You attend to yours. The new line is right and, by heavens, I'll stick to it!"

"We are attending to our business," the countryman replied, "and we'll show you, wealthy though you are, that you can't work any bluff game on us. But," and here he lowered his voice, "Mr. Sinclair, we don't want to quarrel. We came chiefly to tell you that your men in Camp Number Three are cutting the logs on the farm of a poor widow with several children. If you are a man of any heart you will see that the work is stopped at once."

"What, cease for a widow and her brood? Never! There is the Poor House — let her go there; and the Orphanage is the place for the kids if they are not old enough to work. Such people only injure a settlement, and you should be glad to be rid of them. So, gentlemen, as I have much business on hand, I wish to be alone."

"And you will do nothing to help that poor woman?" the three men asked as one.

"No, nothing. Do your best. If you wish to lose your farms, go ahead. Good day."

Christmas came on Thursday, and on Tuesday morning Mr. Sinclair informed Lois that he was going away and would not be back until the end of the week. It was during breakfast that he told her this, and Lois paused in the act of pouring his coffee.

"And you'll not be here for Christmas?" she asked in surprise.

"No. Christmas means nothing to me. I intend to visit my camps. I should have gone before, as no doubt the men are loafing. I am going to surprise them. They'll never expect to see me at this season of the year. The men'll want to take three days off, and I can't allow it. They always come back unfitted for work after their celebrations. They'll do nothing of the kind this year if they expect to work for me."

Lois knew only too well how useless it was to try to reason with her father when he had once made up his mind. She had learned from bitter experience in the past that the less she said the better it would be. Nevertheless, her heart was very sad at the change that had come over her father. Never before had he gone away fit Christmas time, and it was the one day in the year when he was more pleasant than usual. What would be the outcome of it all? she wondered.

That very morning as soon as breakfast was over Mr. Sinclair left for the scenes of his lumbering operations, about fifty miles from the city. He travelled with a horse and sleigh, and on the second day he reached Camp Number Two shortly after the men had finished their mid-day meal and were starting back to their work. No sooner had Sinclair entered the cabin than his eyes fell upon a man lying in one of the bunks.

"Hello, Stevens," he called to the foreman, "who is this taking life so easy, when the rest of us are struggling for our daily bread?"

"Oh, that is Robins, one of our best men," was the reply. "He took sick this morning, and I would have sent him to the shore at once only to-morrow will be Christmas Day and I thought he could wait until to-night when the teams will be going out, and —"

"Going out! Going out, are they?" Sinclair interrupted. "And who gave orders to quit on Christmas Day, I'd like to know?"

"We always quit on that day, sir," Stevens stammered. "It's been the custom for years, and I took it for granted —"

"Yes, that's just the trouble. You take too many things for granted. But I tell you this, Christmas is all nonsense. It breaks up the work, and the hauling season is none too long at the best.

I'll have none of it. You'll work or quit, and that's the end of it."

"But what about Robins?" questioned the foreman, whose thoughts were travelling away to a little group of bright faces anxiously awaiting his home-coming for a jolly Christmas.

"Isn't there any spare team?" Sinclair asked.

"None to spare, sir. We've only the bob-sleds, and they're not much for a sick man to ride on. But," he added after a pause, "we were going to fix up something to-night, sir."

"Confound it all!" Sinclair exclaimed. "What are we going to do? I can't afford to let a double team go, and besides, it would mean a loss of two days. Let me see. How far is it to Camp Number Three?"

"Three miles if you go by way of the cut-off, but four if you go around. The cut-off hasn't been used much by the teams this winter, and it is little more than a foot-path."

"How far is it to the cut-off?" Sinclair asked.

"About two miles."

"Well, look here, Stevens. You drive me to that cut-off, and then get some one to take that sick fellow out with my rig. I'll walk the rest of the way to the camp, and stay there till you come for me."

When the cut-off had been reached, Sinclair started off on a brisk walk in the keen frosty air. He even felt quite young and cheerful as he moved forward. But the trail was rough, and his coat was very heavy, so after walking for some time he began to feel weary.

"This is a long trail," he muttered. "Confound that sick man! What business had he getting laid up and causing all this trouble."

Hardly had the words left his mouth before his foot struck the stump of a small tree, and with a cry of pain he sank upon the snow. Recovering himself he tried to walk, but so great was the agony when his right foot touched the trail that he groaned aloud.

CHAPTER XVI

CHRISTMAS EVE

Peter Sinclair was now in a serious predicament. Fortune had favoured him so long that to be thus blocked by a mean little stump was too much for his excitable nature. He raged and railed against everything and everybody in general. But the tall stately trees were silent witnesses to his passionate outbursts, and poor sympathisers. When sober thoughts at length came to him, he began to realise the seriousness of his position. Out of hearing of the camp, on a trail seldom travelled; a sprained ankle; the short December day closing down, and the unknown terrors of the lone forest. The perspiration stood out in beads upon his forehead as he viewed the situation.

At last he started to limp along the trail, but at every step he staggered into the snow and fell heavily forward. He tried to crawl, but so slow was his progress and so weary did he become that this was soon abandoned. And there he lay, thinking as he had never thought before. His business was forgotten, and several times he remembered the sick man lying in the bunk at Camp Number Two. And all this time the sun sank lower to rest, and long shadows stole among the great trees like fearful monsters creeping upon him. He became cold, too, and his body shivered, while his teeth chattered incessantly.

When it seemed to him that he had lain there on the snow for hours, he heard a noise, and looking along the trail he saw a little red dog bounding straight toward him. How often had he spurned just such a cur with his foot, on the city streets, but never did any creature seem so good to Sinclair as did that lean canine specimen before him.

"Good doggie," he called. "Come here, doggie."

But the animal remained at a safe distance, barking furiously, at the same time casting glances back along the trail as if expecting some one from that quarter. Soon a sturdy figure appeared in sight with a rabbit over his shoulder. He stopped in amazement at the scene before him, unable to comprehend its meaning.

"Come here, sonny," Sinclair called out, fearing the boy would take fright and disappear.

But the lad stood perfectly still as if turned to stone.

"For heaven's sake!" Sinclair continued, "come and help a poor stricken man who can't walk."

At this appeal the boy drew nearer, and seeing that it was only a man lying in the snow, the startled expression faded from his face.

"What's the matter, and watcher want?" he asked.

"I've sprained my ankle and can't walk," was the reply. "Is there any house near? Can't you bring some one to help me?"

At this the lad became electrified into new life. His senses returned, and he grasped the situation in an instant.

"Gee whiz!" he exclaimed. "Mighty lucky I came to my rabbit snares to-night instead of t'morrer. Y'see, that's Christmas Day, and we don't do no work then."

"Lucky for me you came to-night, my boy," Sinclair replied, and then he remembered how he had denounced the day but a short time before. "But I can't stay in this place all night. Can't you get somebody to help me?"

"Y'bet," the boy responded. "Buck and Bright'll help y'outer this fix. Jes' wait a minute."

At this he hurried away, and although he was gone not much over half an hour it seemed to Sinclair like an age before

"Haw, Buck! G'up, Bright! Git up thar!" sounded upon his ears.

Presently he beheld the forms of two panting steers, plunging and wallowing through the snow, each crowding the other in an endeavour to maintain the firm footing on the narrow trail. When they caught sight of the dark object lying before them, they stopped, sniffed the air, and bolted to the right. But the boy with considerable skill, the result of long practice, wheeled them about, and after much shouting and exertion headed them homeward.

"Hi, thar!" he called to the prostrate man. "Kin ye manage t'git to th' sled? These steers is mighty scart, and I must stan' by an' hold 'em."

With a great effort Sinclair began to crawl slowly along the trail, and when about exhausted reached the sled.

"Hol' on now," the boy ordered, as he cracked his whip and the steers started forward. It was a rough trip, over knolls, striking stumps here and there, and squeezing between trees, when the sled had to be freed by much twisting and manoeuvring; but Sinclair thought it the best ride he had ever taken.

"Mother's lookin' fer y'," remarked the lad, when they had finally gained the good road. "She's got the best sofy out, an' was warmin' things up when I left."

Sinclair made no reply. He was cold, stiff, and too much exhausted to enter into conversation. Not until he was stretched out on the big cosy sofa in front of the cheerful fire, after his sprained ankle had been bathed and well rubbed, did he become talkative.

"My good woman," he began, "how can I ever repay you for your great kindness?"

"Oh, that's nothing," she returned with a cheerful smile. "I'm so glad Stephen went to his snares to-night. It's Christmas Eve, you see, and though I'm sorry you're hurt, yet it's nice to have some one with me and the children. It's very lonely here sometimes, and," she added after a pause, "he was here last Christmas. But," she quickly continued, afraid she had said too much to a stranger, "I hope you feel more comfortable now, sir."

"Oh, yes," Sinclair replied. "My foot is quite easy: But would you mind making me a cup of hot tea? I feel so chilly, and the tea will do me a world of good. It always helps me."

As he uttered these words a change passed over the woman's face, which Sinclair was not slow to observe.

"Never mind," he hastened to remark. "I don't wish to trouble you."

"Dear me, sir, it's not that," the woman replied, somewhat confused, as she sat down upon a splint-bottom chair, and plucked at her apron. "It's not the trouble I mind; it's something else. You see, it's this," she continued, while a flush passed over her care-worn face. "He left us last February, after one month's illness, and what with the doctor's bills and funeral expenses it was hard scraping. We tried our best to get along, and ploughed and sowed last spring. But it was a bad year for us. The frost destroyed our buckwheat and potatoes when they were just in blossom; a fine cow died, and the foxes killed our geese and turkeys. But we had our logs, and we always felt that we could fall back on them if the worst came. Then just as we had made up our minds to sell a strip to that new Light and Power Company another blow fell."

"What was that?" Sinclair quickly asked, as a new light dawned upon his mind.

"It was a letter, sir, that I received from Mr. Sinclair, the manager of the city Light and Power Company, and who does a big lumbering business besides. He told me that a new line had been run by a surveyor between the shore lots and the old Dinsmore Manor, and that all of those logs which I had hoped to sell belong to him. He warned me not to sell or cut one, as he would prosecute me at once if I did. His men have already begun work, and I am helpless to stop them. It is no use for me to go to law as I have no money, and it takes money to fight a man like that. Would you like to see the letter, sir?"

"No, no," Sinclair hastily replied. "That man is a dev — excuse me, madam, but I mean he is a hard man."

"Well, you see," the woman continued, "things got so bad that we had to give up every little luxury, and the few dollars we could make from eggs and butter went for flour, clothing and taxes. Tea we found too expensive, and it was given up. That is the reason why I can't give you any to-night, sir. And the poor children are so disappointed. Never before were they without presents at Christmas time. But this year —" Here the woman stopped and put her apron to her face. It was for only an instant, however, for quickly removing it she continued: "But gracious me! here I've been bothering you with my long tale of woe, when you, poor man, have troubles enough of your own. I have some fresh bread, butter, milk and preserves, which you shall have at once," and the little woman bustled away, leaving Sinclair alone with his thoughts.

"Isn't it about time the mailman was along?" the mother asked that evening, after the chores had been done, and the children were sitting quietly in the room for fear of waking the stranger who had fallen asleep upon the sofa.

"I believe I hear his bells now!" Stephen cried, as he rushed to the door. Presently he came running back, his face aglow with excitement. "A bundle, Mother!" he shouted. "A big bundle! Come and help me."

The confusion thus made awakened Sinclair, who opened his eyes just in time to see a good-sized bundle carried into the room, securely bound with stout cords.

"There must be some mistake," exclaimed the surprised woman to the mailman who had entered.

"No, mum," he replied. "It's yours all right. I found it at the shore where a freightin' team left it. I don't generally carry such things. But says I to myself, 'That's fer Widder Bean, and she's goin' to have it to-night if Tim Harking knows anything.' So thar 'tis. I must be off now. A merry Christmas to ye all," and with that the big-hearted man hurried away.

"Dear me!" cried Mrs. Bean. "What can it be, and who could have sent it?"

"Let's open it, mother," Steve suggested. "Mebbe we'll find out then."

Together they all set to work, and after much tugging and labour the knots were loosened and the bundle fell apart.

Then what a sight met their eyes. Clothes of various sizes and quality were neatly piled together; complete suits for the boys; dresses for Betty and Dora, and another for their mother, besides a good supply of underwear for the whole family.

"Well, bless my heart!" Mrs. Bean exclaimed. "Who in the world has done this? There must be some mis —"

"A doll!" shrieked Dora.

"A knife!" yelled Stephen, as he seized the precious treasure, felt its keen edge and examined the handle.

Then a paper fluttered out of the bundle and fell on the floor at Mrs. Bean's feet. As she picked it up and read the contents, a light broke over her puzzled face, and her hand trembled.

"What's the matter, Mother?" Jimmy asked, noting her agitation.

"Nothing, my boy," she replied. "Only I'm so overcome at the good Lord giving us such kind friends on this Christmas Eve. This is such a lovely letter from Miss Sinclair, and she says that all these things are from the Helping Hand Society of St. Saviour's Church. Isn't it good of them?"

A groan from the sofa startled her.

"Is your ankle worse, sir?" she enquired, going to the side of the afflicted man.

"Y-y-es," Sinclair replied; "but I feel better now. I didn't mean to disturb you."

"And look here!" Stephen cried, who had at length reached the bottom of the bundle. "Well, I declare! Two packages of Red Rose tea! Hurrah! Now we kin have some fer Christmas."

"And you, poor man," she said turning to Sinclair, "shall have a good strong cup just as soon as I can make it. It seems to me I must be dreaming," and the excited woman bustled off to the kitchen.

"Fool! fool!" Sinclair mused to himself as he sipped the delicious beverage. "I thought such gifts went only to rogues and lazy rascals. I was wrong. And yet, some of that tea has reached one of the biggest fools and rogues in the whole country, and that is Peter Sinclair."

"And now, children," said Mrs. Bean, when the excitement of the evening had somewhat subsided, "it's getting late. Let's have a Christmas hymn, and then Dora must go to bed. You don't mind, sir, I hope. We always sing several hymns on Christmas eve, and last year he was here to start them, for he had a good voice."

"Oh, no," Sinclair replied. "I don't mind, so go ahead."

The mother started and all joined in; and as the words of "Hark the Herald Angels Sing" floated forth, old memories came drifting into the mind of the silent listener on the sofa. He forgot for a time his surroundings and saw only the little parish church, of his boyhood days, decked with fresh bright evergreens, and heard the choir singing the familiar carols. Several faces stood forth in clear relief; his parents', honest and careworn; his rector's, transfigured with a holy light; and one, fresh and fair, encircled by a wreath of light-brown tresses.

He came to himself with a start, thinking the choir was singing "Glory to the New-Born King," when it was only the little group at his side finishing their hymn. Tears were stealing down his cheeks, which he quickly brushed away, lest his emotion should be observed.

That night, when the house was quiet, Sinclair drew forth a small note-book and wrote a few lines to the foreman of Camp Number Three. "Send word to the other camps as quickly as possible, and tell the men they need not come back till next Monday." He then brought forth a thin book and made out a cheque for no small amount, payable to Mrs. Bean on account.

Little did Peter Sinclair realise that the letter written to the foreman would never reach its destination, and that months would pass before the cheque would be presented for payment.

CHAPTER XVII

THE NIGHT SUMMONS

All through the fall and winter Jasper had been very busy. The planning of the work, the overseeing of the men and ordering the supplies rested upon him alone. He felt the responsibility, and he was determined that as far as he was concerned the company should not be disappointed in the amount of logs cut and hauled to the large "brow" near the falls. He left the woods only when it was absolutely necessary for him to do so. Several times he was tempted to drive to the city when new supplies were needed instead of ordering them over the telephone from Creekdale. He longed to see Lois, even for a few minutes. Such a visit, no matter how brief, would be an inspiration to him in his arduous work. But he had always resisted the temptation, however, and had remained firmly at his post. His desire to see her and to listen to her voice was great. But he dreaded the idea of presenting himself at her home when she might have company, and he would feel so much out of place in their presence. It might embarrass Lois as well, so he reasoned, and it would be better for him not to go.

As Christmas drew near the men began to talk much about going home. Jasper listened to them but took no part in the conversation. All of the men had homes to go to. Most of them were married, and were looking forward with eagerness to the holiday with their families. But to Jasper the season brought little joy. No one was expecting him, and no face would brighten at his home-coming. There was only one place where he longed to go, and one person he desired to see. If he could but feel that her eyes would sparkle and her heart beat with joy at his presence, he would not have hesitated a moment. But he was not sure, and so he decided to remain in camp and keep watch over the supplies while the rest went home. If Christmas Day should be fine, he planned to pay a visit to old David in the afternoon. He might hear something about Lois from the Petersons, so he thought, and that would be some comfort.

Jasper lived in a small snug log cabin which he had built for his own special use. He wished to be alone as much as possible each night that he might think over the work for the next day, and also have quietness for reading. He had supplied himself with a number of books, and these were placed on a small shelf fastened to the wall. So long had he been denied the privilege of good literature that he now came to the feast like a starving man. Hitherto, his mind had craved only solid works of the masters. But of late he had turned his attention more to books of romance, for in them he could find more heart satisfaction than in the others. How he revelled in the outstanding characters of Dickens, Scott, Thackeray and Kingsley. But it remained for Charles Reed to completely captivate him in "The Cloister and the Hearth."

He was reading it this Christmas Eve as he lay stretched out upon his cot. The lamp was at his head and the camp stove was sending out its genial heat. It was a scene of peace and comfort. But Jasper thought nothing of his surroundings as he lay there, for he was lost in the tragic story of Gerard and Margaret. Nothing had ever moved him as much as the sad tale of these two unfortunate lovers. His disengaged right hand often clenched hard as he read of the contemptible ones who plotted to separate them. But how Margaret appealed to him. What strength of character was hers, and how true and unselfish was her love through long, trying years.

At length, laying aside the book, he began to meditate upon what he would do under like circumstances, if Lois' love for him were as deep as that of Margaret for Gerard. He blamed Gerard for what he considered weakness on his part. Why did he not arouse himself and throw off the shackles which bound him? What right had any Church to separate two loving ones, and make their young lives so miserable?

While thus musing Jasper fell asleep. He was awakened by a loud rapping upon the door. With no idea what time it was he sprang to his feet, hurried across the room and threw open the door. As he did so he saw a young lad standing before him. His face was flushed and he was panting heavily as if from a long run.

"Hello! Who are you? And what do you want here at this time of the night?" Jasper demanded.

"I'm Steve Bean, Betty's brother," the boy replied as he stepped briskly into the cabin. "My, that was a hard run!" he added. "I left home jist a quarter to twelve an' I don't think I've been over twenty minutes comin'."

"Is it that late?" Jasper asked in surprise, as he drew forth his watch. "Why, it's half-past twelve! I didn't think I was asleep that long. But, say, boy, what do you want at this time of the night?"

"I want ye to go fer the doctor as quick as ye can."

"Go for the doctor!" Jasper gasped. "Who's sick? Your mother?"

"Oh, no; she's all right. But there's a man at our place who is pretty bad, I guess. I found him last night on that old cut-off when I was visitin' my snares. He had a sprained ankle, an' couldn't walk. I got the steers and toted him to our place. Guess he got a bad cold while he was layin' there in the snow, fer he took awful sick in the night with chills, an' ma's afraid he'll die. She kept Jimmy to help her an' sent me to git you to fetch the doctor."

"But why didn't you get one of your nearby neighbours to go?" Jasper enquired. "You have lost valuable time already."

"H'm, I guess you don't know our neighbours. They're kind enough an' would do all they could. But their horses are about as slow as oxen. So ma says, 'Steve, you jist hustle fer Mr. Jasper. He's got a horse that goes like a streak of lightin'. He'll go all right when ye tell him you're Betty's brother.' So I took the short-cut through the woods, an' here I am. Will ye go?"

"Sure," Jasper replied as he reached for his coat and hat. "But who is that man? And where did he come from?"

"I don't know; never saw him before. He's quite oldish, though."

"Didn't your mother ask him what he was doing there alone in the woods?"

"No; she didn't like to ask him. She thought maybe he was goin' to Camp Number Three, which is not far from our house, an' on our land, too."

Jasper paused in the act of lighting the lantern and looked into Steve's face.

"Why, didn't you go there for help?" he asked.

"What! go to them skunks fer help?" and the boy clenched his fists. "Never! They're stealin' our logs an' we can't do nothin'. De'ye think we'd ask old Pete Sinclair's men to do anything fer us? We'd die first. Jimmy an' me's been waitin' fer some time fer old Pete to come our way. An' when he does —" Steve's clenched right fist shooting out straight before him supplied his lack of suitable words to express the depth of his feelings.

An idea suddenly flashed into Jasper's mind with a startling intensity.

"What does that man look like?" he demanded in a voice which surprised the boy.

"Oh, he's somewhat oldish, as I told ye; rather thick-set; has a heavy moustache, an' looks as if he has always had plenty of good things to eat. I don't know as I can tell ye much more about him."

Jasper had blown out the lamp and opened the door before Steve had finished speaking. He was now very impatient to be away. There was only one man, he felt quite sure, who would be prowling along that lonely trail on a Christmas Eve, and that man would be Peter Sinclair. It was of Lois he thought and not the sick man as he hurried to the stable, harnessed Pedro, and made him fast to the sleigh.

"You go back home, Steve," he ordered, "and tell your mother that I have gone for the doctor."

Pedro did not like the idea of being taken out of his warm stable at such an hour of the night. But when once upon the firm road he gave his noble head a toss and sped along at a fast clip. He had not been driven much of late and was in excellent form. It was a clear star-light night, with not a breath of wind astir. Jasper not only enjoyed the ride in the bracing air behind such a fast horse, but the feeling that he was doing it for Lois' sake filled him with satisfaction. How he longed to speed straight to her with the message. But, no, that would not do. Her father, he believed, was in need and must be cared for first.

It took him somewhat over an hour to reach the doctor's house and to arouse him from sleep. The latter was in no enviable frame of mind when he had admitted Jasper and learned the object of his visit.

"Confound it all!" he growled. "What do people mean by getting sick in the night! Why don't they take the day for it! But I don't see how I can go now. My horse threw a shoe coming home last night, and I wouldn't think of putting her on the road without being properly shod."

"I'll drive you there," Jasper replied, "and bring you back as well. But we must have you to-night, and at once. If he is the man I think he is, you will not regret going."

"Who is he? Any one I know?" the doctor queried, now somewhat interested.

"Yes, you know him. But I shall not mention his name until I am certain. Will you come?"

"Oh, yes, I suppose so," the doctor replied as he moved wearily away to get ready for the journey. "I have had so many night calls of late that I am tired out, and was hoping to have a good rest, especially on Christmas Day."

In less than half an hour Pedro was again bounding nimbly over the road, this time headed straight for Mrs. Bean's ten miles off. Jasper believed that the doctor slept most of the way for he never uttered a word from the time they started until they drew up before Mrs. Bean's house.

The sound of the bells brought Jimmy to the door, and asking him to stable Pedro and give him something to eat, Jasper accompanied the doctor. He was anxious to find out as soon as possible whether his surmise was correct about the sick man. If so, he had his mind all made up what he would do, and there was no time to be lost.

Mrs. Bean was waiting at the door to receive them, and led the way at once into the little sitting room which was warm and cosy.

"Where's that man?" the doctor asked as he threw off his coat. "You might have waited until morning before sending for me. It's no joke to come so far on a cold night like this."

"But I was afraid he would die, sir," Mrs. Bean replied. "He is a very sick man. He's in there," and she pointed to a door which led from the sitting room.

After warming himself for a few minutes before the stove, the doctor entered the small bedroom closely followed by

Jasper. A shaded lamp with the wick turned down stood on a little table by the side of the bed. Though the light was dim, it was enough for Jasper to recognise the man lying upon the bed.

"You know who it is," he remarked in a low voice as he turned to the doctor.

"Good heavens! it's Peter Sinclair!" was the astonished exclamation. "What in thunder is he doing here?"

CHAPTER XVIII

THE WILD NOR'EASTER

Jasper did not remain long in the bedroom. There was nothing there that he could do and he would be only in the way. He found Mrs. Bean in the kitchen putting some wood in the stove.

"Do you know who that sick man is?" he asked.

"No, I have not the least idea," was the reply. "He is a stranger to me, but that makes no difference. The Bible bids us to entertain strangers for they may be angels unawares. Isn't that so?"

"But the Bible doesn't say that they will all be good angels, does it? Suppose the stranger you entertain should turn out to be your enemy, for instance?"

"Why, what do you mean?" and the widow looked her surprise. "How could an angel be one's enemy?"

"Doesn't the Bible speak about evil angels? If people were troubled with them in olden days I guess affairs haven't changed much since. Now, suppose the stranger you have entertained should be your enemy unawares instead of your friend, what would you do?"

"It wouldn't make any difference in my care of him," Mrs. Bean emphatically replied. "I should do just as the Scripture tells me, 'If thine enemy hunger, feed him; if he thirst, give him drink: for in so doing thou shalt heap coals of fire on his head.' That is what I should do."

"Well, I guess you'll feel like heaping on the coals, all right, when you learn the name of your stranger. You had better get a shovelful ready, for I am going to tell you."

Mrs. Bean was busy setting the table for she knew how the men would appreciate a cup of hot tea and some of her fresh homemade bread after their long cold drive. She paused with a plate in her hand and looked keenly at Jasper as he stood with his back to the stove. When he had mentioned evil angels she thought that he was joking. But now something told her that he was in earnest. Suddenly there flashed into her mind an idea which made her heart thump.

"There is only one person in the world who is my enemy, as far as I know," she remarked.

"The man who is stealing your logs, eh?" Jasper queried.

"Yes. But surely he's not in there!"

"Get your coals ready, Mrs. Bean," Jasper bantered. "You can use them right away if you want to."

Mrs. Bean paid no attention to these words. Her worn face grew a shade paler and her hand shook as she laid the plate upon the table. Just then the doctor entered the kitchen.

"We must have a trained nurse at once," he began. "That's a very sick man in there, Mrs. Bean, and he must have the greatest of care."

"I shall do the best I can, sir," was the quiet reply. "No one shall ever say of me that I didn't do my duty. I have tried to do it in the past and shall try to do it still."

"I know you will do what you can, Mrs. Bean," and the doctor's voice was more gentle than usual, "but you must have assistance. No one could expect you to look after the house and take care of such a sick man as that. We must send to the city for a nurse at once."

"What about Miss Sinclair?" Jasper asked. "She should be told of her father's illness. I was planning to phone to her when we get hack to Creekdale. She could arrange for a nurse to come by train, and I could meet her at the station. This is Christmas Day and I'm afraid it will be difficult to get a nurse to come on go short a notice. She would have to come on the suburban this evening, though, as that will be the only train she would be able to get."

"Do the best you can," the doctor replied. "I shall stay here to-day. It would not do for me to leave now until some one comes to help Mrs. Bean."

The sun was just rising above the far-off horizon as Jasper rode into Creekdale. Not a breath of wind was astir, and the only signs of life were the long wreathes of smoke circling up from numerous chimneys. The village nestled on the side of a hill and thus met the sun's early smile while the surrounding valleys were still draped in shadows. To Jasper it seemed as if fairyland had burst suddenly upon his view after his drive through the sombre forest. The snow sparkled like countless diamonds and the white-robed trees stood bathed in glistening glory. It was Nature's silent symphony in honour of the birthday of the great Prince of Peace.

The telephone was at the store and it did not take Jasper long to arouse Andy Forbes and acquaint him with the object of his early visit. The storekeeper was greatly interested in the news of Peter Sinclair's illness. He knew that in a short time various rumours would be circulating throughout the parish. But he would have exact information and would be able to impress all by his hints of superior and first-hand knowledge.

It took Andy some time to get "Central" in the city, and longer still to make connection with the Sinclair home, the number of which he had found in the Telephone Directory. But at length his efforts were rewarded and he handed the receiver to Jasper.

"Guess it's her, all right," was his comment. "Her voice seems mighty shaky as if she's scared most out of her wits."

How far away seemed Lois' voice and how anxious the tone

as before Jasper had even time to explain she asked about her father. Then, as briefly as possible, Jasper told what had happened to him, his illness, and where he was.

"We need a nurse at once," he said, "and if you can get one, send her out on the suburban. I will meet her at the station."

"She will be there," was the emphatic reply. "I know of one who will go without fail. I thank you very much, Mr. Randall, for all your kindness to my father."

Leaving the store Jasper made straight for the Haven where he received a royal welcome. Early though it was they were all astir for a wonderful Christmas tree had been prepared the day before, and there it stood loaded with presents.

"We had it for Betty," Mrs. Peterson explained, though it was quite evident that she and the captain as well as David were as much pleased as the girl.

Besides the presents from one another there was something for each one from Lois. As Jasper watched them unwrap their gifts and listened to Betty's exclamations of delight, a slight feeling of jealousy stole into his heart. He was the only one there beyond the orbit of Lois' circle of remembrance. He was well aware that he had no reason to expect anything, and yet how much any little token would have meant to him, for it would have told him that she had not forgotten him.

"Wasn't it kind of Miss Lois to send these lovely presents," Betty exclaimed, after she had examined everything most carefully. "And there's something for you, too, Mr. Jasper," she added. "I kept it till the last," and a merry twinkle shone in her eyes as she handed him a neatly-tied package.

"Why, who sent me this?" Jasper asked in surprise.

"Miss Lois, of course. She knew that you would be here today, and she asked me to give it to you when you came. This tree is her idea, you see. We would never have thought about it but for her. Isn't she great!" .

Jasper took the package in his hands and held it there like a big awkward school boy. He could not trust himself to speak lest he should betray his feelings. He longed to be away in the quietness of his own cabin that he might open his treasure and that no eyes but his might look upon the gift. But Betty knew nothing of such thoughts.

"Open it, Mr. Jasper," she ordered, "I know you'll be surprised."

Slowly and carefully Jasper untied the red ribbon and opened out the paper wrapping. As he did so there came forth a grey woollen well-knitted muffler.

"Isn't it lovely!" Betty exclaimed as Jasper stood holding it in his hands staring hard upon it. "And I saw Miss Lois begin it herself just before she left for the city. She asked me what I thought you would like for a Christmas present, and I told her that you should have a muffler to keep your throat warm on cold days. She thought maybe you would rather have a book, but when I told her that you could buy books, but not a muffler like she could make, she said that perhaps I was right. Let me see what it looks like on you, for I must write and tell her all about it."

Before this torrent of words Jasper was as helpless as a child. He allowed Betty to unfold the muffler and wrap it carefully about his neck.

"There, isn't that fine, Mrs. Peterson?" she asked. "Mr. Jasper won't get cold now in his throat, will he?"

"I have never worn such a thing in my life," Jasper managed to explain. "What shall I do with it? I couldn't wear that in the woods."

"Oh, but you might need it, Mr. Jasper," Betty insisted. "Anyway, if you don't wear it Miss Lois will be so disappointed. She knit every bit of it with her own fingers, for she told me so. You should wear it because of that if for no other reason."

Jasper made no reply, but taking off the muffler folded it up and laid it upon the table. In fact, he hardly knew what he was doing so full of happiness was his heart. It was fortunate that just then Mrs. Peterson announced that breakfast was ready, for it changed the topic of conversation and gave him time to think it all over.

What a day that was at the Haven! There were so many things to talk about and such a number of questions to be asked and answered that the time sped by all too quickly. David was in excellent spirits, for he learned of the progress the men were making in the woods. Jasper heard, as well, about Lois, and Betty showed him several letters she had received from her. In every one she told of her longing for the spring that she might return to Creekdale.

When Jasper left the Haven he noticed how the weather had changed. The brightness of the day had passed and the sky was a mackerel grey. The wind, drifting in from the northeast, hummed a weird prelude to the coming storm upon the telephone wires stretched along the road.

The journey to the station was a pleasant one, for Pedro, after his rest, swung along at a swift clip. The wind was in their backs and the snow had not begun to fall. Jasper realised that the storm would not hold off much longer, and he wondered how the nurse would mind facing it for fifteen miles to Mrs. Bean's. The muffler that Lois had given him he was wearing. Betty had put it there before he left the Haven with the strict instruction to wear it, because if he didn't Miss Lois would feel badly. Never had he received any present which he valued more highly than this. And to think that Lois made it herself, especially for him, and that it had been so often in her hands. He was almost like a man beside himself as he thought of this, and several times his lips pressed the muffler in the fervency of his emotion.

Reaching the station he had half an hour to spare before the train would arrive. This gave him an opportunity to give Pedro a feed of oats in a nearby stable, for he well knew that a severe battle was ahead of him. Already the storm had set in, gentle at first but increasing in intensity as the afternoon waned. It was snowing hard by the time the train surged up to the station, and as Jasper waited for the passengers to alight he wondered whether it would be advisable to face the tempest on such a night and in the teeth of so furious a storm.

As the passengers came forth what was his surprise to see not a stranger as he had expected but Lois Sinclair. Scarcely had she stepped upon the platform ere Jasper hurried forward. Her face brightened when she saw him and she reached out her gloved hand.

"How is my father?" was her first question. "I have been so uneasy about him."

As they walked along the platform Jasper told her all he could about the sick man, and how the doctor was staying with him, to assist Mrs. Bean until the nurse arrived.

"I little expected to see you," he added, "I am afraid it will be a terrible drive in the face of this storm. But if we wait until morning the roads will be so blocked that we may not be able to get there for several days."

"Let us go to-night," Lois replied. "I can stand the storm, but it is a great pity to give you so much trouble. How far is it?"

"About fifteen miles. You get good and warm in the waiting-room while I go for Pedro. Wrap yourself up well before we start."

In about a quarter of an hour they had left the station and Pedro was speeding up the road with long swinging strides. So far but little snow had fallen to interfere with the travelling, and they made excellent progress. But after they had been on the way for about an hour Pedro was forced to slow down and walk most of the time. Drifts were forming across the road and the snow was blinding. At times they obtained considerable shelter from stretches of woods they passed through. But out in the open the tempest struck them with full force, blotting out everything from view.

But notwithstanding the discomforts of the journey, Jasper was supremely happy. For a few brief hours this beautiful woman by his side was his, and he was her guide and protector. The unexpected had happened and come what might he would always look back upon this drive as one of the happiest times in his life.

Lois, too, enjoyed the drive. She was content to sit there and to feel Jasper's strength by her side, as he guided Pedro through the night. Owing to the storm there was very little conversation. But it was not necessary. They were happy in each other's presence and words were not needed.

The farther they went the heavier became the roads and the more violent the storm. It was cold as well, and once a shiver shook Lois' body, which Jasper was quick to notice.

"Are you cold?" he asked. "I have an extra rug. Let me wrap it around you."

Carefully as if she had been a child, Jasper placed the rug about Lois' shoulders and over her head. Then, taking off the precious muffler he folded it about her body in such a way as to hold the rug in place and thus form a complete shelter from the driving storm. This accomplished, he reached over and drew the sleigh-robe around her body. It was but natural that his arm should remain around her for a while that the robe might be kept in place. Their heads, too, drew closer together. Perhaps it was the storm which caused this movement, for it was difficult to face the tempest. It was merely an incident in their young lives, and yet it caused their hearts to beat faster and their faces to flush, the memory of which they would ever cherish. How easy then it would have been for Jasper to give voice to the promptings of his heart. He felt that Lois cared for him and would respond to his love. But just when he might have spoken Pedro plunged into the ditch, and it took all of his master's attention to get him back on the road without upsetting the sleigh.

"We nearly went over that time," Jasper remarked. Then they both laughed. Why they did so they alone knew. But from that moment they understood each other better than ever before.

It was a hard struggle Pedro put up that night as mile after mile he crept onward. The froth flew from his champing mouth and the vapour rose from his steaming body. The footing was uncertain, the snow deep, and the driving storm almost blinded him. But never for an instant did he hesitate or show the least sign of discouragement. He seemed to realise how much depended upon his exertions this night, and he felt bound to do his utmost. His master held the reins and in his judgment he had perfect confidence, and for him he would have expended the last ounce of his marvellous strength. Nevertheless, his eyes brightened and his weary steps quickened when at length he saw the lights from Mrs. Bean's house struggling faintly through the night. With a sudden spurt he dashed through the gateway and surged proudly up to the door like a hero who had fought a hard battle and had won.

CHAPTER XIX

DEVELOPMENTS

Lois was destined to remain at Mrs. Bean's during January and February. She camped, as she called it, in the room next to the small one occupied by her father, and thus she was always near to wait upon him day or night. Mr. Sinclair's recovery was slow, and at first the doctor almost despaired of his life. It was a bad case of pneumonia brought on by his becoming over-heated while walking along the cut-out, and then getting chilled to the bone lying on the snow. To Lois it was a most anxious time, and during the first two weeks she seldom went out of the house. When at last her father was able to be left alone for a while she spent an hour or so out of doors with Dora and Stephen.

It was a wonderful winter to the Bean family. Never before had Mrs. Bean known what it was to be free from the oppressing spectre of want. No longer was she forced to worry about household supplies; neither was it necessary for Steve to go to the store each week with his basket of eggs and a few rolls of butter. He carried, instead, an order from Lois, and Andy Forbes was only too willing to deliver the goods in person instead of letting Steve carry them as hitherto. Jimmy was working in the woods with Jasper, and every Saturday night he brought his wages home to his mother. Thus the Bean household was well supplied with sufficient food and the widow's heart was made glad.

To some city people the life in a country house, especially in the winter time, would have been very lonely and trying. But with Lois it was different. She thoroughly enjoyed the change, and as soon as she was able to leave her father alone for a few hours she would spend the time out of doors with Dora and Stephen. To them she was a marvellous woman, and they fairly worshipped her. What fun they had coasting down the big hill over the firm crust, and what snow-houses they made when the snow could be packed and moulded into any shape. But to Lois the best enjoyment of all was to accompany Steve on his rounds to his rabbit snares. The forest was a revelation to her. She knew it well in summer, but nothing about its winter moods, such as the weird silence of a frosty morning, broken only at times by the pistol-like report from a distant tree. It startled her at first, and she stood spell-bound listening to its reverberation up and down the long woody reaches.

"The frost does that," Steve explained. "I've heard our house do the same thing on a cold night. Ma says it's drawin' the nails."

Lois liked the woods best when a stiff wind was abroad. She enjoyed hearing it roaring overhead, bending and twisting the tops of the pointed trees. The forest then seemed to be alive, and not so inanimate as on a cold frosty morning. It was more companionable in such a mood, and it seemed to her like a wonderful organ with all the stops out under the control of some mighty unseen master. It was a pleasure to her to stand and listen to the varying sounds. But Steve and Dora knew nothing of such feelings and kept her constantly on the move. The tracks of the rabbits or those of a fox thrilled them far more than Nature's mysterious melodies.

It was a Saturday afternoon such as this that Lois was with Steve and Dora on their regular rounds. They led her this day farther than usual to some new snares that Steve had set. At length they came out upon the trail leading from Mrs. Bean's to the falls, travelled chiefly by Jimmy. Lois was standing on the path with Dora by her side waiting until Steve had set one more snare in a good place he had spied. She presented a picture of perfect health and beauty as she stood there, with the rich blood mantling her face. Jasper was sure that he had never seen any one so lovely as he appeared suddenly in sight around a bend in the trail. He was walking fast with an axe over his shoulder, but he stopped in his tracks when he saw Lois before him. At first he was half tempted to turn back, lest his presence might not be desired. He did not wish to have the appearance of spying upon those before him. But before he had time to decide, Dora saw him.

"Oh, look," she cried, "there is Mr. Jasper."

Startled more than was her wont, Lois quickly turned and her eyes rested upon the young man who was now hastening forward.

"Pardon me," Jasper began, "I am so sorry that I have frightened you."

"Oh, it is not as bad as that," Lois replied with a smile. "I was not frightened, only startled. Anyway, we are glad to see you, for you have deserted us of late."

"It was not my fault, I assure you," Jasper explained. "We have been so busy that I have had no time to come, though I sent Jimmy often, to enquire about your father. I have had to go to the city every Saturday since I saw you last and never got back until late Sunday night. The company is pushing us hard, and now that the portable saw-mill has arrived there is no let-up. To-day I was cruising the woods for some special trees the company wants, and as I came so near I made up my mind to drop in and see for myself how you are all making out."

"And you will come and have tea with us?" Lois asked.

"Yes, if I shall not be in the way. It will be a great change for me."

"We shall be delighted to have you, and I know my father will be pleased to see you, for he gets so lonely at times. He is sitting up now, and likes to have some one to talk to. He has changed a great deal since his illness."

By this time Steve had finished setting his snare, and then they all started homeward. It was quite an event to have a visitor, so Dora and Steve rushed on ahead to tell their mother to set an extra place "fer company." Lois and Jasper had no inclination to hurry. Their hearts were happy in each other's company, and they walked slowly along the trail not talking about anything in particular, and laughing when there was really nothing to laugh about.

Mr. Sinclair was sitting in a big, cosy chair before the fire as Lois and Jasper entered the room. Notwithstanding the change that had come over him and his desire for conversation, he looked upon his visitor with a reserved suspicion.

"You belong to that new company, eh?" he questioned.

"Only as an employee," Jasper replied. "I am merely working for wages."

"H'm, is that so? I thought you had an interest in the concern."

"In a way I have. I am interested in getting out as many logs and poles as I can this winter. But apart from that I am nothing as far as the company goes."

"But you know all about their plans, I suppose, and what they intend to do?"

"Oh, yes, I naturally understand that they intend to supply light and power to the city and the surrounding country, but further than that I know nothing."

"Don't you know who compose the company?"

"No, I have not the least idea."

"Well, that's queer," and Sinclair shifted uneasily in his chair. "Perhaps you can tell me, though, where Crazy David comes in? He seems to be somewhat connected with the whole affair."

"He supplied the plans, so I believe. They paid him, and made him Honorary President of the company."

"And so that's all you know about it?"

"Certainly. The whole affair is as much of a mystery to me as it is to you."

"Confound it all!" and Sinclair stamped his right foot upon the floor. "I'd like to know what's coming over people, anyway. Things are getting so mysterious these days that I'm about crazy trying to puzzle matters out."

"Don't try, father, dear," Lois soothed, placing her arms about his neck. "You must not make yourself worse by worrying over such things now. Supper is all ready, and Mrs. Bean is waiting for us, so let us forget all about such matters for the present."

Jasper stayed for a while that evening, and before leaving he made arrangements with Lois to take her to church in the morning, and then they would stop at the Haven for dinner. That was the beginning of a most delightful time for Lois and Jasper. Every fine Sunday he called for her, and pleasant were the drives they had together.

When Mr. Sinclair was well enough he moved with his daughter into his own house. Lois and Betty had spent several days getting it in order and thoroughly warmed. It was really a comfort to be here, and for the first time he expressed his pleasure to Lois.

"This is a comfort," and he gave a sigh of relief as he sat in a big chair before a bright open fire. "How large and roomy this house seems after living for so long at Mrs. Bean's. But she was good to us and I hope you sent her that money."

"For the logs on her place?" Lois asked.

"Yes. I made out a cheque the night I took ill, but she never got it. This new one is larger and will somewhat pay her for the trouble we have been to her as well as for the logs."

"I mailed it to-day, father, and Mrs. Bean should get it to-morrow."

"That is good. I feel more contented now. But, see here, Lois, you will be very lonely now with only me to talk to. Isn't there any one who could come and visit us for a while? It might brighten us both up."

"I expect Margaret," Lois replied. "She said she would be delighted to come as soon as we moved into our own house. Dick, you know, will bring her in the car just as soon as the roads are settled. It will be so nice to have her."

"Do you think Mr. Randall will forsake us now?" Mr. Sinclair asked.

"Why, what makes you think that he will?" Lois replied.

"I was afraid he might, that's all. I like that young man. But he has peculiar ideas, and will not go where he thinks he is not wanted."

Lois did not reply to these words. She was sitting by her father's side sewing, and she went on calmly with her work. But she was thinking of the great change that had come over her father since his illness. He was so gentle and considerate, and was more companionable than she had ever known him to be. It caused her great joy of heart, and she was so thankful now that she had not left him when he had made life so miserable for her. She was thankful as well that he liked Jasper and welcomed his visits to the house. She, too, had wondered if he would come as often as he did to Mrs. Bean's. When Margaret arrived he might think that he was not needed and would stay away.

Jasper, however, did not stay away. He came as often as before, even after Margaret arrived. He now believed that Lois cared for him and looked forward with pleasure to his visits. Never before had the Sundays seemed so far apart. She was his inspiration in all that he did and she was ever in his mind throughout the week. How delightful it was to listen to her playing upon the piano, and then when she and Margaret sang, as they did so well together, it seemed to him as if heaven had opened and poured upon him its greatest joys. His past trials were all forgotten, and he did not worry about the future.

One balmy spring Sunday evening they were all gathered around the piano as usual singing several of their favourite hymns. Lois was playing, and the soft light from the shaded lamp fell upon her face. Jasper standing near thought he had never seen her look so beautiful. It seemed to him that her face was almost radiant and her eyes glowed with an intense light of holy fervour. Everything in that room spoke of peace and harmony. The singers were happy in one another's company, and no worry troubled them.

As they sang, the shades of night deepened over the land and brighter the light seemed to shine through the large window facing westward. A man standing just outside watched all that was going on within the room. He had approached cautiously and now stood back far enough from the window that he might not be observed should any one happen to look in his direction. To all outward appearance he might have been drawn there out of mere curiosity or by the sound of the music. His lean, smooth-shaven face betrayed nothing, and his steel-grey eyes which rested alternately upon Jasper and the fair young player were expressionless. Well it was for Lois' peace of mind that she did not see that face out there in the night, for it was the same face which had been haunting her for months.

CHAPTER XX

BUSINESS DETAILS

As spring drew near David became anxious for more definite news about the work at the falls. He knew what Jasper and his men were doing and how the portable mill was busy sawing the logs which had been hauled out. But he was impatient to see what he called "the real beginning." It was, therefore, with considerable satisfaction when at last the great start was made. As the weeks passed word reached him of what was going on. He had not yet visited the falls as he did not feel equal to the walk. But he listened eagerly to all that was told him. The reports were truly marvellous of the large number of men engaged upon the "Plant," of the activity at Creekdale and all up the brook. In a few weeks the whole place had been converted into a hive of bustling industry. It seemed as if a magic wand had been suddenly waved over the place to produce such an astonishing change.

In addition to this there were men working between the city and Creekdale as well as along the road leading up-river, putting large poles in place for the electric wires. These poles had been run down the brook and then floated to various places along the river. In this way the work was facilitated. Everything had been well planned, and it seemed as if nothing had been overlooked. Though David could not visit the falls, yet he and Betty often sat by the road and watched the workmen as they dug the deep holes, erected the poles and strung the wires.

One beautiful morning as they came to the road, they saw a man not far off busily sketching a clump of white birch trees a short distance away. So intent was he upon his work that he did not appear to notice the two who were watching him with undisguised curiosity.

"Who is he?" David whispered, fearful lest he should disturb the man.

"He must be that artist who came yesterday," Betty replied. "He has a little tent over there," and she pointed to the right. "I saw him fixing it up yesterday and it looks so cosy. He spoke to me as I came by and seemed to be very friendly."

"And you say that he is an artist?" David enquired.

"Yes. Don't you see him painting now? He told me that he wants to get some pictures of this beautiful place."

"He must see the falls, girl," and David rose from his sitting position. "There is nothing here to equal it, and how nice it would be to have a picture before too great a change takes place up there."

"Suppose we tell him about it," Betty suggested, now much interested in the idea. "Come, I will introduce you."

As the two approached, the artist rose to his feet and lifted his hat.

"Why, it's my little visitor of yesterday," he pleasantly remarked. "I didn't expect to meet you so soon again. Is this your grand-father?"

"Oh, no," and Betty laughed heartily. "This is Mr. David, and I am looking after him."

"I am glad to meet you, sir," and the stranger held out his hand. "I have only arrived lately and of course do not know any of the people here, so you will pardon my mistake."

"It doesn't matter, I assure you," David replied. "Betty is really a daughter to me, so it was no mistake after all. But I hope we have not interrupted you."

"Not at all. I am not doing much this morning, just getting my bearings, as it were. But you have a wonderful view from this hill. I am hoping to get some excellent pictures. I wish I had known of this beautiful spot before."

"Wait until you see the falls," David eagerly replied. "You will find something worth while there."

"Is it far from here?" the artist enquired.

"Oh, no. You can easily find it. There is a good road there now which has been made by the new company."

"Is that the place where the light and power are to come from, of which I have heard so much?"

"So you have heard of it then? I am very glad." There was a pleased expression in David's eyes. It gave him much satisfaction to know that the news of what was being done at the falls had extended beyond Creekdale.

"Oh, yes, every one has heard about the great undertaking which is going on at Break Neck Falls," the artist replied. "I have read much about it in the city papers, and only recently there was a long article describing certain phases of the work and what would be accomplished. I have the paper with me. Here it is, if you care to read it," and the artist drew from his pocket a carefully-folded newspaper, and handed it to the old man.

With much eagerness David took it in his hands, unfolded it and ran his eyes quickly over the article with the big headlines, "A Gigantic Undertaking." Betty stepped close to his side and began to read as well. Her animated face and sparkling eyes showed plainly the keen interest she took in the whole affair, and several times she gave expression to exclamations of delight.

"Isn't it great!" she cried, when she had finished. "And what a lot they tell about you, Mr. David, and how you had that thing in your head for so long when you were very poor."

"Yes, girl," David replied, "and did you notice what is said about the benefit it will be to the city and the whole country?"

In their intense excitement they had forgotten all about the artist. But as they talked like two happy children he was watching them very closely, especially the old man. In his eyes there was a peculiar half-gloating expression, while a partly-suppressed sinister smile lurked about the corners of his mouth.

"May we show this paper to Miss Lois?" Betty asked, turning suddenly toward the artist. As she did so, she started, for intuitively she saw something in the man's face which frightened her. Whatever it was, it instantly dispelled the happiness which possessed her. The artist noticed this, and it annoyed him. He shrugged his shoulder and gave a short laugh.

"Yes, you may keep the paper," he said. "I am through with it. But I must get on with my work now."

They stood and watched him as he walked away carrying with him his easel and camp-stool.

"I am afraid of him," Betty whispered to her companion. Then she shivered as if cold.

"Why, what's the matter?" David asked in surprise. "What makes you afraid of that man? He is only a harmless artist, and he was very kind to us this morning. I feel most grateful for the paper he has given us."

"I know that, but I don't want to see him again," the girl replied. "I saw something in his eyes which I don't like. I can't explain it, but it makes me afraid of him. I hope he will go away soon."

"Tut, girl, that is all nonsense," David chided. "It is just a notion on your part. I like him well enough for a stranger. What harm can he do us?"

During the rest of the morning Betty could not get clear of the feeling of fear which possessed her, and David worried much over her unusual silence. She longed to see Lois that she might talk it all over with her. In fact she had her mind made up to visit her that afternoon when an unlooked-for excitement changed the entire current of her thoughts, and put the artist out of her mind for the rest of the day.

It was just after dinner when the captain and David were out upon the verandah enjoying their pipes, when a big car lurched up and stopped in front of the house. To David's surprise he saw Mr. Westcote alight and come up the verandah steps. He at once rose to meet him.

"I have come to give you a ride in my car," Mr. Westcote informed David, after he had been introduced to the captain, and had handed him a cigar. "It is a pity to take you from such a beautiful place as this," and he cast his eyes over the sloping fields before him. "But, I would like for you to come with me to the city to-day. It is a matter of business, that is, some details which should have been attended to before."

"Has it anything to do with the falls?" David enquired.

"Yes, everything centres there," and Mr. Westcote smiled. "This affair is really important or I should not bother you to-day."

"I can be ready in a short time," David replied. He was eager now to be away, and the thought that he was needed and was in some way necessary to the working out of the plans at the falls gave him great pleasure.

In little less than half an hour the car left the Haven and sped rapidly down the road. David enjoyed the ride, and leaned back comfortably in the soft springy seat.

"You should have a car, sir," Mr. Westcote remarked as he noted how David liked the drive. "It would do you so much good to have a spin every day."

"Why, I never thought of it," was the reply. "But I would not know how to handle a car if I did have one. And besides, it would cost a great deal."

"Oh, you could easily overcome such difficulties. You are a rich man, you know, and could afford to buy a good car and keep a chauffeur to drive it for you. You have not spent all of that money you received, have you?"

"No, no; only a very small portion of it. You see, Betty and I live very quietly, and spend but little. We are planning to build a comfortable house of our own some day. We keep putting it off, though, as we are so happy at the Haven with the captain and Mrs. Peterson."

Nothing more was said about this subject during the rest of the ride, and in about an hour and a half they reached the city and drew up before a large building on one of the business streets. When once inside David looked around with much interest upon the busy scenes which met his eyes.

"This is our main office," Mr. Westcote explained, "and we keep quite a staff. As the work develops it will be necessary to have a building of our own, for we have only the ground floor here. This is my private office," and he motioned to a door on the right. "We will be more quiet there."

David was greatly delighted at all he saw, and he could not restrain the feeling of pride that he was the cause of all this activity. Not the slightest surprise entered his mind at what he observed. There was not even the least shadow of mystery about it all. To him it was but natural that things should be as they were. He doubted nothing; he asked no questions. His plan was so great and reasonable that he accepted everything as a matter of course.

"You have perhaps wondered," Mr. Westcote began, after they were seated, "why I have brought you here to-day. I told you that it is a matter of business details, and so it is. You are Honorary President of our company and, accordingly, you are a large share-holder. You were not aware of that before, and I trust you do not mind our keeping it a secret?"

"No, no; not at all," David replied. "Everything is satisfactory to me."

"That is good," Mr. Westcote continued. "But as you have such a large interest in the company, it is necessary that you should have your will made to save complications in the future. Life is uncertain, you know, and if anything should happen to you it would make it very difficult for us if you did not have your business matters attended to."

"Quite right, quite right," David assented. "I have thought about it somewhat of late, and I am very glad that you have mentioned it. Could we not have the business attended to at once? It will not take long, will it?"

"No, it can soon be done," was the reply. "But first of all it will be necessary for you to state in whose favour you wish to make your will. Then we can have the papers drawn up, and you can sign them before you, leave the city."

"Yes, that will be necessary," and David placed his right hand to his forehead in a thoughtful manner. "I have been thinking that all over, and know the ones to whom I wish to leave my principal share in the falls. You see, I want to have people who will take a keen interest in the undertaking, such as I have, and who will be able to continue the work when I am gone."

"You are quite right," Mr. Westcote replied, though it was evident that he with difficulty repressed a smile of amusement at his companion's words.

"But I am somewhat worried about the others," David continued. "I wish to leave something to my faithful girl, Betty Bean, to her mother, who is a widow, and to Captain Peterson and his wife, for they have a hard struggle to make a living. Now, they are the ones I wish to help as far as I can, but I have no idea what I ought to leave them."

"How much would you like for them to have?" Mr. Westcote enquired.

"Well, it would be nice if they could have a thousand each. That would make them so comfortable. But I am afraid such an amount is out of the question."

"Not at all," was the reply. "You name the amount, and we shall put it in the will. You see," he added, as if it were an afterthought, "the falls will be good for that, and perhaps more, even after you have arranged for the others."

"I am pleased to hear you express such confidence in the undertaking," and David looked into his companion's face. "I little realised that it would pay so well in such a short time. I am very grateful to you for what you have done."

"It will pay you regularly," Mr. Westcote replied. "I may as well tell you that this is one of the most remarkable companies ever formed. Will you now mention the names of the principal ones to whom you wish to leave the rest of your interest?"

"There are only two, but I have such unlimited confidence in them that I feel I am making no mistake. You know them both for they are Jasper Randall, the young foreman, and Miss Lois Sinclair."

"Have you no relatives?" Mr. Westcote asked, concealing his surprise as much as possible. "If you have, would it not be well to remember them in your will?"

"I desire that all I possess in this world should go to the ones I have mentioned," David slowly replied. "We will not talk about relatives, please."

"Just as you say," Mr. Westcote assented, as he rose to his feet. "I shall have the papers drawn up at once. In the meantime, you had better come and stay with me. You will need a good rest after your trip."

It was late in the afternoon the next day before the work upon the will was completed. It was quite an elaborate affair, so David thought, and he had to study it carefully before signing it. When at last all was finished, the car was waiting before the office to carry them back to Creekdale.

"I am going with you," Mr. Westcote remarked as he took his seat by David's side. "I want to see that you get safely home. And besides," he added, "I wish to learn how the work is getting along up there. I have just been telephoning to Mr. Randall, and his report is most encouraging."

CHAPTER XXI

HARNESSED POWER

It was dark by the time they drew near to Creekdale, and as the car rounded a bend in the road David was astonished at the sight which met his eyes. The entire way was brilliantly illuminated by hundreds of electric lights strung along both sides of the road.

David started, sat bolt upright, and clutched his companion by the arm.

"What is this?" he demanded in a hoarse whisper. "Where are we, anyway? I thought you were bringing me home."

"So I am," Mr. Westcote laughingly replied. "We are at Creekdale now. This is the work of your beloved falls. Are you satisfied?"

"Oh!" It was all that the old man could say. He leaned back in his seat and a sigh of relief escaped his lips. It was quite evident that he was strongly moved by what he saw.

Slowly the car moved up the great white way, and at last turned into the gate leading to the Haven. Two large lights had been placed on the gate post, and these shed forth their bright light upon all sides. It was a marvellous transformation which had been made in such a short time. David could not utter a word, so overcome was he. Even when he saw the house ablaze with many lights and the verandah as bright as day, and observed the people there waiting to welcome him home, he seemed like one in a dream. It was only when Betty danced about him and caught both of his hands in hers, that he aroused from his stupefaction.

"What's the matter, Mr. David?" she cried. "Why don't you speak to me, and tell me how you like it all?"

"It is wonderful!" and the old man placed his hand to his forehead, as he always did when greatly affected or puzzled. "Who did all this?"

"It was done for you, Mr. David," the girl explained. "My, we have had a lively time here since you left!"

"And was that the reason why I was taken to the city yesterday?" David asked, while a new light of comprehension dawned upon his mind. "You knew all about this, did you?"

"Oh, no, I didn't know a thing," Betty protested. "But just as soon as you got away Mr. Jasper and a whole crowd of men began to work, and they have been just hustling ever since. Isn't it lovely! And to think that it was in your brain all the time!"

"This is very gratifying, sir," and David turned to Jasper, who was standing by listening with great interest to the conversation between the girl and the old man. "I can hardly believe what I see. I had no idea that you had made such progress at the falls. It will be necessary for me to go and see the works for myself."

"We have a great deal more to do yet, I assure you," Jasper replied. "We have merely begun. We planned this little surprise for your special benefit. We wished that you should be the first one to be honoured. But we have something more to show you, which, no doubt, will surprise you. If you will come with me I will show you what it is."

Leading the way, he conducted them through the kitchen and into an adjoining room used partly as a wood-house and also as a wash room. Each place was brilliantly lighted by means of several electric lamps. He stopped at last before a cream-separator which was new and recently installed. Touching a switch, there was a sudden whirring sound, and the machine began to revolve, slowly at first, but gaining rapidly in speed until it was fairly spinning. After it had been running for a few minutes Jasper turned off the current, and then stood watching the separator until its movements ceased. He next moved across the room to where stood a churn. Again placing his finger upon another switch the churn began to revolve.

During all this time David's eyes were ablaze with joy as he watched all that was taking place.

"It is wonderful!" he remarked. "How have you managed to arrange everything in such a short time? It seems almost magical."

"Oh, we had everything all ready," Jasper laughingly replied. "And just as soon as we got you away we merely had to put the machinery into place. But here is something else," and he turned to the left. "This is a wood-cutting machine, and all you have to do is to turn on the current, so," and he touched a switch, "and behold, your saw is all ready for use. Watch this," he added, picking up a stick, which in an instant was severed in two. "That is the way the farmers will cut their wood. You have thus seen some of the things your falls will do. But there are others we cannot show here, which will revolutionise the entire country."

Scarcely had he ended when Lois entered and stood watching the revolving saw. Jasper was the first to see her, and he noticed that her face was paler than usual and that she seemed to be trembling.

"I am sorry that I am late," she apologised. "I was planning to be here to see these wonderful things, but I was delayed."

"But you can see them all now, Miss Sinclair," David eagerly replied. "Look at the lights along the road and in the house, and the way these machines run. Isn't it wonderful? My visions have come true at last, and my beautiful falls have done it."

Jasper was anxious to know what was troubling Lois. Although she talked and laughed and seemed to be the gayest one there, it was quite evident to him that she was merely acting the part. When she had stayed for about half an hour she spoke to Jasper privately and asked him to accompany her home.

"I wish to speak to you about something," she told him.

Jasper was delighted, and after they had said good-night to the rest they walked slowly down the lighted lane toward the main road.

"This is like fairyland," Lois remarked. "I never expected to see anything like this."

"It was done for David's sake," Jasper replied. "And wasn't he surprised and delighted? I think I was as much excited as he was."

"Have you any idea why the company should do all this for his sake?" Lois enquired. "Who is he, anyway?"

"I have not the slightest idea," was the reply. "Everything has been a profound mystery to me from the beginning. There is something most interesting back of it all, mark my word. Mr. Westcote evidently knows, but he has never enlightened me. Perhaps his daughter knows something."

"If she does she has never told me. Sometimes I think she knows, but is not at liberty to speak. Oh, what's that?" and Lois gave a sudden start. "I thought I heard something among the trees. But I guess it was nothing, only my nerves," and she gave a slight laugh.

"Perhaps it was merely some animal," Jasper suggested. "It may have been a dog or a rabbit. Any slight noise sounds large at night."

"Let us hurry on," Lois urged. "I am afraid that I am somewhat upset to-night. I had such a start on my way to the Haven that I have not got over it yet."

"I saw that there was something wrong with you when you came into the house," Jasper replied.

"Did you? I was hoping that no one noticed it."

"What was the matter?"

"It was a man."

"Oh, was that all? I thought that perhaps it was a bear."

"But a man can be far worse than a bear, Mr. Randall. I would not mind meeting a bear half as much as a brute in the form of a man."

"What, did he frighten you, or try to harm you in any way?" Jasper stopped short in his tracks and waited for an answer. He was beginning to understand now that Lois' fright was something not to be treated lightly.

"Oh, no," Lois hastened to explain. "He didn't even speak to me. But I saw him cross the brightly-lighted lane leading to the Haven. He plunged among the trees and disappeared."

"Did you know him?" Jasper asked, now much interested.

"Yes. I met him once in the city at Mrs. Dingle's party. He is an English artist, Sydney Bramshaw by name, and he affected me then like a terrible night-mare. I could not get him out of my mind for weeks. I have never been able to explain it, and never experienced anything like it before."

"Do you know anything about the man?" Jasper asked.

"No, and that is the strange thing about it. I had a slight conversation with him then and his words disgusted me. Apart from that I know nothing."

"It is strange," Jasper mused as if to himself. "We sometimes do get queer impressions about people, do we not?"

"But I never had anything like this before. It seemed to me when I first saw that man that he was Satan in disguise. A queer idea, was it not? I felt that in some unaccountable way he had crossed my path for evil, and I have that same feeling now."

They had reached the house by this time and were standing near the verandah steps. It was a chilly night, and the sky was overcast with not a star to be seen. A tremor shook Lois' form as she stood there.

"You are cold," Jasper remarked, "and you should go in the house at once."

"Will you come in?" Lois asked. "It is not late and father will be pleased to see you."

"Not to-night, thank you," Jasper replied. "I was working nearly all last night at the Haven, and so must get some rest. I am living in my little old cabin now, and it is really good to be there again. It seems more like home to me than up the brook. But, there, I must not keep you any longer or you will catch cold. Do not worry too much about that man. If he begins to trouble you, he will have to reckon with me."

Jasper walked slowly away from the house along a path leading to the main road. He was thinking seriously of what Lois had told him about Bramshaw. He could not understand her strange aversion for the man, and he wondered if there were really anything in such a presentiment. He made up his mind that he would be on the lookout and if the fellow became the least objectionable he would deal with him then in no gentle manner.

As Jasper drew near to the main road a feeling suddenly possessed him that he was being followed. He looked back but could see nothing. Laughing at himself for what he considered his foolishness, he continued on his way. But it was not so easy to banish the impression he had received, and every once in a while he glanced around as if expecting to see some one not far off. Once he thought he heard the sound of foot-steps in the distance, and he stopped to listen but heard nothing more.

Reaching at last the path which led to his cabin, he was about to enter upon this when an idea came into his mind. It was suggested by a thick clump of hazel bushes by the side of the road. As quick as thought he darted behind these and crouched low upon the ground. From this position it was possible for him to watch the road without being observed. He wished to find out whether any one was really following him, or if it was merely imagination on his part.

He had not been there long ere he heard faint footfalls upon the road, which grew more distinct as he listened. He was now sure that his surmises had been true, and it made him angry. He knew that it was not an ordinary pedestrian, for why had he come after him along the path leading from the Sinclair house? It must be some one stalking him, for what purpose he could not imagine.

Peering forth from his concealed position Jasper was ere long able to see the dim form of a man slouching cautiously along, keeping well to the side of the road where the trees and bushes were the thickest. He even brushed the hazel bushes in passing and Jasper held his breath lest he should be detected by his breathing. He was sure now that the man had been following him with no good intentions, and his first inclination was to rush forward and find out what was his business. He resisted, however, thinking it better to remain where he was and see what the night prowler would do next.

Not long did he have to wait for the man, coming to the path leading across the fields, stopped and looked carefully around. The dim form of the little cabin could be seen in the distance, and for this he at once started. There were no trees now to hide him, and he started on a run across the open space. Jasper, seeing this, sprang from his hiding place and hurried forward. By the time he reached the path the man was nowhere to be seen. He had evidently reached the cabin, and was no doubt at the door or listening at the window. Jasper knew that it was now time for him to act and he at once bounded across the field straight for his cabin. He had scarcely reached it when the prowler came suddenly around the corner, and the two met. In an instant Jasper reached out his hand and caught the man by the shoulder and demanded what he was doing around his cabin at that time of the night. With an angry oath, the other tried to free himself from the tightening grip, and when he failed to do so he struck Jasper a blow right in the face with the clenched fist of his right hand.

"Take that, you damned fool," he growled, "and mind your own business."

Jasper did not wait to argue. In a twinkling he threw himself full upon the man. His blood surged madly through his veins, for the blow stung him to fury. His opponent, though he tried to put up a fight, was as a child in Jasper's hands, and soon he was sprawling upon the ground with Jasper sitting upon his body.

"Now, then," the victor calmly remarked, "as you would not answer my question in a civil manner while standing on your feet, perhaps you will do it here on the ground. And you will do it before you get up, remember that, so you might as well speak first as last. Who are you, and why were you following me up the road and prowling so suspiciously around my cabin?"

"I'm a stranger here," was the low reply, "and I was looking for a place to spend the night. Will that satisfy you?"

"No, it will not," Jasper emphatically replied. "I believe that you are lying. What is your name?"

"Jim Dobbins," was the somewhat hesitating answer. "I am seeking for work with the Light and Power Company and got astray."

"Now, look here," and Jasper rose to his feet, "it's no use for you to string off such lies to me. Your name is Sydney Bramshaw, the artist. I know who you are, but why you are acting this way I do not know. So get up now, and clear out of this. If I catch you at any more such pranks I'll break every bone in your body. You had better mind what you do while in this place, and keep out of my sight after this."

Without a word the prostrate man rose to his feet and stood for an instant as if he would speak. He was trembling with rage, though in the darkness Jasper could not see the ugly expression upon his face. Presently he turned and glided away swiftly from the cabin, and was soon lost to sight.

Jasper stood for a while and peered through the night. He was almost tempted to follow the man to be sure that he really departed and was not hiding among the bushes but a short distance away. He called himself a fool for letting him off so easily. He should have kept him until morning to be sure that he would do no mischief under cover of darkness. At length, however, he entered the cabin and threw himself upon his cot. He wished to think it all over and keep awake lest the man should return and wreak vengeance upon him in some under-handed way. He felt sure now that Lois' opinion of the man was correct, and that for some unaccountable reason he had a contemptible enemy to deal with, who would stoop to almost anything to carry out his evil designs, whatever they might be.

CHAPTER XXII

IN THE PATH OF DESTRUCTION

It was only natural that the people of Creekdale should have been greatly excited over the progress made at the falls. They watched everything with the keenest interest which reached its highest point on the night of David's arrival home. To see the road so brilliantly illuminated was both wonderful and puzzling. They all knew that it was done for "Crazy David's sake," and they could not understand why such a fuss should be made over his return to the place.

"It beats me," Andy Forbes remarked to a number of men gathered before the store. "I'm mighty glad to have the lights there for they make things around here as bright as day. But why is it done? What has Crazy David got to do with it? You would think he was a king coming home instead of a half-cracked old man."

"But he supplied the plans, didn't he?" one of the men asked in reply.

"The plans be jiggered!" and Andy gave a contemptuous toss of his head. "What value do you suppose were his plans? I don't believe the company ever looked at them."

"There must be something, though," Ned Travis replied. "David's living in luxury now, and if the plans were not back of it, I'd like to know what is. It isn't natural for a big company with unlimited means to throw away money on an old man like that just for charity."

"How's Jim Goban feeling these days?" Andy asked. "I haven't seen him of late."

"He's a very sick man," Billy Goban answered, at which they all laughed. "He curses himself every minute day and night for letting Crazy David out of his clutches. He believes that if he had kept him he would have come in for a big share of David's good luck."

"Serves him right," Andy mused as he gazed thoughtfully at the array of lights before him. "He should be ashamed of himself, and so should we for that matter for selling that old man to the lowest bidder. It'll be the last time such a thing takes place in this parish if I can help it, and I guess I can. It's most degrading, and should be stopped."

While the people of Creekdale were intensely aroused over the marvellous progress of the Light and Power Company, the world beyond was becoming much interested in what was taking place. The day after David's arrival home the city papers devoted considerable space to the developments at the falls. They told about the mysterious company and the old man who had supplied the plans. They gave a most vivid account of the lighted way and the examples of the harnessed power at the Haven. They, like the people of Creekdale, could not understand why such a fuss should be made over David. They hinted that there was some mystery back of it all, the solving of which would be watched with considerable interest.

But the papers had much more to say. They spoke of the great benefit the city would receive from cheaper light and power, and how the new company would lower the rates, and perhaps force the city company out of business altogether. They deemed it a day of great things when people would not be compelled to pay such prices as hitherto, and how industries of all kinds would increase and flourish. A table of rates was appended showing the difference between the rates of the old company and the new.

It was with much satisfaction that David read these accounts to the captain as they sat out upon the verandah. He was a happy man that day, and when he was through with his reading he leaned back in his chair and remained silent for a long time. The captain watched him somewhat curiously as he puffed away at his pipe. Presently he took the pipe from his mouth and allowed it to go out, which was a most unusual thing for him. He even stared at David as if he had never seen him before. What his thoughts were he kept to himself, but he observed the old man now more closely than ever and studied his face most carefully.

They had been sitting on the verandah for about half an hour, when Sydney Bramshaw strolled up to the house, with his easel under his arm. He looked none the worse for his experience with Jasper and was most affable as he accosted David, who at once introduced him to the captain.

"You have a beautiful place here, sir," he remarked to the invalid. "I have been fascinated with the scenery and have done considerable work since my arrival. May I have the privilege of sketching this delightful cottage? It will make a fine picture, I am sure."

"Sketch away all you like," the captain replied. "It is a beautiful spot, if I do say it, and it can't be beat anywhere."

From the moment the captain had set eyes upon the artist he was sure that he had seen him before. Just where it was he could not at first recall, but suddenly it flashed into his mind, and with it a train of thoughts which excited him more than was his wont. He looked at David and then at the artist, and for a moment he closed his eyes as memories drifted upon him. What was this man doing here? he asked himself. He longed to question Bramshaw, but desisted, determined to await future developments. Nevertheless, he was very quiet during the rest of the day, which made his wife and Betty think that he was not well.

"You are not sick, are you?" Mrs. Peterson asked.

"Not at all," was the reply. "I am only thinking."

"Maybe he's got something in his head just like Mr. David," Betty suggested.

"Maybe I have, girl," the captain laughed. "But I'm afraid the thing that I've got won't make as much money as his. Where is Mr. David now?"

"He's with that artist over there, watching him sketch this house. He likes the man, for he talks to him so much about the falls. I don't like him; his face frightens me."

The captain made no reply to these words but gazed meditatively out over the fields long after Mrs. Peterson and Betty had left him. He was trying to piece together a number of fragmentary incidents which were revolving in his mind, and to ascertain how they were related.

"I'm sure 'twas on that trip," he muttered, "But darn it all, why can't I remember what he said. He was always talking and boasting about one thing and another. Hello, by jingo, I've got it!" and the captain gave such a whoop that both Mrs. Peterson and Betty came running from the kitchen to see what was the matter.

"It's nothing," the captain growled, disgusted with himself for attracting attention when he wanted to be alone, "I was just thinking, that's all. Can't a man whoop when he wants to without everybody rushing around him like mad?"

"It all depends on what kind of a whoop it is, Robert," his wife replied. "We couldn't tell whether you had gone out of your mind or had fallen off the verandah."

"It's that thing in his brain which did it, Mrs. Peterson," Betty explained. "Mr. David acted queer sometimes, though he never hollered out. It must be something great, Captain," she added, "which made you yelp like that."

"It certainly was, girl," and the captain smiled. "I feel better now, though, so you women needn't worry about me."

The next morning David told Betty that he had made up his mind to visit the falls. He said that he wished to see for himself the wonderful changes which had been made there. Betty was delighted and at once set to work to prepare the luncheon they were to take with them.

"We'll find a nice cosy place along the brook and have a picnic there," she told Mrs. Peterson.

"I'm afraid there will not be many cosy places," was the reply. "You must be prepared for great changes up the brook."

David and Betty were like two children off for a holiday as they left the Haven and walked gaily down the lane toward the main highway. It was a perfect morning, and the perfume of clover from the expansive meadows scented the air. Birds were darting here and there or twittering from the branches of the trees. A short distance from the road, and partly concealed, a white tent nestled among the trees, though no sign of the artist was to be seen. Betty breathed a sigh of relief when they were past. She did not wish to see Bramshaw, to whom she had taken such a violent dislike. She wondered where he was at that time of the morning. Perhaps he was still asleep, she thought, for she knew that he prowled about late at night.

The tent was a small one, such as is generally used by campers. It was in a beautiful situation, and it was so placed that it commanded an excellent view of the Haven and the lane leading to it. It was a common occurrence for people from the city to camp along the river during the summer months, and people did not wonder about this one among the trees. They all knew that Bramshaw was an artist of some note, and they felt rather pleased that he had come to Creekdale to obtain some pictures.

"I am glad we didn't meet that artist this morning," Betty remarked after they had left the tent out of sight.

"I cannot understand your dislike to the man," David replied. "He has been so civil to us both, and he is very fond of hearing about the work at the falls, and how the whole community will be benefited."

"I can't help it, Mr. David," and Betty twirled the sunbonnet she was carrying in her hand, as was often her custom. "He may be all right, but I don't like him. I wish he would go away and never come back. Isn't it strange how some people spoil everything? We are so happy this morning because we are going to the falls together, and yet as soon as I think of that man I shiver. I don't understand it at all."

"You'll get over it in time, Betty," David replied. "But, see, what a change they have made in our path. Why, it's a regular road now."

"I don't like it one bit," Betty protested. "It isn't half as nice as it was before. I hope they haven't touched my rock. If they have, somebody's going to get a big scolding."

Talking thus and passing remarks upon everything they saw, the two moved slowly along the newly-made road. Several freighting teams passed them and the drivers looked with interest upon the old man and the bright-faced girl.

"They all know you, Mr. David," Betty remarked. "Did you notice how the men lifted their hats!"

"They did it to you, girl," was the reply. "Why should they do such a thing to me?"

"Because you are great, that is why. They all know of the wonderful thing you had in your head. Oh!" she suddenly exclaimed, stopping short in her tracks.

"What is the matter?" David asked.

"They have taken away my rock! Look, there are only little pieces of it left."

"They needed it, no doubt, for the works up there, Betty. You must not mind when it has been put to such good use."

Betty, nevertheless, felt badly, and for a while she ceased her chattering and walked along quietly by her companion's side. At length they came to a place where the road left the path and swung to the right.

"Isn't this nice!" Betty exclaimed. "Some of our dear old path is left, anyway, and we can follow it and forget that any changes have been made."

The path ran close to the brook and after they had followed this for several hundred yards through a growth of young birches and maples, they came to a clearing which had been made since they were last there. Above them was the road, and on its lower side was a large pile of big poles ready to be rolled into the brook.

"I wonder what they left them there for?" David enquired.

"Oh, I know," Betty replied. "Mr. Jasper told us, don't you remember, that they left a lot of poles to be used along the brook. They must be the ones."

"So he did tell us that," the old man mused. "Your memory is better than mine. Suppose we sit down here and rest a while. That walk has tired me."

"There's a nice place right in front of that big stump close to the brook," and Betty pointed with her finger. "We can rest there and eat a part of our lunch."

When they had reached the place Betty began to unpack the basket. First of all she spread down a white cloth, and then laid out the sandwiches and cake. Then she paused, and a look of dismay overspread her face.

"We forgot to bring anything to drink!" she exclaimed. "I had the milk all ready in the bottle and came away without it. What shall we do?"

"Oh, never mind," David replied. "We can drink some of this brook water, can we not?"

"No, it's nasty. It's too warm. I know," and she reached for two tin cups. "There's a nice cool spring just up the brook. I have often got water there. You keep off the flies from the food. I won't be a minute."

Leaving David, Betty hurried up along the edge of the brook until she reached the spring bubbling out of the bank. Filling the cups she made her way back as carefully as possible so as not to spill any of the water. She had just reached the edge of the clearing when a strange sound fell upon her ears. It startled her, and looking up, her face blanched with terror, for coming down the steep bank was one of the large poles which had been separated from its companions. It was only a few seconds in making the descent, but in that brief space of time a world of thought crowded into Betty's excited brain. She saw David sitting right in the track of death, unconscious of impending doom. Betty tried to shout, to rush forward to rescue him, but no words came from her lips, and her feet seemed glued to the ground. Rapidly the pole sped down the bank, and then just when but a score of feet from the helpless old man it struck the large stump in its onward sweep. With a wild bound it leaped high and like a mighty catapult hurled itself through the air over David's head and fell with a terrific crash into the brook below.

At first a wild scream of terror escaped Betty's lips, followed instantly by a cry of joy as she rushed forward, seized the hand of the bewildered old man and led him to a place of safety near the edge of the forest. Then her strength deserted her, and she sank down upon the ground and wept like a child.

"Oh, Mr. David, Mr. David," she sobbed, "you were nearly killed. Oh, oh, oh! Wasn't it awful!"

"There, there, Betty, don't feel so badly," and David stroked her hair in a gentle manner. "I'm all right now, so why should you cry?"

"But I can't help it," the girl moaned. "I was sure you would be killed, and I could do nothing to save you."

"Strange," her companion mused, "what started that log just as I was sitting there. It must have been loose and ready to start at the least motion."

"Let us go home," and Betty rose suddenly to her feet. "I don't want to stay here any longer. The place is not like it used to be. I do not feel safe. There seems to be danger everywhere."

Hurrying as fast as possible across the open space and casting apprehensive glances up the bank lest another pole should take a sudden notion to come down, they soon reached the woods beyond.

"There, I feel safer now," Betty panted. "Those poles can't touch us, anyway."

"I did want to see the falls," David replied, "and I am quite disappointed. But I do not feel able to try the trip again as it tires me too much."

"Suppose we ask Mr. Jasper to drive you there," Betty suggested. "I know he will be only too pleased to do it. Isn't it funny we didn't think of that before?"

"That is a good idea," David assented. "Maybe he will do it tomorrow. But what's the matter, girl?" he demanded, looking with surprise upon Betty, who had suddenly stopped and was staring down upon the brook through an opening among the trees.

"Look," she whispered, pointing with her finger, "there is that artist sketching down below. He doesn't know we are here, so let us be as quiet as possible."

"Well, why should he startle you?" David enquired. "He is not troubling us. I'm not afraid of him. In fact, I feel inclined to go and have a talk with him."

"Don't, please don't," and the girl laid her right hand imploringly on his arm. "Let us go home at once, for I feel shaky all over."

"Very well, then," David assented. "But I wish you would get over your foolish notion about that man. He is merely a harmless artist who has come to this place to get some good pictures. Why can't you be sensible?"

CHAPTER XXIII

RESCUED

Jasper had charge of fixing the poles and stretching the wires for light and power between the city and the falls, as well as throughout the country wherever it was planned to extend them. Gangs of men were at work along the lines, and Jasper was kept busy moving from place to place giving instructions and supervising everything. The entire responsibility rested upon him, and he wished to prove worthy of the trust.

The afternoon when David and Betty were up the brook, Jasper remained closer than usual to Creekdale, where a number of men were working. Opposite them a small island nestled out in the river, called "Emerald" Island by reason of its rich covering of fir, pine and birch trees. As a rule, Jasper paid strict attention to his duties, but to-day his mind often wandered and he would stand gazing out over the water to the island beyond.

As the afternoon wore away he became quite restless and watched the river most anxiously. A wind had sprung up, which, gentle at first, increased steadily into a gale. The water soon became rough and great white-caps rolled up-stream, especially heavy where the tide was strongest.

At length, leaving his men he went to the shore and stood close to the watery edge. He looked more down the river than formerly, as if expecting some one from that direction. But occasionally he cast his eyes off toward the island and breathed more freely after each look. He often consulted his watch as he now paced up and down the beach.

"What can be keeping that fellow?" he muttered. "He should have been here an hour ago. Surely he's not tied up on account of the wind. I gave him strict instructions to come back as soon as possible. If he does not — hello, there he is now," and his face brightened as he gave a sigh of relief.

Coming up the river was a big boat used for rafting purposes containing one man. Volumes of spray leaped high as she surged through the water driven by a seven horse-power engine. This craft was used for towing logs and poles, and for the carrying of supplies to the various camps.

"You're late, Tom," Jasper remarked as the boat's bow touched the shore where he was standing. "I expected you an hour ago."

"It was the wind, sir," was the reply. "A number of logs broke loose from the raft and I had a hard time to collect them. There's a heavy sea runnin' below the Bar."

"It's bad out there, too," and Jasper pointed off toward the island.

"Sure thing," the man replied, turning partly around. "There's a boat leavin' the island now. Surely it's not goin' to try to run over."

"Where is it?" Jasper demanded.

"Look," and Tom stretched out his long right arm, "ye kin just see it. There, it's plainer now."

The only answer Jasper made was to give the boat a vigorous push from the shore, leap aboard, seize the wheel and order Tom to start the engine. In a few seconds they were cutting their way rapidly through the water straight for the big white-caps beyond. Tom asked no questions, but attended to the engine. It was all in the day's work to him, and this was much easier than towing logs.

From the moment he had seized the wheel Jasper had not taken his eyes off of the little boat away in the distance. He could see that it was in the rough water and was pitching about in an alarming manner. It seemed to be beyond control and was drifting rapidly toward the rougher water of the main channel.

"We are going very slow, Tom," he remarked. "Can't we do any better?"

"She's runnin' full speed," was the reply. "I'd like to slow down a bit, for we're gettin' soaked."

"Never mind the water, Tom. I wish you could make her go as fast again. Oh! did you see that?"

"See what?"

"The way that little boat pitched. I thought she had swamped."

It did not really take them more than ten minutes to run across that stretch of water, but to Jasper it seemed much longer. The boat pounded and threshed her way forward, shipping water at every plunge, keeping Tom busy with the small suction pump. At last, however, it was easy for Jasper to see two women sitting in the drifting boat. That they were helpless and had given up all attempt to reach the shore was quite evident. One was seated astern, and the other was holding the oars in her hands, but making no use of them. Jasper's heart beat quicker as he watched her, for he well knew what a struggle she must have made before giving up in despair.

"They're women!" Tom exclaimed in astonishment. "What in the devil are they doin' out here!"

"Shut up, and attend to your engine," Jasper sternly ordered.

They were quite close now, and the women saw them. As they approached Jasper could see Lois' face turned toward him and it was very white.

"Sit still," he shouted, and then he motioned to Tom to slow down. "Stop her," he presently ordered, and soon they were drifting up close to the little boat.

It took Lois and Margaret but a few seconds to step on board of the rafting boat, and then their own craft was taken in tow. There was no time for words now, as Jasper had all he could do to handle his own boat, for she was rolling heavily as he swung her around and headed for the shore. Running almost broadside to the waves a great deal of water was shipped, which kept Tom busy at the pump.

Jasper had no time to pay any attention to the women, but he intuitively knew that Lois was watching him. He was really happier than he had been for days, and he was so pleased that he had been of some service to the woman he loved. This was the second time he had rescued her from the water, and his mind went back to the experience up the brook below the falls. There was no Sammie Dingle present now to mar his pleasure, for which he was most thankful.

It did not take the boat long to run to the Sinclair shore, and here in a snug place, safe from the wind, she was beached.

"We can never thank you for what you have done for us to-day," Lois remarked as she and Margaret walked with Jasper to the house. "You have saved our lives."

"Don't thank me," Jasper replied. "It was a pleasure for me to do what I did."

"But how did you know we were out there?" Margaret asked.

"It was Tom who saw you first and pointed your boat out to me. He is the one you should thank."

"But why was Tom looking toward the island?" Lois enquired. "Your explanation does not satisfy me."

"Do you imagine that I was spying upon your little outing?" Jasper questioned.

"Not exactly spying. I don't like that word. But you must have known that we were there."

"Yes, I did. I saw you go over this afternoon, and when the wind sprang up it was only natural to suppose you would have trouble in getting home. That is all there is about it."

"And so you kept watch, and then came to our assistance?"

"Yes."

Lois said no more just then, but walked quietly to the house. She was doing considerable thinking, however, and when she and Margaret went upstairs to change their wet clothes, she again referred to the matter.

"It is just like him," Margaret remarked. "He knew that we were over there and that our lives would be in danger on the water. Not many men would have thought of such a thing."

Lois made no reply, but there was a deep happiness in her heart. She believed that Jasper had been thinking of her throughout the day and that she was always much in his mind. Margaret somewhat divined her thoughts and twined her arms around her neck.

"I believe he thinks a great deal of you, dear," she said, "and I am so glad. It is only natural, for who could resist you? You are as sweet and loveable as can be. If I were a man I am sure I would fall in love with you the first time I met you."

"You did it, anyway, didn't you?" Lois asked, in order to hide her embarrassment. "But there is the car," she added. "I wonder what brings father home so early?"

Going downstairs, they found Mr. Sinclair and Jasper seated upon the verandah in a corner protected from the wind by heavy vines.

"You are early to-day, Father," Lois remarked as she gave him the customary kiss. "We generally have to wait dinner for you."

"It is quite necessary that I should get back early, from what I have heard about you young women," was the reply. "It is hardly safe to leave you alone."

"So you know all about our narrow escape, then," and Lois looked enquiringly into his face. She believed that Jasper must have been telling him, and it somehow disappointed her. She did not think that he would be the first one to talk about the rescue he had made.

"Oh, yes, I learned all about it before I got home," Mr. Sinclair explained. "The men down the road saw it all, and then when Tom took the boat back he gave them the full details. You must be very careful after this, Lois, about going over to the island. You might not always have a rescuer handy as you had to-day."

Lois did not reply. She was glad that Jasper had not told, and she was sorry that she had judged him wrongly. She might have known better, so she mused.

Mr. Sinclair was in excellent spirits. He had changed a great deal since his illness and had become more like a father to her than he had ever been before. He entered more into the life of his family, and his old sternness passed away. Lois wondered what brought him back so early from the city. She asked no questions, however, feeling sure that he would explain the reason in due time.

She did not in fact have long to wait, for after they were all seated at dinner Mr. Sinclair looked quizzically into his daughter's face.

"I know you are puzzling your brain why I came home so early," he began. "Now, are you not?"

"I certainly am," Lois laughingly replied. "Margaret and I have been having all kinds of surmises."

"I've done a great stroke of business to-day," Mr. Sinclair continued, "and it has lifted a heavy burden from my mind. Can any of you guess what it is?"

"Bought a new tract of timber, Dad," Dick replied. "I can't think of anything that would please you better than that."

"No, it's not that."

"Maybe you've found some work for Dick to do," Lois suggested. "That would certainly be a great stroke of business."

"Come, come, Lois," her brother remonstrated. "You seem to think that I have nothing to do."

"Haven't I good reason to think so?"

"No, it's not that," Mr. Sinclair intervened. "You're a long way off."

"Have you bought out the new Light and Power Company?" Jasper asked.

"No, no," and Mr. Sinclair chuckled as he went on with his dinner. He was enjoying immensely the little game.

"I think I know what it is," and Margaret looked intently into his face. "You have sold out to the Break Neck Light and Power Company."

"How in the world did you know that?" Mr. Sinclair asked in surprise. "Why, I thought it was a dead secret."

"So it was in a way," Margaret smilingly replied. "But, you see, I am supposed to know a little of what is going on."

"And your father told you about it, did he?"

"Yes. I have known for some time that he was hoping you would sell out, and thus avoid trouble."

"Is it possible, Father," Lois asked, "that you have sold out all your interest in the City Light and Power Company?"

"We've all sold out, and at such a figure that we are much satisfied."

"Oh, I am so glad," and Margaret clasped her hands before her. "I was afraid that there might be trouble between you and father, and I did not want that."

"There is no danger of that now," Mr. Sinclair replied, "though there was at one time. I never believed that the matter could be so satisfactorily arranged, for I had no idea that the new company would be willing to come to our terms."

Margaret said nothing more, and while the others talked she took no part in the conversation. She very well knew why the matter had been so amicably settled, and she smiled to herself as she thought of the several long conversations she and her father had had together. But for her interference nothing would have been done, she was well aware of that. She remembered how stubborn her father had been when she first suggested the idea to him. But after he had considered it most carefully he realised what a good business proposition it would be.

"I believe Margaret is getting home-sick," Dick remarked.

"Why, what makes you think that?" she asked, somewhat startled by the question.

"Because you are so quiet. You haven't said a word for the last five minutes."

"She hasn't had much chance," Lois laughingly replied. "You have been doing most of the talking, Dick."

"Have I?" and the young man opened his eyes wide in apparent amazement. "But I am going to be silent now and let Margaret tell my fortune. She is a dandy at that," and he handed over his cup as he spoke.

"Oh, I have told your fortune so often," was the reply, "that it is getting to be an old story now."

"Won't you tell me mine?" Jasper asked, passing his cup. "I should like to know what's in store for me."

Margaret took the cup in her hand and gazed at it thoughtfully for a few seconds.

"Do you really wish to know?" she asked.

"Certainly."

"Well, then, I see great trouble ahead of you."

"Whew!" Dick whistled. "This is getting serious. You'd better be careful, Spuds."

"Yes," Margaret continued, "I see a big black cloud, and it entirely surrounds you."

"Does it pass away?" Lois questioned, now much interested.

"I can not altogether tell."

"He's going to have a nightmare," Dick bantered, at which they all laughed.

"I hope there's nothing in your prophecy," Jasper remarked. "If I were at all superstitious I might worry a great deal over what you say."

"Look here, Lois," and Dick turned to his sister, "is there a hole in that tea-strainer? For pity sakes get a new one, and don't let so many grounds get through in the future. We don't want any more clouds."

When dinner was over they all went out on the verandah. It was a beautiful evening, for the wind had subsided, and the river stretched out before them like a huge mirror.

"How I should like to be out there now," Lois remarked, as she gazed pensively upon the water. "Suppose we go for a row?"

"I should think you'd be sick and tired of the river after your experience to-day," Dick replied. "I prefer the car to a boat any time."

"With all the enjoyment of dust, noise, and smell of gasoline thrown in," his sister sarcastically retorted.

"I guess you were most thankful to smell gasoline to-day, though, when Spuds picked you up in that old tub of his. Now, weren't you?"

Before Lois could reply Betty suddenly appeared before them. Her face was flushed, and she was panting as if she had been running fast.

"I have only a minute to spare," she explained, "for Mr. David doesn't know I have left him. He wants to see you, Mr. Jasper, and so I have come before it gets too late. I am afraid to come out after dark now."

CHAPTER XXIV

GATHERING CLOUDS

Jasper did not like the idea of leaving such agreeable company and going with Betty. It was so pleasant to be near Lois, and he was hoping that they might have a quiet little conversation together. Why could not David wait? There was surely nothing of great importance that he wished to see him about. No doubt he wanted to ask him some questions concerning the progress of the work at the falls. He could call in on his way home and have a chat with him.

These thoughts ran quickly through his mind as he sat there watching Betty. But something in the girl's face told him that he had better go at once, and so he rose from his chair.

"Won't you come back again?" Lois asked. "It is go early that surely Mr. David will not keep you all the evening."

"I'm afraid not," was the reluctant reply. "I shall go over to my cabin and get a good sleep. I was up late last night looking after that raft of poles which we took down river to-day."

Lois had the feeling that something was wrong, and she longed to go to the Haven and find out what it was. She was almost tempted to leave the rest and accompany Jasper and Betty. She banished this idea, however, thinking that after all there was nothing over which she should worry. But in a twinkling there flashed into her mind the words Margaret had so lightly spoken over the tea-cup. "I see a big black cloud, and it entirely surrounds you." Why did those words come to her now? she asked herself, and why should she have that strange foreboding of impending trouble? So strong was this impression that she was inclined to hurry after Jasper and give him warning. She did nothing of the kind, however, but during the remainder of the evening she was quieter than usual and took little part in any conversation.

Jasper walked by Betty's side along the road leading to the main highway.

"How did you know where I was?" he presently asked her.

"We saw you this afternoon out on the river saving Miss Lois and Miss Margaret."

"Why, where were you?"

"Mr. David and I were up on the hill. We had just come back from a walk up the brook. Mr. David was tired after his excitement, and so we sat down to rest. It was then that we saw you."

"What made Mr. David excited?" Jasper enquired. "I suppose it was the great change he saw at the falls, was it?"

"Oh, no, not that. It was the rolling log which did it. You see, Mr. David was nearly killed this afternoon."

At these words Jasper stopped short and looked keenly into Betty's face.

"Nearly killed! What do you mean?" he demanded.

"Yes, that was it." Then in a few words the girl told him what had happened up the brook that afternoon, and of old David's narrow escape.

For a while Jasper walked slowly along the road after Betty had finished. He was greatly puzzled, for he could not believe that any log would become loosened at the exact moment when David was directly in front of it unless there was something to start it on its downward course.

"Did you see any men working near the logs when you were there?" he at length asked.

"I didn't see any," was the reply. "But we met several teams on our way up."

"And you saw no one near the place at all?"

"We didn't see any one near where we were going to have our lunch, but as we were coming home we saw the artist down by our brook."

"You did? And where was he?"

"Not far from Pyramid Rock. I don't think he saw us, for we hurried by as fast as we could."

"Why did you do that?"

"Because I'm afraid of him."

"What, did he ever do anything to frighten you?"

"No. But he makes me shiver all over. I can't understand why it is."

Jasper found David crouched in his big easy chair near the open window facing the falls. His eyes brightened as the young man entered and sat down by his side.

"It is good of you to come," David began, "for I have been anxious to speak to you ever since we came back from up the brook. You may go," and he motioned Betty to the door. "I wish to be alone for a while with Mr. Randall."

He waited until the door had closed behind the girl, and then turned his eyes upon his visitor's face. Jasper noted the worry there, and at once connected it with his experience up the brook that afternoon.

"Has Betty told you?" and David laid his right hand gently upon Jasper's arm.

"About the rolling log, and your narrow escape this afternoon?"

David nodded.

"Yes, she told me about it on our way here. I am so thankful that you were not hurt."

"I might have been killed! It was nothing less than a miracle that I escaped."

"It has shaken you up a great deal, so I see. But you will be all right after a good night's sleep. Your nerves are somewhat unstrung now."

"Perhaps so," the old man mused. "But I feel uneasy. It may be the shock, as you suggest. But there is something in my heart that I cannot explain. I never had such a feeling before, and I thought that perhaps you could help me."

"In what way?" Jasper asked, as David paused as if groping for the right words.

"It appears as if everything is about to slip away from me. I seem to-night as if about to start on a long mysterious journey, and that I shall never return. People call me crazy, and perhaps they have good reason for doing so. You may think the same, and especially so now as you listen to my words. But I cannot help this peculiar notion that possesses me and almost overwhelms me with strange forebodings. It may be the outcome of a mind diseased, who knows? My great concern, though, is in connection with the work at the falls. I have the feeling that in some way I am necessary to its welfare. I do not wish it to stop, and I want you to promise me to-night that if anything should happen to me that you will take my place, and be keenly interested in it."

"I do not see how I can take your place, for that is not in my power. But take a deep interest in all that goes on up there I certainly shall, and be as deeply interested in its progress as you have been."

"Ah, you can never be interested in it as I am," and David's eyes glowed with the intensity of his old-time devotion. "Can any one be as much interested in the growth and progress of a child as its parents? My child is up there," and he stretched out his arm toward the falls. "For it I have longed and suffered. It is bone of my bone and flesh of my flesh. My heart's blood is there."

Jasper now felt certain that the old man's mind was really unbalanced. He attributed it to the excitement of his narrow escape that afternoon. A good sleep would refresh him, and he would be all right in the morning. He rose to his feet and took David's hand in his.

"I must go now," he said. "We both need sleep. I was up late last night, and so must go home early to get a good rest. You had better do the same."

"I don't want to sleep," David emphatically replied. "My mind is too much upset to rest. But if you must go let me walk a short way with you. Perhaps the cool night air will refresh me. Wait a moment until I put on my coat and hat. Betty will be angry if I go without them."

Then he suddenly paused and caught Jasper fiercely by the arm.

"Do you hear them?" he asked. "Listen," and he held up his right hand.

In the old man's eyes had come a peculiar light, and his manner reminded Jasper of the first night he had met him on the road when he had rescued him from the speeding auto.

"Do you hear them?" David repeated. "My beautiful falls, my beautiful falls. What sweeter music than the sound of your rushing water. People have been deaf to your luring voice. I alone have listened and understood. They called me a fool and said I was crazy, ha, ha! But they know better now. They have seen what my beautiful falls can do. Light and power! Light and power! The world transformed. Burdens lifted from weary shoulders; homes transformed, and the hearts of all made glad."

He was standing in the middle of the room as he uttered these words, and Jasper noted how the fire of excitement was increasing in intensity.

"Come," and he laid his hand upon his companion's arm as he spoke, "let us go for a walk."

"Hush! Listen!" he cried, unheeding Jasper's words. "There it is again! Do you hear it? It's coming from the valley; it has winged its way across the sea. Ha, ha, he will hear it and tremble. But, wait, he is not there; he is in hell. Yes, that's where he is — in hell! Where else could he be?"

David's voice had risen to a shriek as he uttered the last words. Jasper stared at him in amazement. What did he mean by such strange utterances? Surely the man was out of his mind.

"Come," he again ordered, "let us leave the house and go for a walk. You will feel better out in the cool air."

Taking him by the arm Jasper led him out upon the verandah and down the steps. The twilight was deepening fast, and a quiet peace had settled over the land. Away to the right the trees on the high hills were clearly silhouetted against the evening sky. At any other time Jasper would have stood and revelled in the beauty of his surroundings. But now he was too much concerned about the man at his side to think about such things. From the time they left the house until they reached the main highway David talked incessantly. He was greatly excited, and gesticulated at almost every word.

At length he stopped, placed his right hand to his forehead, and looked around.

"What have I been saying?" he asked in a calmer voice. "It seems to me that I have been in a strange country seeing all kinds of things."

"You are all right now," Jasper replied. "You certainly have been raving at a great rate."

"Have I?" the old man queried, and he lapsed into a momentary silence. "Peculiar feelings come over me at times. The fresh air of night has done me much good. I shall walk a short way with you along the road."

David was now a pleasant companion, and Jasper enjoyed talking to him. He enquired about the progress of the work at the falls and asked numerous questions. Not once did he refer to the dark forebodings which had possessed him at the Haven, and Jasper believed that he had forgotten about them.

"I think I shall return now," he said after they had walked some distance.

"Shall I go back with you?" Jasper asked.

"Not at all. I shall enjoy the walk alone. You are tired and should get home at once. So, good night. I hope to see you again soon."

Jasper stood and watched him until the darkness swallowed him up. Then he made his way along the road to his own lonely house. He was very tired, but he found it difficult to get to sleep. The strange words which David had uttered kept running constantly through his mind. When he did at last fall into a fitful slumber, he was beset by a dreadful monster, which was slowly crushing him to pieces while he was unable to do anything to save himself.

He was aroused from this nightmare by a loud pounding upon the door. At first he imagined it was some one coming to his relief. Half dazed he groped his way across the room, threw open the door and peered out into the night.

"Who's there?" he demanded.

"It's only me," came a voice which he recognised at once as Betty's. "Oh, Mr. Jasper, have you seen Mr. David?" she asked.

"Seen Mr. David!" Jasper exclaimed in surprise. "I haven't seen him since I left him last night on the road near the Haven. Didn't he go home?"

"No, he didn't, and that's the reason I'm here. I waited up for him and when he didn't come back, I started out to find him."

"You stay there a minute," Jasper ordered, as he closed the door and turned back into the room. Lighting a lamp, he was astonished to find that it was near midnight. It took him but a few moments to dress, and then he again threw open the door and stepped out into the night.

CHAPTER XXV

MYSTERY

By the light streaming through the doorway Jasper could see that Betty's face was very pale. She was greatly agitated as well, and her teeth chattered as she spoke.

"You have been running hard," Jasper remarked. "You had better come in and rest awhile."

"No, no," the girl protested. "Don't let us wait a minute. We must find Mr. David!"

"Are you sure he isn't home?" Jasper asked.

"Yes, I am sure he isn't there."

"But he may have slipped in and you didn't hear him."

"No, no, he couldn't have done it. I was listening and watching every minute for him to come back. I am certain I would have seen him."

"Does Mrs. Peterson know where you are?"

"No. She was asleep when I left. I only intended, to come a short distance for I was sure that I would meet Mr. David coming back. But when I didn't, I came all the way here. Oh, let us go at once."

Jasper stepped back into the room, and put out the light. He was about to close the door when he paused.

"Wait a minute," he said, "until I get my lantern. We can't do anything without a light. Mr. David may have fainted by the side of the road. He is an old man, you know."

It did not take Jasper long to get the lantern, and soon they were speeding across the field toward the main highway. He noticed that Betty kept very close to him, and as they drew near the Haven she seemed to be trembling violently. She started often, and Jasper wondered what was the matter with her.

"Were you not frightened to come all the way alone?" he asked.

"Not at first," was the reply. "But I was frightened after a while and I ran hard."

"What frightened you? Were you afraid of the dark?"

"No — yes," Betty faltered. Jasper wondered at her answer, but made no comment.

All along the road they watched most carefully, thinking they might find David. Especially careful was this search as they neared the Haven but not a trace of him could they find.

The Petersons were greatly concerned over the missing man. The captain suggested that the neighbours should be notified and a search-party should start out at once. As this seemed the only thing to do, Jasper hurried to the village and aroused Andy Forbes from his slumbers. It took the storekeeper several minutes to grasp the significance of the affair, and Jasper had to do considerable explaining.

"So you tell me that Crazy David is lost?" he at length queried.

"Certainly. Isn't that what I have been trying to tell you? We must get a search-party out after him at once. I fear that evil has befallen the old man. He may be wandering off in the woods somewhere, as his mind seems to be uncertain at times."

"I'm afraid we can't do much to-night," and Andy scratched his head in perplexity. "However, I'll see what I can do. Maybe I can get a bunch of men together before morning."

"That's good," Jasper encouraged. "You round up the men here, and I'll go to the camp down the road. There are several men there and I'll get one of them to hurry to the falls and bring in all the men. I feel responsible for the welfare of David as I had strict instructions to look after him. If anything has befallen him I shall never forgive myself."

It took Jasper over an hour to go to the camp and bring back a half dozen men. In the meantime a dozen or more had left the village with lanterns to begin the search. These he met up the road. They had searched every nook and corner, but had found no trace of the missing one.

"It's no use hunting when it is so dark," Andy informed him. "We might as well look for a needle in a hay-stack. I move that we wait until morning."

This suggestion was carried out, and while most of the men went back to their homes in order to get something to eat, Jasper made his way to the Haven. Mrs. Peterson met him at the door and her face bore a worried expression.

"Have you found him?" she enquired. "We have been so uneasy."

"No," was the reply. "We must wait until morning. It is no use groping about in the dark. Where is Betty?"

"She's in Mr. David's room. I am so anxious about her. She has been crying and wringing her hands ever since you left. I cannot tell what has come over the girl."

"She is fretting about David, no doubt."

"Yes, that may account for some of her grief," and Mrs. Peterson's eyes rested thoughtfully upon the floor. "But there's something else troubling her, mark my word. She's been nearly frightened to death over something, and the way she sits and shivers at times is hard for me to stand."

"But won't she tell you what's the matter?" Jasper asked.

"I have asked her over and over again, but she always shakes her head, and falls to sobbing and moaning worse than ever. Poor child, I feel so sorry for her."

"It is strange," Jasper mused. "May I see her? Perhaps it is only the excitement that is troubling her."

Betty's face brightened somewhat as Jasper entered the room. This was for only an instant, however, and then she buried her face in her hands and sobbed as if her heart would break.

"Betty, Betty, what is the matter?" Jasper asked. "Tell me what is worrying you?"

"It's about Mr. David!" she moaned. "He's lost and I'm sure he's dead!"

"But we hope to find him," Jasper soothed. "Just as soon as it is light enough we are going to continue our search for him. He must have wandered away into the woods, and no doubt we shall soon find him. There is something else troubling you, is there not? Won't you tell me what it is?"

But the girl shook her head, and try as he might Jasper could not induce her to talk. She was determined to remain obstinately silent.

There was but one person to whom Jasper felt he could turn for assistance, and that was Lois. He had thought of her before, and wondered if she had heard the news of David's disappearance. He felt that it was unlikely as no one would think of carrying the news there. As he stood for a few minutes looking upon Betty who was sitting before him the very embodiment of abject misery, he believed that Lois was the only one who could comfort her, and perhaps induce her to reveal the cause of her unusual state of agitation. Telling the girl to be brave, and to keep up hope for David's safe return, he left the Haven and hastened down the road toward the main highway, and then took a short cut across the field toward the Sinclair house. Far off in the east light was breaking above the horizon, and he knew that in a short time the search would again begin for the missing man, and he must be there.

Not a sign of life could he observe around the place, and he wondered how he could awaken Lois and not disturb the whole household. As he drew near the verandah he noticed that a light shone from one of the upstairs windows. Whether it was Lois' room or not he could not tell, but scarcely had he stepped upon the verandah and tapped gently upon the door, ere it was opened and Lois stood before him, dressed in her out-of-door clothes.

"What's the matter?" she asked before Jasper had time to say a word.

"Have you heard anything?" Jasper enquired,

"No, nothing," was the reply. "But I saw the lights near the Haven and along the road and felt sure that something was wrong."

Jasper noted that Lois' face was very pale, and that she was trembling as if cold. He did not know that she had been unable to sleep owing to the strange presentiment which had come to her the previous evening. So strong had this at last become that she had risen and looked out of the window facing the Haven. It was then that she saw the moving lights, and her worst tears were confirmed.

"David is missing," Jasper told her, "and we are waiting for daylight to have another search for him."

"David is missing!" Lois slowly repeated, as if she had not heard aright. "Have you any idea where he is?"

"No. I left him last night on the road near the Haven. He may have wandered off somewhere into the woods. But Betty is feeling very badly, and I have come thinking that perhaps you might be able to comfort her."

"I shall go at once," Lois replied. "I am so glad you have come for me, as I was almost frantic wondering what was going on."

As they made their way toward the Haven Jasper told Lois more about Betty and her state of agitation.

"What is the cause of it, do you suppose?" Lois asked. "Do you think it is in connection with Mr. David?"

"Not altogether, I am quite certain. There is something else on her mind. She might explain to you what it is when she would tell no one else."

They had just reached the gate leading to the Haven when Andy Forbes, accompanied by several men, swung up the road.

"I must leave you now," Jasper told Lois, "and assist in the search."

"Please let us know as soon as you find any trace of Mr. David," Lois replied. "I shall stay with Betty for a while."

It was quite light now, and as the men walked along the road they searched most carefully every nook and corner, but all in vain.

"He is not anywhere here," Andy remarked. "But he may have wandered into the woods along that old winter road. I suggest that we follow it for a while. He may be wandering about in there. We can comb the woods if he's not on the road."

The men moved very quietly, keenly alert, each hoping to make the discovery first. To Jasper there seemed something uncanny about the way they moved so silently onward at that weird morning hour. A spirit of depression came upon him, and his companions appeared like enemies. He felt that in some unaccountable way they believed that he was to blame for all the trouble, and that he should have taken more care of the old man.

After they had gone some distance along the old road and had found nothing, they stopped and held a consultation as to what they should do.

"Suppose we divide up and search through the woods," Jasper suggested. "Andy, you and Dave come with me, and we'll work back on this side of the road, while the rest of the men do the same on the other."

Acting upon this suggestion, they at once plunged into the woods and took up their positions several rods from one another. Jasper was nearest the road. Next to him was Dave, while Andy was farthest off. Walking abreast among the trees, they were thus enabled to examine every portion of the ground. In a way it seemed almost a hopeless task, but there was nothing else for them to do. They knew that other men would be scouring up and down the main road, as well as through the fields, and in fact every place where David might have strayed.

They had been thus searching for some time and were not far from the main highway, when they heard loud shouting from the men on the other side of the old wood-road. Feeling sure that they were needed, the three men hurried forward in the direction from whence the sounds came. Jasper led, and his heart beat fast as he bounded through the woods, unheeding scratches upon his face and hands from the rough branches which brushed his body.

It took him only a few minutes to accomplish this, and he suddenly came upon the men grouped around something which was lying upon the ground. When his eyes rested upon the form of David huddled there, he gave a half-suppressed cry, and brushing the men aside, dropped upon his knees by the old man's side.

"Is he dead?" he asked in a hoarse whisper.

"Dead as a door nail," Jim Goban replied. "Guess he's been dead fer some time by the look of things. Mighty bad piece of business this, I call it."

"Do you suppose he was killed?" Jasper enquired.

"Sure. There's no doubt about that from the mark on his head. He's been knocked down like an ox."

A shiver shook Jasper's body at these words, and he straightened himself up. He did not notice that several of the men were watching him closely and observing his every word and action. "Who could have done such a diabolical thing?" Jasper mused, as if to himself. "Let us examine the ground very carefully to see if the man who did this deed left any trace. He might have dropped something."

"We have looked," Jim replied, "and we found this."

Jasper's eyes had been searching the ground, but something in Jim's voice caused him to turn suddenly, and as he did so his heart almost stopped beating and his face turned ghastly pale, for there in the man's out-stretched hand was an envelope with his own name upon it.

"Where did you find that?" he gasped, as he reached out to take it.

But Jim drew back, while an expression of exultation gleamed in his eyes.

"No, I guess I better keep it," he replied. "It might come in handy later on. We found it right there," and he pointed to a spot near where the dead man was lying. "Guess we all saw it at once."

A sickening feeling suddenly overwhelmed Jasper, and he felt faint. He looked keenly into the faces of the men standing near, but their eyes were averted. Did they believe him to be guilty of such a foul deed? he asked himself. Something told him that they did, and the less he now said the better it would be. He wanted to get away from their presence to think it all over.

"You better carry the body to the Haven," he at length suggested in a voice as calm as possible. "I'm afraid I can't be of any more service."

With that, he turned and walked rapidly away, leaving the men staring after him with suspicious, wondering eyes.

CHAPTER XXVI

UNDER SUSPICION

Never in the entire history of Creekdale had there been such intense excitement as when word was received of the murder of old David. At first people could not believe it was true, and thought there had been some mistake. But when the men who had found David related the story then all doubt was set aside. The store was crowded that afternoon with excited men who had gathered to hear the smallest detail, and to discuss with one another the whole affair. It was Sandy Miller who described how he had made the discovery, and then shouted for his companions.

"Was the letter lying near?" Andy Forbes asked.

"I didn't notice it at first," was the reply, "as I was so overcome by the sight before me. It must have been lying there all the time, for Jim Goban saw it at once."

"Where is that letter now?"

"Jim has it, I guess. It wasn't a letter, but merely an envelope with 'Jasper Randall' written plain on the outside. You should have seen that fellow's face when Jim showed it to him."

"But do you think that proves anything?" Andy enquired.

"Wouldn't like to say. But you know as well as I do how suspicious the thing looks, and how much the lawyers will make out of it."

"Is the body at the Haven now?" one of the men asked.

"We took it there," Andy replied. Then he paused and looked around upon his audience. "I hope I shall never have to take part in such a business again," he continued. "I can't get the face of that girl Betty out of my mind, and her wild cry is still ringing in my ears. I thought she would go crazy for sure when she heard what had happened."

"She was very fond of the old man, so I understand," Ned Purvis remarked.

"She certainly was. They were just like father and daughter. But I must say that Miss Sinclair was a regular brick. She took charge of everything at once and seemed to know the right thing to do. But, my, her face was pale, and you should have seen her eyes — when she turned them upon Jim Goban."

"What did she do that for?" Ned questioned.

"Because Jim showed her the envelope and hinted that Randall was the guilty one."

"Did she say anything?"

"Never a word. But her eyes said enough, and I saw Jim flinch as if he had been struck in the face."

"The women folks say that her and him are pretty thick," Steve Clemwell drawled. "Maybe that's the reason why she's goin' to stick up fer him. They've been seen drivin' together, and he's been often at her house."

"But what reason would Randall have for murdering Crazy David?" Andy asked. "They've always been the best of friends, and they've never had a quarrel as far as I know."

"But the old man had money, so it was reported," Ned replied. "Andy here knows something about that."

The storekeeper, however, shook his head. He was not anxious now to appear to know more than he really did. He alone of all the men was feeling keenly for Jasper.

"Mark my word, men," and he looked around solemnly upon those before him, "there's a deep mystery connected with this affair. You have taken for granted that Randall is guilty because that envelope was found near the body. But

I think we had better keep our mouths shut, for if we don't some of us may get into trouble. There's going to be a big time over this, and it's best for us to wait and see what will be the outcome. When the detectives get to work they won't leave a stone unturned, and the smallest detail which bears upon the matter will be put into evidence.

"When will the detectives begin work?" Ned asked.

"I don't know, and I don't suppose any of us will, for that matter. They're not going to inform the public of their movements, and maybe we'll never know they've been here. But they'll find out all there is to know, or I'm much mistaken."

"D'ye s'pose they'll arrest that chap on suspicion?" Steve enquired, as he cut a slice from a plug of tobacco he was holding in his hand. "I've heered they ginerally do that furst of all so as to make no mistake."

"Most likely they will," Andy replied. "I wonder where he is, anyway. I haven't seen him since he left us in the woods."

"Maybe he's cleared out," Ned suggested.

Scarcely had he finished speaking ere Jasper entered the store. His face was very pale, and he walked at once toward Andy.

"I want to use the phone," he told him.

"All right, go ahead," and the storekeeper motioned to a small closet-like compartment in one corner of the room. Andy prided himself upon this place which he had built with his own hands. As there were generally people in the store he found it important that the ones using the telephone should be as private as possible. It was for his own protection as well as for others that he had built it.

Jasper at once crossed the room, entered the place and closed the door tightly after him. He well knew that the ears of all would be strained to the utmost to hear what he was saying. It took him only a short time to call up Central in the city and to get into communication with Mr. Westcote. His message was very brief.

"There is great trouble here, and you must come as soon and fast as you possibly can. Come at once to my cabin, and bring the best lawyer in the city. I will explain everything then."

That was the message, and in reply Mr. Westcote told him that he would leave immediately in his car, travel as fast as possible, and bring his own lawyer with him.

Jasper then crossed the room and paid the storekeeper the price of the message. There was a dead silence while he did this, which Jasper was not slow to notice. He spoke to none of the men gathered there, in fact did not even look at them, but left the store as soon as possible.

From the time the blow had fallen and he realised that he was a man suspected of murder, he seemed to be dazed.

He had gone to his own cabin and had tried to reason the whole thing out. But the more he thought the more puzzled he became. There was no doubt that David had been murdered, but who had done the deed, and for what purpose? Only one person came to his mind, and he recalled what Betty had told him about the old man's narrow escape from the rolling log. Though he felt that Sydney Bramshaw had something to do with the affair, he had no definite proof. He naturally connected him with the murder. But what object would the man have for doing such a dastardly deed? He wondered much about the envelope, and how it got there. He had never been to that spot before, and he was quite certain that David did not have it with him. Somebody, then, must have obtained possession of the envelope and dropped it near the body in order to cast suspicion upon him. But why should any one wish to involve him in such a serious crime?

Long and carefully Jasper considered the matter in an effort to solve the problem. But the more he thought the greater was he puzzled. He realised that he must have assistance as that envelope and the fact that he was on the road with David the night of the murder would tell strongly against him. He naturally turned to Robert Westcote as the one man who could help him and would stand by him in his time of need.

He felt very lonely and wretched as he left the store and walked slowly up the road. He did not wish to go back to the silence of his own cabin. If he could only speak to some one and feel that all were not against him it would be some comfort. He thought of Lois, and wondered if she were at the Haven. He was certain that she would not believe him guilty of such a cowardly deed, but would stand by him to the last. Yes, she was the very one, and he would go to her at once. His step quickened as this impulse possessed him and he hurried rapidly along the road, with swinging strides.

"Hello, you seem to be in a great hurry."

Jasper started at these words, stopped short and looked in the direction from whence the voice came. As he did so his face darkened, for there, sitting before his easel not far from the road, was Sydney Bramshaw.

His brush was poised in hand as if he had merely paused in his work of sketching a bunch of birch trees a short distance away.

"You seem to be in a great hurry," the artist repeated, evidently enjoying the forbidding expression upon Jasper's face.

"Well, what of it?" was the curt reply. "It's a free country, isn't it?"

"That all depends," and Bramshaw laid down his brush in a thoughtful manner. "It might be free to one and not to another. You and I can do about as we please to-day, and no one will try to interfere with us. But it isn't the same with the one who put that poor old man out of business last night. He isn't free in the sense we are."

"So you've heard about it, have you?" Jasper questioned.

"Oh, yes. The whole country is wild with the news. I have been talking to a number of people and they are greatly worked up over the cowardly deed. Poor old David! He certainly was an innocent cuss."

"When did you first hear about it?" Jasper enquired.

"Not until late this morning. I am a sound sleeper."

"You surely must be. I don't see how any man could sleep with all the noise the men made passing along the road last night. Were you up late, eh?"

"What do you mean?" and an angry light leaped into Bramshaw's eyes. "I wish you to know that I went to sleep with the birds last night."

"I am glad to hear of it. You didn't always keep such good hours, especially one night when I caught you prowling about my place. Perhaps a hint to the wise was sufficient, and you have changed your manner of living."

"D — you!" Bramshaw cried, rising to his feet. "I was willing to be friendly with you, but you insult me to my face."

"That's much better than insulting you behind your back, isn't it? You are sure who does it and you can act accordingly."

"Is that a challenge to fight?"

"Take it any way you like. I am anxious to get my hands on somebody to-day, for I want a little exercise. I'm getting tired of doing nothing."

"But there's nothing to be gained by fighting," Bramshaw protested. "What reason have we for fighting?"

Jasper gave a sarcastic laugh, and looked the artist up and down.

"You certainly wouldn't gain much by fighting, but I would. Sydney Bramshaw, I believe you are a miserable sneak, ay, and worse, and it would be a great satisfaction for me to get my hands on your measly carcass just for two minutes."

Under the impulse of the moment Jasper had left the road
and approached close to the artist. The latter shrank back and
his face paled at the action of his formidable opponent.
"Bah! I wouldn't touch you," Jasper sneered. "I wouldn't
spoil your nice clothes and your soft delicate hands. Oh, no.
Go on with your work of painting the beautiful things in
nature."

For a few seconds Jasper stood and looked upon the man
cowering before him. He longed to pierce his very soul that
he might learn whether his suspicious were really true. He was
tempted to startle him with a question about that envelope.
But, no, he felt that it would be better to consult the lawyer
before saying anything.

Leaving the artist, Jasper regained the highway with a bound,
and hurried onward. It did not take him long now to reach the
road leading to the Haven, and his angry mood passed like
a cloud from the face of the sun when he saw Lois standing
there beneath the shade of a large tree. Her eyes brightened
when she saw him, and without a word she held out her hand.
For a few heartbeats neither spoke, but their eyes met, and
Jasper knew by the look that Lois gave him that she at least
was true and believed in him.

"You know all?" he stammered.

"No, not all," was the quiet reply. "But I know enough to
make me certain that the people in this place are wrong in
their suspicions."

"Whom do they suspect?" Jasper eagerly asked, thinking that
perhaps he might learn something new.

"Don't you know?"

"Yes, I'm afraid I do," Jasper bitterly replied. "But I can
endure it if I know that you believe me to be innocent."

"I certainly do, no matter what others think."

"What proof have you?"

"Your life; isn't that proof enough?"

"It may be to you, but I'm afraid it will count but little at the trial."

"At the trial!" Lois repeated in amazement. "Surely you'll not be —"

"Arrested?" Jasper assisted, as Lois' voice faltered.

"Yes, that's what I mean."

"I'd like to know what's to prevent it. Wasn't I with David the night he was murdered, and wasn't that envelope with my name on it found by his body? Do you for one moment imagine that I can hope to escape a severe grilling and perhaps conviction with such evidence against me?"

"But it isn't right," and Lois stamped her foot impatiently. "It's only circumstantial evidence, and that shouldn't count."

"But it does. It has convicted many men before this. But tell me, did you learn what is troubling Betty?"

"It's about Mr. David, you know. She grieves very much over his death. She loved the old man dearly, almost as if he were her own father."

"I know she feels badly. But isn't there something else troubling her as well? Didn't you notice it?"

"I did, but Betty would tell me nothing. I believe she has been frightened in some way, for at times she started up in terror, and her whole body trembled. I wonder what it can be!"

Before Jasper could reply, an auto swung up the road and stopped near them. There were two men in the car and almost intuitively Jasper knew that they were detectives. They looked keenly at the two standing beneath the tree, and then asked the way to Captain Peterson's. Jasper told them, and without another word they turned to the left and sped up to the house.

"Who are they, do you suppose?" Lois asked.

"They must be detectives," Jasper slowly replied.

"Oh!" It was all that Lois could say as she stood watching the car until it drew up before the Haven.

"I shall go back to my cabin now," Jasper remarked. "I expect Mr. Westcote shortly, and so I must be there when he arrives."

Slowly they walked along the road to the gate leading to the Sinclair house. For a while neither spoke. Jasper realised that it would be a long time ere he would again be with her who was so dear to him. Perhaps never, for who could tell what the lap of the future might contain? Lois was thinking of the same thing, and her heart was very heavy. There came to her mind the words Margaret had so lightly spoken over the tea-cup. Why had she not warned Jasper? she asked herself over and over again. Never before had she fully comprehended what this man really meant to her. He was the first one who had ever inspired her with the spirit of courage and endurance. Not once had she heard him whine or complain but, in her presence at least, he had always appeared as master of his fate. Now he was going from her, and she might never see him again. But no matter what happened she was sure that he would bear himself manfully, and fight to the very last.

Having reached the gate, they paused. Both knew that the moment for parting had come and strange feelings stirred their hearts. Jasper thought that Lois never looked so beautiful. Oh, if he were only certain that she loved him. If he could only take her in his arms and tell her of his love, and feel that his great love was returned; then he could go down into the dark valley of trouble, and perhaps death, with a braver heart. But, no, it would not do for him to tell of his love now with such a shadow hanging over his head. There were many things he longed to do, but all he did was to step forward, seize Lois' right hand in his, and press it fervently to his lips. Instantly he realised his boldness.

"Forgive me," he cried, "but I could not help it."

"There is nothing to forgive," Lois quietly replied, though her heart was beating fast and her face was more flushed than usual. "You had better go now, for Mr. Westcote may come at any moment. Good-bye, and may God bless and keep you."

That was the hardest parting Jasper had ever known. But as he walked up the road a new spirit possessed his soul. He knew what it was to fight, for he had fought all his life long. But now he had the vision of a fair woman to sustain him, and for her sake, and to show her that he was worthy of her trust he would still fight the fiercest battle of all. What the outcome would be he could not tell, but he was determined to bear himself in such a manner that Lois would never be ashamed of him. He well knew that even a defeated man might be more of a conquerer than those who triumphed over him. And even as he walked there flashed suddenly into his mind a vision of the Man of Sorrows bearing his cross. Why had he not thought of Him before? he asked himself. There was his example to follow; there was the One who was the victor even on the cross, and there was the One to whom he could now turn for comfort in the hour of his great need.

CHAPTER XXVII

IN THE TOILS

It was with a heavy heart that Lois made her way slowly toward the house. She felt that many changes would take place before she would again see Jasper. Not for an instant did she consider him guilty of murdering old David. But she was well aware that others would think differently, and would be only too ready to condemn Jasper upon the slightest evidence. An idea suddenly flashed into her mind, which caused her heart to beat quicker. Some one was guilty of the murder, and that person must be found, whoever and wherever he was. Was there not something that she could do? she asked herself. Jasper must be saved, and who else would take such a real heart interest in the matter as herself? She knew that a woman was not expected to undertake work of such a nature. But Lois Sinclair had very little respect for social customs if they stood in the way of duty.

During the day she had thought much about the murder and had tried to unravel the mystery connected with it. Who was there in the place likely to commit such a cowardly deed, and what would be his motive? Old David had not an enemy, as far as she knew, and he had injured no one. It was necessary for her to probe deeper still, and as she neared the house her mind brooded over this question. She chided herself that she had not asked Jasper's opinion. Perhaps he had some suspicion, for even upon the slightest clue important results might depend.

Lois had reached the steps leading to the verandah when she happened to stop and look down toward the river. As she did so, she started, for there near the shore, with his easel before him, was Sydney Bramshaw. Had she known of the stormy scene which had taken place between him and Jasper about an hour before she would have been more surprised to see him where he was. He was seated facing the house, and thus could observe all that took place about the building. If he saw Lois he gave no sign of recognition, but seemed to be entirely occupied with his work.

The sight of this man had a remarkable effect upon Lois. She had seen him but little of late, and to behold him now when she was thinking so much about the murder was most startling. She entered the house as if nothing unusual were agitating her mind. But with the door closed behind her, she hurried upstairs, where she found Margaret sitting in her room engaged upon some fancy-work. It was a bright sunny room, and the girl sitting there by the open window presented a beautiful picture of peace and youthful charm.

"What is the matter, dear?" she asked, pausing in her work, as she noted the troubled expression upon Lois' face.

"Look," and Lois pointed toward the river, "there he is near the shore."

"Well, what of it?" Margaret enquired with a smile. "One would think that you had never seen a man before."

"But not such a man as that, Margaret," and Lois sat down by the girl's side. "Something tells me that he had much to do with the murder of poor old David."

"Whatever put such a foolish notion as that into your head?" and Margaret looked keenly into Lois' face.

"Sydney Bramshaw is merely a harmless artist, and wouldn't hurt a fly."

"So you have always said. You may be right, but my heart

tells a different story, and it is hard for me not to believe it. I am going to find out, anyway, if there is any justification for my suspicion of that man."

"You!" and Margaret looked her astonishment. "Why, what can you do?"

"Perhaps nothing. Anyway, I am going to try. Something must be done at once if Mr. Randall is to be saved." Lois then told Margaret all about the finding of David, of the envelope lying near the body, and how the people were accusing Jasper of the murder.

When Mr. Sinclair and Dick came home they brought with them a copy of _The Evening News_, which contained a long account of the murder. Lois' hand trembled as she took the paper and saw the big startling headlines. She feared lest Jasper's name should be mentioned in connection with the affair, and she breathed a sigh of relief when she saw that it did not appear. The article merely said that a certain person was suspected and that the detectives were working on the case.

"I'm afraid Spuds is in hot water," Dick remarked, as they all sat down to dinner.

"What makes you think that?" Lois asked in a voice as calm as possible.

"Oh, from what people are saying. It's known all over the country that he was with Crazy David that night, and that they left the Haven and walked along the road together. That in itself looks suspicious, for Spuds was the last person seen with old David."

"Who saw them together?" Lois enquired, "and how did that information get abroad?"

"The Petersons, I suppose, or that girl Betty told it."

"But do you suppose some one else saw them together? Have you thought of that?"

"I don't catch the drift of your meaning," and Dick looked enquiringly at his sister.

"Suppose there was some one else near the road that night watching Mr. Randall and David as they walked along? And suppose, further, that when the old man was going back alone to the Haven some one had killed him?"

"Good heavens, Lois! you make my blood run cold. Why should you suggest such a thing?"

"But you don't believe that Mr. Randall killed David, do you?"

"No, no! I couldn't for a moment think that Spuds would do such a thing."

"Well, then, some one must have done it in a way similar to what I have said."

"Sure, I never thought of that. But who do you suppose did it?"

"That's for us to find out."

"Us?"

"Yes, why not? Isn't it right to stick by our friends in their time of need?"

"But what can we do?"

"That remains to be seen."

"But what about that envelope, Lois? How do you I suppose it got there? That looks queer, doesn't it?"

"That's another part of the mystery to be solved, that's all."

The next day was an exciting one, for all kinds of rumours were afloat, and at times Lois hardly knew what to believe. But there were several things about which there was no doubt. She learned that an inquest had been held over David's body, and that it had been decided that David Findlay had met his death at the hands of some unknown person or persons. There was nothing more left to be done but to give the body a decent burial.

The funeral was held that afternoon, and it seemed that the entire parish turned out. It was a fine mild summer day, but notwithstanding that the farmers left their fields and attended the funeral. Lois and Betty walked together to the church, and as they passed Jasper's cabin they looked across the field, thinking they might see some one there. But not a sign of life could they behold.

The service in the church was brief and solemn, and Betty found it very difficult to control her feelings. At the grave side she broke down completely, and Lois had to lead her away to a quiet spot.

"Poor Mr. David!" the girl moaned. "I shall never see him again. He was so good to me."

"There, there, dear," Lois soothed. "If he were alive he would not wish you to feel so badly. He is at rest, anyway."

"I know that, but I miss him so much. Oh, why was he taken?"

For some time they sat there, Betty sobbing out her grief, and Lois trying to sooth her, at the same time wondering what had become of Jasper. If he had not gone away it was strange that he was not at the funeral. The people leaving the grave passed close to the spot where they were sitting, and many were the curious glances cast in their direction. Several women stopped to speak to them, among whom was Mrs. Wadell, noted all over the parish for her fondness for gossip, as well as for meddling in the affairs of others.

"So ye feel bad, do ye?" and she fixed her piercing eyes upon Betty's tear-stained face. "I wouldn't feel bad fer such as him," and she jerked her thumb toward the grave.

"But I do," Betty protested. "He was good to me, and now he is gone."

"I guess ye'll like him better now that he's gone," Mrs. Wadell remarked. "I know I should, anyway, if he'd done as handsome by me as he's done by you."

"Why, what do you mean?" Betty asked in surprise.

"Why, about the money he's left ye. It's a snug sum, so I understand, and I suppose it'll make ye put on mighty fine airs, so's ye won't speak to common folks any more."

Lois now became much interested in the words of this garrulous old woman, and she was anxious to know more, and where she had obtained her information.

"How did you hear that?" she asked.

"Land sakes, don't ask me sich a question as that, Miss," was the evasive reply. "How could I begin to tell ye where I hear things, fer the air is full of all kinds of stories to-day. But I guess it's true all right."

"I didn't know that Mr. David had made a will. That is a surprise to me."

"And indeed it is to everybody else, Miss. We didn't think that Crazy David had anything to leave. Why he was sold as a pauper to Jim Goban in this very parish about a year ago. But that isn't the only thing that surprises me."

"What, is there something more?"

"There surely is, Miss. It's reported that he's left a hull lot to that Randall feller. I guess he knew how to work his cards all right with the old man. He didn't take an interest in him fer nuthin', oh, no. People don't generally do sich things these days fer love."

"Mr. Jasper hadn't anything to do with that will," Betty angrily protested. "He didn't know anything about it, neither did I."

"Oh, you wouldn't know," and the old woman gave a sarcastic chuckle. "He wouldn't want people to know what he was doin'. He was cute enough fer that. And then to think that he should kill Crazy David to git his money. Why the poor old man couldn't have lived much longer, anyway."

"You lie!" and Betty, trembling in every limb, sprang to her feet. "Mr. Jasper didn't do it. I tell you he didn't, and you have no right to say such things."

"Come, Betty," Lois remarked, rising to her feet and taking the girl by the arm, "let us go home."

"Ye may not believe me," the old woman called after them as they walked away, "but ye'll soon find out fer yerselves, and then maybe ye won't talk so big and mighty."

Betty was going to reply, but Lois checked her.

"I wouldn't say anything more, dear," she advised. "We must expect people to talk and imagine all sorts of things. Let us be brave and hope for the best."

"But I can't bear to hear them say such awful things about Mr. Jasper," the girl sobbed. "I'm sure he didn't get Mr. David to make his will, and then kill him to get the money."

"So am I, Betty. But I'm afraid we'll be the only ones who think so. We'll stand by him, anyway, and do all we can for him, won't we?"

Lois suddenly stopped and her face went pale. They had now come in sight of Jasper's cabin, and near it were several men. On the road were most of the people who had been at the funeral. That they were greatly excited was quite evident. In an instant Lois realised the meaning of it all, and she clutched Betty by the arm in the intensity of her emotion.

"They are going to arrest him!" Her voice was hoarse, and she spoke scarcely above a whisper.

"Who?" Betty asked in surprise, not fully comprehending the meaning of her words.

"The constables are after Mr. Randall," Lois explained. "There they are now!" she cried. "They are coming from the house, and he is walking between them."

"Are they going to put him in prison?" the girl asked.

"Yes, I'm afraid so."

With a wild cry, Betty sprang forward and rushed up the road. Lois followed, wondering what the girl was going to do. She reached the crowd just as Jasper and the constables approached, and stood there a silent watcher. What could she do? she asked herself. Would he see her, and know of her sympathy?

Jasper was walking with a free easy motion, closely guarded by the two constables, one of whom was Jim Goban. His face was pale and he looked very careworn, but he held his head erect and kept his eyes straight before him. Betty standing near, rushed suddenly forward and caught him by the hand.

"Oh, Mr. Jasper," she cried, "we know you didn't do at, and I want to tell you so."

Taken by surprise, Jasper paused and looked at the girl.

"Thank you," he replied. "I am glad you believe in me."

"And so does Miss Lois," Betty explained. "She's standing right there," and she motioned to the right.

Jasper turned, saw Lois, and their eyes met. Not a word did they say, but in that fleeting glance the expression that he saw in the eyes of the woman he loved gave him great comfort and courage.

"Git out of the way, girl," Jim Goban brutally ordered. "What d'ye mean by stoppin' us in our duty? We'll miss the boat if we don't hurry."

CHAPTER XXVIII

LIGHT BREAKS

Lois stood and watched Jasper and the constables until a bend in the road hid them from view. Then taking Betty by the hand, she moved away from the crowd. She could not bear to listen to their animated discussions as to what would happen to the prisoner, for she was well aware that most of them believed him to be guilty. She walked quite fast until the path across the field was reached. This led along the edge of a grove of young maples and birches, and here was a restful seclusion from all prying eyes.

"You must come and have dinner with me, Betty," she said, speaking for the first time since leaving the crowd. "You will be lonely at the Haven now, and I would like to have you for company, as Miss Westcote has gone to the city."

"Oh, may I?" and the girl lifted her tear-dimmed eyes to her companion's face. "How nice that will be, and we can talk together about him, can't we? I must go home soon, for mother will be anxious to see me. She hasn't been well lately and wasn't able to get to the funeral. I must do what I can to help her."

"You will not have to work out any more, I suppose," Lois remarked.

"Why?" the girl asked.

"Because of the money Mr. David has left you. You remember what Mrs. Wadell said, don't you?"

"Oh, yes," and Betty fixed her eyes thoughtfully upon the ground. "I have been thinking about that. But do you think I should use that money on myself?"

"Why, certainly; what else should you do with it?"

"But Mr. Jasper will need it, will he not?"

"In what way?"

"Won't he need a lawyer to help him? I know it costs so much to get a lawyer for mother has told me so. We must do all we can to save him."

A mistiness came into Lois' eyes as Betty uttered these words. She suddenly stopped, put her arms lovingly around the girl, and tenderly kissed her.

"You precious dear," she cried. "How sweet it is of you to think of him, and I am most grateful to you. But I do not think you need worry about paying the lawyer. I am sure Mr. Westcote will look after that."

"Oh, do you think he will?" and the girl breathed a sigh of relief. Then her face clouded, and that worried expression again came into her eyes.

"What will they do with Mr. Jasper?" she enquired.

"I can't say," was the low reply.

"Will they keep him in prison a long time, or will they —?"

"Don't say that word!" Lois cried, clutching Betty firmly by the arm. "I know what you were going to say, and I can't bear to hear it."

They were walking slowly now along the narrow path, bordered by waving grass. Birds sang in the trees to their left and butterflies flitted here and there over the broad fields. It was a scene of peace and contentment. Nature was in her most attractive mood and seemed to care nothing for the cares of struggling humanity. At any other time Lois would have rejoiced in the beauty around her and would have revelled in the glory of earth and sky. But now it was otherwise. How could she be happy when her heart was so heavy? She knew the cause, and she was not ashamed to confess it to herself. In fact, it brought a slight ray of comfort to feel that she was suffering with him.

They had almost reached the house when a boy was seen approaching. He carried a note in his hand, which he gave at once to Lois.

"It's from Mr. Forbes," he explained, "and he told me to hustle, and take an answer back as quick as I can."

Lois read the note, which simply stated that she was wanted at the telephone.

"Tell Mr. Forbes that I shall be there shortly," she told the boy, at the same time handing him a coin for his trouble in carrying the message.

Hurrying into the house in order to leave word with the maid where she was going in case any one should call, Lois started with Betty for the store. There was no more loitering now as she was anxious to learn who wanted her on the phone. It was rarely that any one called her up, and she was hoping that it might be Margaret to tell her that she was coming back that evening.

On their way they came to the grove at the top of the hill not far from the Haven. Here Betty stopped, and stood as if hesitating what to do.

"I think I shall leave you, Miss Lois," she said.

"What, are you not going with me to the store?"

"No, I guess not. I will see you later. I want to go to my room now to think something over."

She was trembling as she said this, and Lois wondered what was the matter with her. Then an idea flashed into her mind. Was she afraid to go past the artist's tent? she asked herself. There could surely be nothing else which would cause her to leave her and go to the loneliness of her own room. She said nothing to Betty, however, of her thoughts, but bade her good-bye and hurried on her way.

Coming at length to the spot where Bramshaw had been living, she glanced to the left as if expecting to see him. But no sign of him did she see, and great was her surprise to find that his tent was gone. She rubbed her eyes, thinking that she had not seen aright. But, no, there was no mistake. Bramshaw had gone, and had taken all his belongings with him. This was strange, and as she walked along she began to muse as to where he had gone and the purpose of his hasty departure. Had it anything to do with the murder of old David? she wondered.

Lois was thinking of these things as she reached the store, where she met Andy Forbes.

"Do you know what has become of the artist?" she enquired.

"Isn't he up the road?" Andy asked in reply.

"His tent has been removed, and so I suppose he has gone with it."

"Gone!" he exclaimed in surprise. "Why, when did he go?"

"I haven't the least idea."

"Well, I guess there must be something in it after all," Andy mused as if to himself.

"In what?" Lois questioned, wondering what the man meant.

"I'll tell you in a minute, Miss Sinclair, but you'd better read this first," and the storekeeper handed her a piece of paper. "It's the telephone message," he explained.

Lois took the paper in her hand, and read. It was from Mr. Westcote, containing a request that she should go to the city the next day if she possibly could, as he wished to see her on important business.

"Why didn't you send this with the boy?" Lois enquired, some-what annoyed. "It would have saved my coming here."

But Andy did not notice her annoyance, for something seemed to be troubling him.

"Would you mind coming into the house?" he asked. "My wife will look after the store for a few minutes. There is an important matter I wish to speak to you about."

Opening the door to the right, he ushered her at once into a small sitting-room. It was a cosy place, and here she found Mrs. Forbes, a bright-eyed little woman, seated at the window facing the road, doing some sewing. Lois knew her very well as one of the quiet thoughtful women, of Creekdale, and who was of such great assistance to her husband.

"It is too bad to disturb you," Lois apologised, when Andy had asked her to look after the store for a short time.

"Oh, I do not mind," she pleasantly replied. "I am so glad you have come, for I have been most anxious for Andy to have a talk with you. Sit down, please," and she motioned to a chair.

Andy did not sit down but walked up and down the room, as was his custom when greatly excited. Presently he paused and looked keenly into Lois' expectant face.

"It's something very serious I've got to tell you, Miss Sinclair," he began. "In fact, it's so serious that I have been doubting for some time whether I should tell anybody about it. But when I told my wife this afternoon she advised me to tell you, and so that's the reason why I asked you to come here."

"Has it anything to do with the murder case?" Lois asked, now much interested.

"Yes, I believe it will have, and that is what makes me so worried, because I don't want to get tangled up in that nasty affair."

"Tell me what it is," Lois suggested, impatient to learn what it really was.

"Well, it has to do with that envelope."

"Oh!" Lois was more interested than ever now.

"Yes, that's what it is about. You see, Randall came to the office one day last week, and there was a letter for him from his company. I know that much about it for their name was on the top left hand corner. Randall opened the letter right in the store and dropped the envelope on the floor, and didn't pay any more heed to it. I've seen him do the same thing several times and so I didn't pay any special attention to it. Now, Randall hadn't been gone very long before that artist came for his mail. There was nothing for him and he seemed very surly and said a few cuss words about people not writing. As he was standing there talking I saw him stoop and pick up the envelope Randall had dropped. He didn't know that I saw him doing it, for I was busy with the mail though I was watching him all the time out of the corner of my eye, for I never liked the fellow. I saw him glance at me, and when he felt sure that I didn't notice what he was doing he slipped that envelope into an inside pocket of his coat."

When Andy began his story Lois was sitting with her hands clasped before her and her eyes fixed full upon his face. But before he had finished she had risen to her feet greatly agitated.

"Are you sure that is the same letter that was found by David's side?" she asked in a hoarse whisper.

"I couldn't swear that it was," Andy slowly replied. "Anyway, it looks very much like it, and the name of the company is on the left-hand corner, just as it was on the one which Randall dropped on the floor and Bramshaw picked up."

"It must have been the same one," Lois emphatically declared. "Oh, I am so thankful that you have told me this. I am sure it will go a long way toward saving Mr. Randall."

"I can't swear though that it's the same envelope," Andy repeated.

"But you will be willing to swear to what you have just told me, will you not?" Lois asked.

"Sure. I'd swear to that any time and anywhere."

"Thank you," and Lois breathed a sigh of relief. "I feel quite certain that it will be valuable evidence."

"Now, I wonder what that chap wanted that envelope for?" Andy mused.

"To leave it by old David's body, of course, and to throw the blame on Mr. Randall."

"Yes, that no doubt was his idea. But why did he want to do that? And if he committed that deed, why did he do it? What object did he have in murdering an innocent old man who never injured anybody, as far as I know?"

"That is the puzzling thing which must be solved," Lois replied. "But I must go home now, Mr. Forbes, and I thank you very much for what you have told me this afternoon."

She left the store with a lighter heart than she had entered it, and walked briskly up the road. She somehow felt that what Andy had told her would be of great value in freeing Jasper and bringing home the crime to the right person. But something more must be done, and she knew that it would be quite necessary to find the motive which prompted Bramshaw to pick up that letter and to commit the deed.

As Lois came to the road leading to the Haven, she found Betty waiting there for her. The girl seemed brighter than she had been since the night of the murder, and Lois wondered what was the cause of it. Had she heard some good news? she asked herself.

"Oh, Miss Lois," Betty cried, "I have been waiting a long time for you and I thought you would never come. May I go home with you?"

"Certainly, I shall be delighted to have you. But you look brighter, Betty, than you did when I left you. Have you heard anything new?"

"Oh, yes, Miss Lois, I have," the girl replied. "The captain told me that he has gone away."

"Who?" Lois enquired.

"The artist! Just think of that! He has cleared out, and taken everything with him."

"Why should that make you so happy, Betty?"

"Because he can't hurt me now."

"Why, did he ever try to hurt you?"

"Oh, yes, he said he would kill me if I told on him."

"Kill you!" Lois exclaimed, stopping short. "If you told on him! I do not understand you."

"Hush," and the girl raised a warning finger and looked apprehensively around. "Don't speak too loud. I am really afraid yet. But I know he can't hurt me because he has gone."

"No, he won't hurt you, Betty. I will see that he doesn't. Tell me when he said he would kill you."

"The night I went to meet Mr. David."

"Oh!"

"Yes, I was hurrying along the road just up there when I heard some one coming toward me. I was sure it was Mr. David, and so I rushed up to him and called out his name. Instead of Mr. David it was the artist, just think of that! My, he was surprised when he found who I was. He was so excited that he caught me by the arm so hard that I cried out with pain and fear."

"He did?"

"Yes; and he said he would kill me if I ever told that I had met him there on the road that night. He said that nothing could save me from him, and oh, how he did curse and swear what he would do. He made my blood run cold."

"And did you promise that you wouldn't tell?" Lois asked.

"No, indeed I didn't! I jerked myself suddenly away from him and ran home as hard as I could. He ran after me, but he didn't catch me. I was so afraid to look for Mr. David after that. I stayed in the house till near midnight before I went out again."

"So that was what was troubling you so much, was it?" Lois asked.

"Yes. I was afraid that he would kill me. I guess I'm a coward anyway. But when I saw the constables take Mr. Jasper away this afternoon I made up my mind to tell you all about it. I don't mind now if the artist does kill me if I can save Mr. Jasper. Anyway, I am glad that he has cleared out."

"Don't be afraid, Betty, he will not hurt you at all," and Lois put her arms lovingly around the girl. "I am so thankful that you have told me this. Come, now, and let us go home."

CHAPTER XXIX

LOIS GOES TO THE CITY

Betty's story filled Lois with still greater hope, and she was anxious to see Jasper's lawyer that she might tell him what she had learned. For most of the night she thought about the matter, and she tried to find some reason why Bramshaw should commit the murder. She thought, too, of Jasper, and wondered how he was bearing himself in his lonely cell. She longed to speak to him and tell him of the discovery she had made. She knew that his mental suffering must be great, and she did want to help him to bear his trouble.

Lois learned from her father and Dick upon their arrival from the city what a strong feeling was abroad against Jasper. People condemned him in no measured language, and denounced him as a dastardly villain who deserved the severest punishment. Mr. Sinclair told of the conversation he had with several people along the road, and how all were loud in their severe denunciations. Even the city papers, following the popular cry, had editorials about the murder. Though they did not mention Jasper by name, yet their allusions were so pointed that no one could mistake their meaning. All united in condemning the criminal and declaring that the deed was all the more abhorrent owing to the age of the murdered man and the friendly relations which had existed between him and his suspected assailant.

All this was very hard for Lois to endure. It annoyed her to think how willing people were to condemn a man and judge him worthy of death before he had received a fair trial. She had a secret satisfaction, however, in the information Andy and Betty had imparted to her. It buoyed her up with the hope that it would greatly assist in freeing Jasper and clearing him entirely from all blame. It was only natural that she should desire to see the ones who condemned him so severely put to an ignominious silence. She smiled almost bitterly as she thought how they would come about Jasper with their smooth, oily words of congratulation when he again came into their midst.

In the morning Lois went to the city with her father and Dick. She enjoyed the ride in the fresh air and she was somewhat sorry when she alighted from the car in front of her father's office. Dick wanted to drive her around to Mr. Westcote's house as he was most anxious to see Margaret. He had not met her for two days, and to him it seemed a very long time. But as Lois had some shopping to do, she preferred to walk.

"I'll be around this afternoon, though," Dick told her.

"Oh, I know you will," was the laughing reply. "Shall I tell her?"

"Yes, do, Lois. She's great, isn't she?"

"She certainly is, Dick. But I must hurry away now," she added as she saw that her brother was anxious to talk more about Margaret.

It did not take Lois long to do her shopping, and she was just leaving the store when she met Mrs. Dingle face to face. Had she seen her sooner she would have made a desperate effort to escape her. But there was nothing for her to do now but to submit with the best grace possible.

"Oh, isn't it lovely to see you, dear," Mrs. Dingle effusively cried, as she gave her a peck-like kiss upon the right cheek. "We have been talking so much about you lately. Sammie is fairly crazy to see you, and you must be prepared for a visit from him as soon as he learns you are in town. I am so thankful that I have such a dutiful son. He is quite a comfort to me, and I am sure any woman would be proud to have him for a husband. There are so many bad men these days that we appreciate a good one when we find him. We knew that you would come back to the city."

"What made you think that?" Lois enquired as Mrs. Dingle paused an instant for breath.

"To get away from that horrid country place, of course, where that terrible murder was committed. I hope they have that villain securely locked up."

"What villain?" Lois asked.

"Why the one who killed that poor old man for his money."

"No, he is not locked up yet."

"But I heard that he is. Surely he hasn't escaped!" and Mrs. Dingle held up her well-gloved hands.

"No, he isn't in prison yet," Lois calmly replied. "But there is an innocent man there, though, I am sorry to say."

"Do you mean that uncouth fellow Sammie was telling me about?"

"I am not referring to any uncouth fellow, Mrs. Dingle, but merely to Mr. Jasper Randall, a gentleman and a friend of mine."

"Oh, I didn't know that," and Mrs. Dingle looked her surprise as well as her embarrassment. "All I know is what Sammie told me."

"What did Sammie tell you?" Lois voice was sharp as she asked the question.

"I can't remember all. But he said that he was brought up on a farm, had to work his way through college, and that sort of thing, you know. As he is not of our set, of course I did not pay much attention to what Sammie told me."

Lois was both angry and disgusted at this woman. Oh, how she longed to tell her something that she would not soon forget. How she was tempted to place Jasper and Sammie side by side and compare them; the one an insignificant, brainless, useless, overdressed nincompoop; the other a strong, self-reliant, masterful man, fighting against fate with face to the front and head erect.

"Excuse me, Mrs. Dingle," she said, "I am in a great hurry this morning. And I am afraid if I stay I may say something to hurt your feelings. Mr. Randall is a friend of mine, and I have great respect for him. I have always made it a point of being loyal to my friends, and adversity is the test of friendship."

Mrs. Dingle stared in amazement after Lois. She could not understand what had come over the girl, and at luncheon she discussed the matter with Sammie.

"You must see her at once, dear," she told him. "It would not do to lose her, for her father is very rich and she is his only daughter. I am afraid she thinks a great deal of that uncouth fellow who has been arrested."

"Hm," her son grunted. "Don't you worry one bit. Spuds'll be fixed all right. The noose is hanging over his head and just ready to drop, I was talking to some of the fellows to-day and they say that he's a goner, and that nothing can save him. Oh, by the way, Ma, I saw Bramshaw to-day."

"You did!" his mother replied in surprise. "Why I thought he had left the city."

"So he did; but he's back now all right."

"Where did you meet him?"

"Just as he was coming out of the C. P. R. ticket office. He was in a great hurry and had no time to stop and talk."

"You must find out where he is staying, Sammie, and invite him to come and see us. He is a very distinguished young man, you know; an artist of wide reputation, and it makes a favourable impression to have such a man visit us.

He is a gentleman, and not like that uncouth man who committed that terrible crime at Creekdale."

"But I don't believe he'll be here long, Ma," Sammie replied.

"Why, what makes you think that?"

"I guess he's leaving the city. He must have been at the office getting his ticket when I met him. No doubt he is going on this evening's train."

"He is visiting some of the big cities, no doubt, Sammie. A man like that could not be expected to remain in a small place like this. People must be anxious to see the man who has painted such famous pictures."

"Have you seen any of them, Ma?" her son asked.

"Oh, no. But he has told me about them, and they must be great from what he said. He has sold a great many at large prices, but the most valuable he keeps in his mansion in England, so he informed me. He said that he regretted that he had not brought several with him, but the risk was too great, and the pictures were so big that it was difficult to transport them so far."

"H'm," Sammie grunted, as he went on with his luncheon, and nothing more was said then about the artist.

Lois found Margaret at home and they had luncheon together. There was only one topic of conversation, and Lois told of the information she had received from Andy and Betty Bean.

"Have you any idea what your father wishes to see me about?" she asked. "I am quite curious to know."

"I really don't know," and Margaret shook her head. "He generally tells me his secret plans because he knows that I will not divulge them."

"You will go with me to his office this afternoon, will you not?"

"Certainly, if you care to have me. Father generally gets his luncheon out and is somewhat late getting back to his office.

Wait a minute, dear, while I phone and tell him you are here."
Margaret was gone only a few minutes, and when she
returned she resumed her seat at the table.

"Father will be back in his office at one-thirty," she began,
"and he says that I may go with you. Lois, I have something
important to tell you." Here she dropped her voice and looked
apprehensively around the room. "Since you told me about
that letter and Betty's fright I have been doing some serious
thinking. You say that Sydney Bramshaw has left Creekdale?"

"Yes. He cleared out, tent and baggage."

"Have you any idea where he is?"

"No. But I am afraid he is far away by this time."

"Well, he isn't. He's in the city now."

"In the city!" Lois repeated in surprise.

"Yes. I met Sammie Dingle on the street this morning, and
he told me that he met Bramshaw coming out of the C. P. R.
ticket office."

"Oh!"

"Yes, that's what he told me. I did not think anything about
it at the time, but I see things in a different light now. He must
be planning to leave the city on the evening train, and if he
once gets across the Border it will be difficult to find him. You
should tell father all you know, and I am sure he will take
action at once."

"And will he have Bramshaw arrested?" Lois asked.

"What else will there be to do? It would not do to let him
escape with such evidence against him. It will be necessary
for him to explain about that letter and his suspicious actions
and threat to Betty. We have really no time to lose. My, I am
getting interested and excited."

"For my part," Lois replied, "I believe he is the guilty man.
But I cannot understand the motive of his crime. If we knew
that it might lead to greater discoveries. You see, in reference

to that envelope it will be merely one man's word against another. Andy will swear that he saw him pick up an envelope which Mr. Randall dropped on the floor, but he cannot swear that it is the same one that was found by the side of the murdered man. Bramshaw will also swear that he never met Betty that night on the road. His lawyer will not overlook anything, mark my word. It will be only circumstantial evidence after all, and it may not have much effect."

"Keep up courage, Lois," Margaret encouraged. "You have accomplished a great deal in a short time, and I know that father's lawyer has not been idle."

"Has he found out anything yet?" Lois eagerly asked.

"I am afraid not. There has not been much time, you see. But he is a very able man and will leave no stone unturned. But, come, dear, it is time for us to get ready. We must not keep father waiting as he is very busy these days."

CHAPTER XXX

A STRANGE COMMISSION

Robert Westcote did not go to his luncheon the day of Lois' visit to the city. He intended to go but was unexpectedly detained. He had been very busy all the morning in his office. His lawyer had been with him for some time, and when he was at last alone he turned his attention to a type-written manuscript lying on the desk before him. This consisted of several sheets of legal paper, attached to which was an official seal which had been recently broken. This was the third time that Mr. Westcote had read it and when he was through he sat for a while in deep thought. He paid no attention to the click of the typewriters in the adjoining room, and so engrossed was he that he did not at first hear a tap upon the office door. When it was repeated, he started from his reverie and called to the visitor to enter, thinking that perhaps it was one of the clerks. It was not his habit to be caught off guard, for he prided himself upon his alertness and strict attention to every business detail.

The office door slowly opened, and instead of a clerk, there stood before him a man dressed in rough working clothes. He recognised him at once as one of the men employed at the falls, and whom he had met on several occasions. It was Mr. Westcote's kindness and courtesy which always won for him the hearty support of his employees. They knew that they would receive justice and consideration at his hands and that he did not look upon them with contempt and as inferior beings. Mr. Westcote at once arose from his chair and held out his hand.

"Why, Dobbins," he exclaimed, "this is a surprise. I did not know you were in the city. How are things going on at the falls? Nothing wrong, I hope? Sit down, please," and he motioned him to a chair.

"The work is going on all right, sir," Dobbins replied, as he took the offered seat. "But I have come to see you, sir, on very important business. It has troubled me so much that I have not been able to sleep ever since Randall was arrested."

"Oh, I see, it has to do with that murder case, has it?" Mr. Westcote asked, now greatly interested.

"I wouldn't like to say that, sir," and Dobbins twirled his hat in his hands. "But it might throw some light upon the matter. You see, somebody killed old David. That's certain, isn't it?"

Mr. Westcote nodded his assent.

"Well, if you knew for sure that somebody had tried to but a short time before, it would make you rather suspicious of that somebody, wouldn't it?"

"I should say so!" Mr. Westcote exclaimed. "But do you know of any one who made the attempt, Dobbins?"

"You can judge of that, sir, when you hear what I have to say. It was this way. The day of the big wind I was sent to the shore to get a piece of mill belting, which was to come from the city on the afternoon boat. I had almost reached the brow of logs on the edge of the clearing when I stopped to get a drink from that little spring by the side of the road. I sat down for a minute or two under the shade of a small thick fir tree to fill my pipe, when happening to glance to my left I saw a man running up the road. I at once saw it was that artist fellow, and curious to know what he was running for I moved back a little behind the fir so's he couldn't see me. He stopped right by the logs and peered down the bank. Then he looked cautiously around and, picking up a stick, he pried loose one of the logs lying on top, and which was almost ready to go anyway. As soon as he had done this, he dropped the stick and ran like a streak of lightning down the road, and that was the last I saw of him."

"Well?" Mr. Westcote questioned as Dobbins paused and wiped the perspiration from his forehead with a big red hand-kerchief.

"This is the part, sir, which I am ashamed to tell," the man continued. "I heard the crash of that log down the bank and the splash in the water. Then there fell upon my ears a shriek of terror. I knew it was a woman's voice and I leaped from my hiding place and peeked down the bank. And there I saw old David and that girl Betty Bean standing there frightened almost out of their senses. Say, I wasn't long getting back under cover again, for I knew that if they saw me they would say for sure that I had rolled that log down the bank on purpose. I didn't dare to go to the shore on the road so I cut up through the woods and came out another way. I didn't dare to say a word about it for fear I might get into trouble. But when young Randall, who is a chap we all think a lot of, was arrested for the murder of that old man I couldn't sleep a wink. If that art-ist fellow tried to kill old David once he would try again, and put the blame off on some one else. At last I could stand it no longer and so made up my mind to tell you all I know. You can judge now, sir, for yourself."

Mr. Westcote was greatly excited at this story, though out-wardly he remained very calm. Twice during the narration he had glanced at the manuscript lying upon the desk, and once he had reached out his hand as if to pick it up. For a few seconds he remained silent when the story was ended. Then he rose to his feet and reached out his hand.

"Dobbins," he began, "I wish to thank you for what you

have told me to-day. You have done a good deed by thus
unburdening your mind. Will you be willing to swear to what
you have just told me?"

"Swear! Indeed I will. I'll swear on a dozen Bibles any time
and anywhere."

"That's good," Mr. Westcote replied, as he bade him good-
day. "We shall need you before long, if I'm not much mistaken, so be ready."

Dobbins had scarcely left the office when Lois and Margaret
arrived.

"My, how the morning has gone!" Mr. Westcote remarked as
he greeted Lois with a hearty shake of the hand. "I suppose
we had better get down to business at once, as no doubt you
wish to go home this afternoon. I hope you will pardon my
sending for you and giving you all this trouble."

"I do not mind in the least," Lois replied, "for I am sure it
has something to do with the murder, and I am so anxious to
learn whether you have found out anything new."

"Only something this morning, Miss Sinclair, which may be
of considerable value. I trust that we may unearth more in a
few days."

"Oh, don't wait for a few days, Mr. Westcote," Lois pleaded.
"You must act at once, this very afternoon, if the criminal is
to be caught."

"How can we, Miss Sinclair," was the reply, "when we are
not sure who the real criminal is?"

"But I know, and I think you will agree with me when I tell
you my story. Listen."

Lois then related what she had heard from Andy Forbes
and Betty Bean. She told her story well and Mr. Westcote was
keenly interested not only in what she told him, but in the
animated look in her eyes and the varying shades of expression which passed over her fair face. He considered Jasper a

lucky fellow in having such a beautiful woman striving so hard for his release.

When Lois had finished, Mr. Westcote turned to his desk and drew the telephone toward him. "What you tell me, Miss Sinclair," he said, "is very valuable, and I must see my lawyer at once. Excuse me a moment." After he had called up the lawyer and asked him to come at once to his office, he hung up the receiver and sat for a few seconds lost in deep thought. "Yes, we had better do it at once," he remarked as if to himself. "It will not do to run any risk."

"Do what, Father?" Margaret enquired.

"Have that Bramshaw detained. I have received some additional information to-day, and with what Miss Sinclair has just told me it should be enough to arrest any man. Now, I must come to the question I wish to speak to you about," and he turned to Lois. "You have told me your story and in return I shall relate one perhaps of a more startling nature."

"In connection with this same affair?" Lois eagerly asked.

"It has a direct bearing upon it. It has to do with the mystery which has been surrounding the life of old David."

"And does it clear it up?"

"Wait, please, until I am through, and you can judge for yourself," Mr. Westcote smilingly told her.

"I shall be as patient as Job," Lois replied, as she settled herself in her chair as comfortably as possible.

"My story might seem strange to you," Mr. Westcote began. "In fact, it has always seemed strange to me, and sometimes I think that I shall wake up and find it nothing more than a dream. Well, without going into details, which would not interest you, it is sufficient to say that I came to this country over two years ago on one of the strangest commissions ever given to man. I was handed two sealed papers numbered 1 and 2,

with strict orders to break the seal of paper Number 1 only
upon my arrival in Canada, and then I should find my instructions in reference to Number 2."

"What were the instructions?" Lois eagerly asked, as Mr.
Westcote paused for a few seconds as if considering how to
proceed.

"That will come later," he replied. "I must tell you about
Number 1 first. You promised to be patient, you know."

"Excuse me, I know I did," Lois smilingly confessed, as she
glanced at Margaret, whose eyes were twinkling with amusement.

"I was naturally anxious to know what my orders were," Mr.
Westcote continued, "and shortly after my arrival here, I broke
the seal of Number 1. Then I learned that I was to search for
an old man who was living in this country under the name of
David Findley. No effort or expense was to be spared. Money
would be provided without stint through one of the city banks.
When the old man was found he was to be kept in complete
ignorance of the fact that I had been searching for him. The
hard part was that I should undertake to assist him in such a
way that he should not have the slightest idea that anything
was being done on his behalf. There was not to be the least
semblance of charity, and whatever was done for him had to
appear to be the natural payment for value received. If the old
man had any special hobby or scheme, no matter how wild,
so long as it was legitimate, I was to undertake to see that
it should be carried out, no matter what the expense. If the
scheme proved feasible, so much the better, and strict business methods were to be used to make it pay. But if not, the
old man's every lawful wish was to be gratified. One of the
strict instructions was that he should be induced as soon as
possible to make his will. This was to be done in such a way
as to arouse no suspicion, but that he should consider it as a

matter of business detail, so that his fond scheme, or whatever it might be, would not suffer in case of his death.

"You can readily understand, Miss Sinclair, the magnitude of the undertaking. At first I thought that I had been made the victim of a madman, and was tempted to return to England at once, and have nothing to do with the affair. But the amount of money placed at my disposal in the bank settled all scruples and started me forth upon my strange quest. I even began to enjoy the adventure of the whole thing, and the mystery attached to it lured me on. I searched far and wide for David Findley and at last, owing to an accident to my auto, located him at Creekdale, living as a pauper. By the description given in paper Number 1 I knew that he was the man for whom I had been searching. After that, matters moved along very smoothly. He had a fond scheme, too, which served my purpose splendidly. He was wrapped up in the idea of converting the water of Break Neck Falls into light and power for the benefit of the entire community. I consulted with the best engineers, and they said the scheme was most feasible, and so we began work. David was paid a sum of money for his plans, which satisfied him, and he was made Honorary President of a company which has never really existed. The money at my disposal made everything easy. You know the rest, and why should I go further into details? It would be unnecessary for me to tell you of the faithful and excellent work of Mr. Randall. He has been of great assistance to me, and without his aid my task would have been much harder than it has been."

When Mr. Westcote paused Lois looked enquiringly into his face.

"May I speak now?" she asked. "I have been very patient, have I not?"

"Indeed you have, Miss Sinclair," and Mr. Westcote smiled. "You may ask anything you like."

"Surely you have not told me all. I thought you had merely begun when you stopped. Who was David Findley, anyway, and what does paper Number 2 contain? I am most curious to know the end of this strange story."

"Oh, I forgot to tell you a very important thing," and Mr. Westcote laughed. "My instructions in paper Number 1 told me not to open Number 2 until after the old man's death. Then I should learn all about him and the mystery of my strange commission would be solved."

"Do you know yet?" Lois eagerly asked. "Have you broken the seal?"

"Yes, I broke it this morning, and have read the contents of the paper three times. I am going to read it to you now, for that will be better than if I tell it to you in my own words."

CHAPTER XXXI

PAPER NUMBER TWO

Mr. Westcote was about to begin the reading of the manuscript lying before him, when his lawyer was announced.

"Excuse me for a moment," he said, "I must speak to Dr. Turnsell at once."

"Suppose we go out for a while, Father," Margaret suggested. "You will wish to see him privately, I suppose."

"Remain just where you are," was the reply. "It is not necessary for you to leave."

When they were alone Lois and Margaret discussed what Mr. Westcote had just told them.

"Isn't it strange?" Margaret began. "Did you ever hear anything like it before?"

"No, I never did," was the reply. "But did you know about it?"

"Oh, yes. Father told me, of course, but I had to promise that I wouldn't say a word about it. And I didn't, did I, not even to you? I longed to tell you all I knew, but that would not have been right."

"I wonder what that paper contains," and Lois motioned to the desk. "It, no doubt, will explain everything. I wish your father would hurry back."

"Here he is now," Margaret replied. "He wasn't long with Dr. Turnsell."

"I am afraid that I shall have to leave you young ladies for a while," Mr. Westcote informed them as soon as he had closed the door behind him. "My lawyer wants me to go with him. It is too bad as I wished to read that paper to you."

"Why cannot we read it ourselves?" Margaret asked. "You surely will not keep us in suspense any longer."

"Why, certainly," was the reply. "That will do just as well. Strange that I never thought of that. Suppose you read it, Miss Sinclair," and he handed the manuscript to her. "I shall come back as soon as I can, so you had better wait here until I return unless I am too late."

"Hurry up, Lois," Margaret urged, when they were once more alone. "I can't wait another minute."

Lois was nothing loath, and in a clear, well-modulated voice she began:

"I, Simon Dockett, feeling keenly the weight of years, and knowing that my days on earth are but few, desire to unburden my soul and make amends as far as possible for a grievous wrong I have committed. That wrong can never be fully rectified in this world. If money could do it, then it would flow like water; if a troubled conscience and a wearied and a burdened soul could atone for what I have done, then surely I have made atonement enough. They greatly err who say that a man can sin and yet have peace of mind. I tell you it is hell; yes, hell here, and hell in the world to come.

"I have heaped up riches in my life, enough to satisfy the most avaricious. But at what cost have I acquired them, and of what comfort are they to me now? I am old, lonely, and menials serve me because of my money. How much better are my so-called friends? They fawn upon me with their lips, but deceit is in their hearts. They laugh at me behind my back, and joke about 'Old Dockett' and his money. In all the world there is none who loves me, but many who hate me. One especially there is who desires my death, thinking that he will get my money. That is part of what my riches have cost me, though not all.

"I have a brother, and when we were young our hearts were as one. He was gentle and thoughtful, while I was rough and impetuous. My one object was to make money for self, his, to assist others. Once I loved him as my own soul. But gold got into my heart and changed everything. I became a machine, nay, more, a brutal thinking machine, with gold as the one object in life.

"All natural affections died in me, and I think I would have betrayed my parents for gold, but thank God they were beyond my power. My only brother, Henry, however, was not, and him I betrayed, deceived and ruined. All that he had became mine, and I considered it shrewd business. He left England and I was glad that he was out of my sight. I have never seen him since, but I have kept track of him.

"Had my brother cursed me when I robbed him, it would have been easier for me in after years. But he reproached me not, except with his eyes, and the look that he gave me as we parted has haunted me ever since. I tried to forget what I had done to him, and plunged deeply into business. But all in vain. I could not banish the wrong I had committed, and my brother's face with the reproachful eyes was ever before me day and night.

"At last I could endure it no longer, and so resolved to make what amends I could. I found out where my brother was living, wrote to him, and sent him a considerable sum of money. He returned it, and that made me angry. But I knew that my brother was right, and I also learned that he would starve rather than accept a penny from me or help in any form.

"For several years I made no further attempt to assist him. But the remorse gnawing at my soul could not be silenced. I reasoned that I had done what I could to rectify my wrong, but that gave me no peace. Finally I resolved that I would help him in such a manner that he should never know that I had anything to do with it. I knew that he was living in Eastern Canada, but just where I was uncertain.

"After weeks of careful consideration I made arrangements that all that I possess should go to my brother Henry after my death. In the meantime I planned with my solicitors that a man of exceptional ability and unimpeachable character and integrity should be sent to Canada, backed with sufficient money, to find my brother and to devise some means of assisting him, and carrying out his every legitimate wish without his ever knowing that I was behind the scheme.

"I have also provided that he should be given two sealed papers, the first setting forth his instructions, which he is not to open until his arrival in Canada. He will then learn that this second which I am now writing must not be opened until after my brother's death, should he outlive me. If he should die first then this paper is to be returned to me with the seal unbroken. The man chosen for this special undertaking must not know anything about me, and he is not to have the least idea who my brother really is. When I am dead, my solicitors will notify the man so that he may break the seal of this paper immediately after my brother's death.

"My solicitors have full knowledge of my business affairs, and they will continue to manage them after my death. In case of my brother Henry dying without having made a will, they have full instructions as to the disposal of my property. Only one other living relative I have, and he is my sister's son, Melburne Telford. He cherishes the hope that my money will go to him after my death. In this, however, he is mistaken, for I have taken a great dislike to the young man. He is absolutely worthless, and travels over the country as an artist. I have given him considerable money at various times, for my dead sister's sake. But he has been very ungrateful, and lives a most evil life. He believes that my brother Henry is the only one who stands between him and my money. But I have so arranged that he shall not receive one penny of it, though he is not aware of the fact.

"I have now done all in my power to make amends for past wrongs to my only brother. I should like to see him again, and to hear from his own lips words of forgiveness. But that can never be. People have called me hard, and good reason have they had for such an opinion. But they have not known all. When I am gone and this story is told, perhaps they may think somewhat differently of me. But whether they do or not will not affect me then. I have made my bed, and so I must lie in it.

(Signed) "SIMON DOCKETT, Liverpool, England."

When Lois had finished, she laid the paper upon the desk and remained silent for a few seconds. The last part of the confession was what interested her most of all. She felt sure that Melburne Telford was none other than Sydney Bramshaw. But how was she to prove it? Where could the person be found who could identify him? she asked herself.

"What do you think of the story?" Margaret asked, as she studied Lois' face in an effort to divine her thoughts.

"It is most interesting," was the reply, "and it explains things I could not understand before. But how are we to prove that Sydney Bramshaw is really Simon Dockett's nephew?"

"Perhaps father may know more about it than we do," Margaret suggested. "He must have received notice of Simon Dockett's death."

Lois was about to reply when a sudden thought flashed into her mind, which caused her face to flush with excitement.

"What is it, dear?" Margaret questioned, noticing her agitation.

"Don't press me for an answer, please," and Lois rose to her feet. "I shall explain everything to you later. I must get home at once. A new idea has come into my mind, which makes me very restless."

As she was standing there, Mr. Westcote entered. His face bore a worried expression which Lois and Margaret were not slow to notice.

"Have they caught him?" Lois eagerly asked.

"No, not yet, but he will be taken no doubt at the station. You have finished reading the paper, I see," and he glanced toward the desk. "What do you think of it?"

"We have found it most interesting, but some of it quite puzzling."

"What part?"

"Where it speaks about Simon Dockett's nephew. Who is Melburne Telford, do you think?"

"Ah, that is where the present trouble lies, Miss Sinclair. I firmly believe that this Sydney Bramshaw is the man, but how are we to prove it without bringing people all the way from England? I thought there was a man in the city who could identify him, as he had done business with the Dockett Concern, as it is commonly called in England. My lawyer and I hunted him up this afternoon, but he told us that he never knew before that Simon Dockett had a nephew. Now if we could only unearth some one who knows that Sydney Bramshaw is in reality Melburne Telford then our case is complete."

"I believe I know the right man," Lois remarked in a low voice. "He is living at Creekdale, and if you will take me there at once we can have a talk with him. I know he will assist us all he can, and we can depend upon what he says."

"We shall go at once," Mr. Westcote replied. "I shall order the car immediately. You had better come too, Margaret."

Lois was now in a great whirl of excitement, and she could hardly wait for the arrival of the car. Mr. Westcote told the chauffeur to make good time, and though they travelled fast it seemed to Lois a long time before the Haven appeared in sight.

The captain and Mrs. Peterson were greatly surprised when the car swung up to the Haven and the young women and Mr. Westcote alighted. The captain was lying in his big chair upon the verandah with his wife knitting by his side.

"Well, this is a surprise," he exclaimed as he shook hands with his visitors. "I thought you were all in the city, and had forgotten your country friends."

"Oh, we can never forget you, Captain," Lois smilingly replied. "We have come on purpose to see you, and so you should feel very much elated and be on your best behaviour."

"Sure, sure, indeed I shall. But what do you want to see me about?" he enquired. "Has it anything to do with that murder case? I am most anxious to hear the latest news."

"I have come to ask you to get your thinking-cap on," Lois replied.

"My thinking-cap! Why, bless your heart, it's always on, day and night."

"That's good, Captain. But first I wish to ask you a few questions."

"Drive ahead, then, I'm ready."

"You have often sailed to Liverpool, have you not?"

"Sure. Know the place well."

"You knew also of the Dockett Concern there, didn't you? I have heard you mention that name."

"Yes, indeed I did. Knew old Simon Dockett himself, and saw him often. My, he was a cranky cuss, if ever there was one. He had a whale of a tongue, and knew how to use it."

"Did you know anything about his family?"

"Not much. He never married, as I guess no woman would have him. But I know for sure that he has a nephew. He sailed once on my ship, and that was the first time I met him. He was a gay one."

"Do you remember his name?" Lois was much excited now.

"Sure; it was Melburne Telford. I couldn't forget that for if he told it to us once on that trip he told it a hundred times. He was always boasting that he was the nephew of old Simon Dockett, and that he was to fall heir to his wealth."

"Have you ever seen him since, Captain?"

"Not until he struck this place, travelling under the name of Sydney Bramshaw. I knew him, though he didn't know me," and the captain smiled as he ran his hand over his bearded face. "I didn't have this then. At first I couldn't exactly make out where I had seen the fellow before, but when I remembered I gave such a whoop that the women folk thought I had gone out of my mind, and came running in to see what was wrong."

"So that was the matter with you that day, was it?" Mrs. Peterson asked as she paused in her knitting.

"Yes, that was it, and poor little Betty thought I had something in my head like 'Mr. David,' ho, ho!"

"But why didn't you tell us who Sydney Bramshaw really was?" Lois asked.

"At first I thought I would. But then I decided to await developments, and see what the fellow was doing around here, and why he was sailing under another name. If I told what I knew it would have been gabbled all over the place in no time, and the chap would have been looked upon with suspicion. He seemed to be harmless enough, and so I thought I might as well hold my tongue for a while anyway. But since he's gone and you've asked me point blank about him, I can't see any harm in telling what I know."

"Would it surprise you, Captain, to learn that Melburne Telford, alias Sydney Bramshaw, is David Findley's nephew?" Mr. Westcote asked.

"His nephew!" the captain exclaimed. "Old David's nephew!"

"Yes, that's who he is, and David and Simon Dockett were brothers."

"Good heavens!" the captain ejaculated. "What's the meaning of it all, I'd like to know?"

"Let me tell you," Mr. Westcote replied. "It is only right that you should know."

As briefly as possible he related the story of the two sealed papers, the captain and his wife listening with the keenest interest. He told also of Bramshaw's suspicious actions.

"And do you mean to tell me that old David was murdered by his nephew?" the captain asked in amazement when the story was finished.

"It looks very much like it, doesn't it?"

"It certainly does. My, my, who'd have thought such a thing!" and the captain leaned back overcome by what he had just heard.

Before the visitors left, Mrs. Peterson spread a little table with a spotless cloth, and brought forth some of her fresh bread, cake and preserves.

"It is no trouble, I assure you," she replied in answer to Lois' remonstrance. "You must have a cup of tea before you leave, and I thought it would be nice out here on the verandah."

"That looks good to me," Mr. Westcote remarked as he drew his chair up to the table. "I haven't eaten a bite since morning. I was all ready to go to the restaurant when Dobbins came to see me, and then you girls arrived. If this keeps up much longer I shall be a skeleton. But I must not remain too long," he added, as he consulted his watch. "I must be back in the city before the C. P. R. leaves."

"May I stay with Lois?" Margaret asked.

"Why yes, if you will not be in the way."

"She must stay," Lois replied. "I could not get along without her now. You will keep us informed, I hope, of how you make out."

"Yes, I shall write to-night, and if anything of great importance turns up I shall let you know at once."

CHAPTER XXXII

THE TABLES TURNED

The agony of mind that Jasper suffered in leaving his cabin and meeting the people of Creekdale on their return from old David's funeral was only a part of the trial he endured on his journey to the county jail. On the wharf, while waiting for the arrival of the steamer, he was subjected to the pitiless stares and gibes of men, women and children. News of the arrest had spread from house to house, and people had flocked to the wharf to have a last look upon the suspected man. Jasper stood with his face to the river watching the steamer off in the distance, which was rapidly approaching. The actions of the crowd disgusted him. There was not one friendly voice lifted up on his behalf. Jim Goban strutted up and down keeping close watch upon his prisoner, and gloating over his task. He was having his revenge now for the blows he had received on the day of David's release.

When once on the steamer Jasper believed that he would be free from all curious eyes. In this, however, he was mistaken. There were many on board and all soon learned that the "terrible murderer" was in their midst. Jasper was kept down below near the engine room and it was remarkable how most of the people on that boat found it necessary to pass him quite often. He could hear some of their comments as they moved away.

"What a bad face he has," a woman remarked.

"Yes," her companion replied, "he surely does look like a

desperate character. Wasn't it awful for him to kill that poor old man?"

Jasper's face was really hard and stern; how could it have been otherwise? Where was all their Christian charity? he asked himself. Where was the spirit of justice? Those people knew that he had not yet received a fair trial, and why were they so willing and eager to believe him guilty?

Old Simon Squabbles was on board, and though he said nothing to Jasper, he expressed his views to several men a short distance away.

"It's nothin' more than I expected," he boasted. "I knew he would soon reach the end of his tether after the experience I had with him. I had him workin' fer me, an' when I wouldn't pay him fer loafin' in the potato patch, he got as mad as blazes an' said things I wouldn't like to repeat."

Jasper endured such remarks without a word. He did not feel like making any reply. In fact, he realised how useless it would be, and the less said the better.

The limit of his bitterness was reached when a woman approached and began to speak to him about his soul, and the danger of hell fire. She dilated glibly upon the awfulness of sin, and even offered to pray for him.

"Keep your prayers for yourself," Jasper retorted, stung almost to fury by her impudence. "You'll do more good if you pray for these snivelling hypocrites," and he motioned to those standing around him.

"Isn't it awful!" and the woman held up her hands in horror. "You should be afraid to speak that way, and you in such danger. Read this, poor man," and she held forth a tract she had been holding in her hand.

Jasper glanced at it and read the heading, "Flee from Hell Fire." He took it, and then crushing it in his hand, threw it from him.

"I've had enough of this," he cried, "and I'll stand no more. Leave me alone, is all I ask. Hell can be no worse than what you people are dealing out to me now."

Jasper's look and attitude caused those near him to shrink back, and during the rest of the voyage he had peace from the clatter of tongues, at least.

It was a great relief to him when at last he was lodged in the cell of the county jail. Here he was alone and free from all curious eyes, and he had time and quietness for thought. His heart was nevertheless heavy as he sat there in his solitude. He brooded over all that had taken place, and the one and only ray of brightness which came to him in his misery was the thought of Lois and the vision of her standing where he last saw her with such deep sympathy expressed in her eyes.

The following day Mr. Westcote's lawyer came to see him, and they had a long talk together. Dr. Turnsell was greatly impressed by Jasper and the straightforward manner in which he told about his visit to David the night of the murder.

"We shall do the best we can for you," the lawyer informed him as he bade him good-bye. "We have tried to get you out on bail, but so far have been unsuccessful."

This visit somewhat encouraged Jasper. He knew that able men were working for him and that Mr. Westcote would spare no money on his behalf. As he sat there in his cell he thought over his past life and of the many struggles he had made to succeed. He brooded over the injustice he had received from so many simply because he was poor and forced to fight his own battles against almost overwhelming odds. "And is this the end?" he asked himself. "Will all my efforts amount to nothing?" He thought of several of his college companions, sons of rich men, who knew not what it was to fight in order to win their way, and who were now occupying important positions in life. He knew what they would say about him now. "Poor

Spuds," would be their laconic comment. "He was always an odd one, anyway." Yes, that was the way they would talk, and then dismiss him from their minds.

The afternoon slowly passed, and after a while he rose and paced up and down his small room. He looked through the barred window and saw the clouds sweeping across the "long savannahs of the blue." How precious freedom seemed to him, and he longed to be once more in the open. He thought of Lois, and wondered if she were thinking of him. Perhaps she was out on the river in her little boat watching those same clouds. There would be no one near now to rescue her should the water get rough.

Jasper was interrupted in his reverie by the entrance of the jailor. He carried a letter in his hand, which he gave to the prisoner, and then retired and bolted the door.

Jasper glanced at the writing and his heart gave a great bound as he at once recognised Lois' handwriting. Quickly he tore open the envelope and drew forth the letter.

"Dear Mr. Randall," it began, "I am sending you this little note to remind you that all your friends have not forgotten you, and that we are doing what we can on your behalf. Keep up courage. I am very hopeful now and feel sure that everything will turn out right. I know you are innocent, and am confident that you will soon be free. Good-bye.

"Yours in haste,

"Lois Sinclair."

Next to Lois herself nothing could have been more welcome to Jasper than that letter. He pressed it fervently to his lips, and read it over and over again. It brought a great comfort to his burdened heart. He was sure now that Lois was thinking of him and doing what she could for his release. He wondered what she had discovered, and mused much upon the words "I am very hopeful now."

Jasper slept well that night and awoke in the morning greatly refreshed. He wondered what the day would bring forth, and as he paced up and down his room in order to get a little exercise, he squared back his shoulders and held his head high. He felt fit and ready for battle and longed for activity of some kind. As the morning hours wore slowly away he became restless and impatient. The silence of his room was affecting his nerves, and he thought with a shudder of men who were condemned for life to solitary confinement. What more horrible punishment could be meted out to any man? He was sure that he would go mad in a few days.

Jasper could eat but little of the meagre dinner the jailor brought him. He was hoping that there would be a letter or some message for him, and when there was none he felt sadly disappointed. How long would it be before he had any word from the lawyer? he wondered.

He was brooding at the table when the door again opened and to his great joy and surprise Mr. Westcote entered. Jasper sprang to his feet and seized the hand held out to him.

"Are you quite repentant now?" Mr. Westcote smilingly asked.

"Quite," was the reply. "I think this dose will do me all my life. I am willing to do anything you ask me, even to blacking your boots."

"That's good, so obey me at once and leave this confounded hole."

"What, go with you?"

"Certainly. What else would have brought me here but to take you away?"

"To the court-room, I suppose," was the bitter rejoinder.

"Not at all. But come now, and I will explain everything on our way to the city. My car is just outside."

How good Jasper felt to be once again out of doors, and

he expanded his chest and inhaled great draughts of the fresh air.

"My, that's great!" he exclaimed. "It will take me a long time to get the poison of that cell out of my lungs, and —"

"The bitterness out of your soul, eh?" Mr. Westcote quietly asked, as Jasper paused.

"Yes, that's what I was going to say. But I'm afraid it will be a much harder thing to do. I've been the sport of fools so long that the bitterness of my soul has become a chronic disease."

"Tut, tut, don't talk that way any more," Mr. Westcote chided. "Jump on board now, and let us be off. I'll tell you something that will sweeten your soul and make life worth living."

To Jasper it seemed almost like a dream as he leaned back and listened to what his companion told him about the net of evidence which had been woven about Sydney Bramshaw. He did not mention Lois in connection with the affair, but related the incidents of the letter, the threat to Betty Bean, and old David's narrow escape from the falling log. He told him also about the two sealed papers, and who David Findley and Sydney Bramshaw really were.

"This is certainly remarkable!" Jasper exclaimed, when Mr. Westcote ceased speaking and took a cigar from his pocket. "But where is Bramshaw now?" he asked. "Surely he has not been allowed to escape."

"Indeed he hasn't. He's in the city jail, that's where he is."

"Oh, I see." It was all Jasper could say.

"Yes, he was arrested last night as he was about to board the C. P. R. for New York. His grip was searched and letters of a most incriminating nature were found. Why, the fellow must be a fool to have kept them with him. Almost any man in his right mind would have destroyed them at once."

"How did he take his arrest?" Jasper enquired.

"At first he put up a big bluff and threatened all sorts of things.

But after a night in the lock-up and a thorough grilling this morning, he broke down and begged for mercy. He was confounded by the net which had been woven about him, and the look of terror in his eyes was really pathetic."

"And has he confessed to murdering old David?" Jasper eagerly asked.

"Not exactly. But he has come so near to it that not the shadow of a doubt is left about his guilt. I believe that he will confess all shortly in the hope that he may escape the death penalty by doing so."

Jasper remained silent for a while apparently studying the scenery as they sped on their way. But he saw nothing of tree, flower or rich rolling meadows. His thoughts were elsewhere, and his next question revealed the working of his mind.

"To whom am I indebted for the collecting of all that valuable evidence?" he questioned. "Some one must have been very busy."

"You are indebted to several," was the reply. "But Miss Sinclair has been the most active."

"So I imagined," was all Jasper said and he once more lapsed into a silence which he did not break until the car drew up before Mr. Westcote's office. He knew now that Lois cared for him, and his heart thrilled with joy as he thought of the efforts she had made on his behalf. How he longed to see her and thank her for what she had done.

The surprise which came to Jasper upon his speedy release and vindication was nothing compared to the shock he received when Mr. Westcote told him about old David's will.

"Surely he has not left everything to me!" Jasper exclaimed.

"No, not all; merely half after a few bequests have been disposed of. Then you and Miss Sinclair are to share alike."

"I don't seem to comprehend it all yet," and Jasper placed his hand to his forehead in a bewildered manner.

"It's only natural that you shouldn't. It will take you some time to grasp the significance of the bequest which has been made to you. Your responsibility will be very heavy, but from what I know of you I believe that you will be equal to the undertaking."

"I shall do the best I can," Jasper replied. "I am too much dazed at present to think it carefully over. For a man to be freed from all suspicion of a terrible crime, and then to find himself heir to a vast fortune all in one day is enough to turn any one's brain."

A knock sounded upon the office door, and Dr. Turnsell at once entered. He shook hands with Jasper and heartily congratulated him.

"I have come to tell you," he added, "that Bramshaw has made a full confession of his crime. He is a nervous wreck, and this morning he broke down completely."

"I am very thankful that he has confessed," and Jasper gave a sigh of relief. "Wasn't it lucky that he was caught before he got over the Border?"

"You have to thank Miss Sinclair for that," Mr. Westcote replied. "But for her prompt action I am afraid we would be frantically searching for Bramshaw now."

"And I would be still in jail," Jasper mused.

"Undoubtedly. Now, it seems to me that Miss Sinclair should be informed of what has happened as soon as possible. Suppose we slip up and tell her?"

"That will be great," and Jasper sprang to his feet. "When can we start?"

"At once. The car is waiting outside. I knew that you would be anxious to go, and so ordered the chauffeur to be ready."

CHAPTER XXXIII

THE REAL HAVEN

Lois rose early that morning and attended to numerous household affairs. It was necessary for her to keep busy, as her mind was always calmer when her hands were employed. She had the feeling that the day would be an unusual one, and that much would happen before its close. She could not rid her mind of this idea, and she mentioned it to Margaret over the breakfast table.

"Do you believe in premonitions?" she asked.

"In a way I do," was the reply. "Strange things happen sometimes, you know. I, too, have a peculiar feeling this morning that we are to hear great news today. Everything is so still just now, with not a leaf nor a blade of grass aquiver. See how the fog rests upon the river through which the sun is trying to break. There will be a heavy wind this afternoon, mark my word. I have often noticed it to be so. It is the rule rather than the exception. And it may be the case with us. The quietness of the morning may give place to excitement before night."

"You are quite a philosopher," Lois laughingly remarked.

"Not at all, dear. I am merely an observer, and I notice that what happens in nature around us is often true in our own lives. The law which governs the waves of the ocean affects in a similar manner the ripples of a tiny pool. I am going to make a prophecy now."

"Let it be a good one."

"Certainly. I am going to predict that this afternoon will bring us the excitement of joy, and that there will be a happy company seated at this table for dinner. How is that for a prophecy?"

"I hope it will come true," Lois replied with a smile.

"Do you care for a walk this morning?" she asked.

"No, I think not. I have some needle-work to finish, and I do so like that shady corner of the verandah. But don't you stay in on my account."

"I'm afraid I couldn't content myself in any one place this morning," and Lois gazed thoughtfully out of the window. "I am so restless that I must be on the move. I shall visit the Haven first and then go for the mail. We should hear something from your father."

Lois enjoyed the walk up along the shaded lane, and when she was almost to the main highway she sat down under a large tree and looked out upon the river. The last trace of fog was slowly lifting and not a ripple disturbed the surface of the water. She longed to be out there in her boat and made up her mind to go for a row during the afternoon. She thought of the day Jasper had rescued her and Margaret. What was he doing now? she wondered. Perhaps he was sitting in his lonely cell thinking of her. The thought brought a flush to her cheeks and a sweet peace to her heart. No doubt he had received her letter, and that would tell him that she had not forgotten him.

She found the captain in his accustomed place upon the verandah.

"You are early this morning," was his salutation as he took the pipe from his mouth.

"Why shouldn't I be?" she asked, as she sat down by his side. "Wouldn't it be a pity to stay indoors a morning like this?"

"Sure it would. But you are lucky to be able to walk about. Look at me; nothing but a cripple who must stick to this one place with never a chance of moving around."

"But you don't need to, Captain. People come to see you, and you know all that is going on. You held quite a reception yesterday afternoon."

"Indeed I did. And I have been thinking very much about what I heard. It is wonderful. I do hope they have caught that rascal."

"Have you seen Betty lately?" Lois enquired.

"We expect her to-night. She is coming to stay a few days with us. It will be good to have her here again, for we miss her very much."

"Have you any idea what she is going to do?"

"Her mind is set upon being a nurse, so I understand. She'll make a good one, mark my word. The way she took to old David and looked after him was a marvel."

Mrs. Peterson now came from the house and joined in the conversation.

"You must excuse me, dear," she apologised, "but I haven't had time to dress up this morning. Betty is coming to-night, and I want to get some cakes and pies made."

"You won't have to work so hard when you get your money," Lois replied. "I suppose you have heard nothing more about it?"

"Only that we're to get a thousand a year. Isn't it wonderful! It seems that it must be all a dream. At first we couldn't understand where so much money was to come from. But after what Mr. Westcote told us it is all clear. Betty and her mother are to get the same amount each, so I believe. Poor old David! We little realised what he would do for us when we took him to board. I did hear that Mr. Jasper is to come in for a large share. I hope he does, anyway, for he deserves it."

"Have you heard who will get the balance of the money,

property, or whatever it is?" Lois asked.

"Why, certainly. Don't you know?" Mrs. Peterson asked in astonishment.

"No, I have not the least idea."

"Well, isn't that strange! Why, the bulk of the property is to go to you and Mr. Jasper."

At these words Lois' eyes opened wide with amazement, and she felt that she had not heard aright.

"To me?" she gasped.

"So I understand. We didn't mention it to you, thinking that you knew all about it. But isn't it wonderful what strange things have happened in such a short time?"

Lois made no reply, for her mind was too much agitated. She wished to be by herself that she might think over this remarkable piece of news. Bidding the captain and his wife good-bye, she walked slowly down the road toward the store. Surely there had been some mistake, she reasoned. Why should anything have been left to her? What had she done to merit it? She wished that David had not done such a thing. It would mean a great responsibility, and she did not feel equal to the task.

Reaching the store, her attention was diverted for a time by the brief note she received from Mr. Westcote telling of the arrest of Sydney Bramshaw. This was very gratifying news, but she longed to hear some word about Jasper, and whether he would be released. This and what Mrs. Peterson had told her about the will occupied her mind all that afternoon. She was unusually silent, and Margaret was afraid that she was not well. She spent a couple of hours upon the river, but the water becoming rough she was unable to remain out any longer.

"Your prediction has come true, Margaret," she said when she had reached the house. "It is very rough out there now. You were quite right as regards the water, but I guess that is about as far as it goes. It is almost dinner time and here we are just as quiet as we were this morning."

"There is plenty of time yet," and Margaret looked up from her work with a smile. "I have had such a delightful day," she added. "See, I have done all this," and she held up a piece of needle-work for inspection.

"I wish that I could settle down to something definite," Lois sighed. "I have never been so restless in all my life as I have to-day. I have the feeling that something wonderful is about to happen, and that a great change is to take place in my life. If I were superstitious I should be quite uneasy."

"Is it a feeling of dread?" Margaret asked.

"No, not at all. I cannot explain it, for I never experienced anything like it before."

This conversation was suddenly interrupted by a long succession of raucous honks up the road, and in a few seconds a car swung around the corner of the house and stopped before the verandah.

Lois had risen and stepped forward. But she stopped short in amazement when she saw Jasper in the car, seated by Mr. Westcote's side. Her father and Dick were in the front seat, but she hardly noticed them. Jasper was free! That was the one idea which filled her mind. It seemed almost too good to be true. Just what happened next she was not altogether certain. She welcomed them all and listened to their voices, but she seemed to be living in a dream from which she would suddenly awaken. She took her place as usual at the head of the table, but made so many mistakes that Dick laughed at her.

"What's the matter, Lois?" he enquired. "You're surely strong on hot water. You've given me a cup of it instead of tea, and the rest you poured into the milk pitcher."

"Did I do that?" Lois asked in surprise. "Well, I guess I'm

rattled, anyway. You have told me so many things during the last half hour that my brain is all in a whirl."

Jasper was as much excited as Lois, though outwardly he remained calm. He said very little, and let Mr. Westcote tell how their car had broken down and but for the timely arrival of Mr. Sinclair and Dick they would not have been able to reach their destination. He recalled his feeling of dismay when they were stalled, and he feared that he would not be able to see Lois that night. He did want to tell her how grateful he was for what she had done for him. But now he was near her and yet he had not told her. He had thought over the proper words he would say, but when he had taken her hand as she met him at the verandah steps, he did not utter them.

After dinner they all went out upon the verandah, and what a delightful time that was. It was a happy company, and for a while all cares were banished. It was a balmy evening, the wind of the afternoon having subsided, and all nature was hushed in repose as the shades of night began to steal over the land. It was the hour of enchantment, and while Mr. Sinclair and Mr. Westcote discussed matters relating to the work at the falls, Dick and Margaret strolled slowly down to the river.

Jasper and Lois thus found themselves sitting alone on the verandah steps.

"Suppose we pay a visit to the Haven," Jasper suggested. "It is a perfect night for a walk, and I know the captain and his wife will be glad to hear the news. Your father won't mind our leaving him, will he?"

"He won't realise that we have gone," Lois laughingly replied. "He is very happy just now."

Jasper and Lois were in no great hurry to reach the Haven. Their hearts were happy, and as they walked slowly along Jasper told Lois all that had happened to him since the day of his arrest.

"I can never thank you enough for sending me that letter of encouragement, and what you have done for me," he told her.

"Don't try to do so," Lois replied. "It was a joy to me to be able to do something."

They were standing beneath a big maple tree, and Lois was plucking at a wild flower she had just picked. Jasper suddenly reached out, caught both her hands in his and held them tight.

"Lois, Lois," he breathed, and his voice was intense with emotion, "I want you for my very own. I cannot live without you."

"Oh, look, you have crushed my flower," Lois remonstrated, while a nervous little laugh escaped her lips.

"That is too bad," and at once Jasper released her hands and placed his arms around her.

"Lois, I love you," he murmured. "I have loved you for years. Can you love me in return?"

In reply Lois lifted her flushed face to his and their lips met. The seal of their betrothal was set, and their young hearts were as one. Time to them was nothing now in the rapturous joy of their sweet pure love. Their past doubts, cares and trials were all ended. They had started forth to reach the Haven nestling on the hill and they found on the way the real Haven which they had long been seeking — the enchanted Haven of Love.